# THE WAR PLANNERS

ANDREW WATTS

Severn River
PUBLISHING

Severn River Publishing

This is a work of fiction. Names, characters, businesses, places, events and incidents are either the products of the author's imagination or used in a fictitious manner. Any resemblance to actual persons, living or dead, or actual events is purely coincidental.

ISBN: 978-1-951249-34-2 (Paperback)

## ALSO BY ANDREW WATTS

**The War Planners Series**

The War Planners

The War Stage

Pawns of the Pacific

The Elephant Game

Overwhelming Force

Global Strike

**Max Fend Series**

Glidepath

The Oshkosh Connection

Books available for Kindle, print, and audiobook. To find out more about the books or Andrew Watts, visit

AndrewWattsAuthor.com.

# 1

In war, truth is the first casualty —Aeschylus

*Present Day*

They came at night, just after David got home from work. No warning. Just two large, unsmiling men wearing suits, standing outside the front door of his home.

"Can I help you, gentlemen?" He held the door about halfway open.

"You're David Manning."

"That's right."

"Honey, who's there?" David's wife, Lindsay, called from the kitchen.

One of the two behemoths flashed an ID card. "We've been asked to escort you..." He used a tone of voice like he was trying to remind David of something that he was expected to have already known.

"Excuse me?" David saw the CIA crest on the ID and opened the door a bit further. "Escort me where?"

One of them looked at the other. "Did you not get the phone call?"

"I guess not."

"You should have gotten a phone call."

David frowned. "About what?"

"David?" His wife was walking toward him. Her voice was soft. Concern in her eyes as she scanned the faces in the doorway. Her arm was outstretched toward David, handing him his work phone.

It was buzzing. *Unknown Caller.*

He took the phone, looking at the men in the doorway. "Excuse me." They nodded for him to answer the call.

"Hello?"

"Mr. Manning, good evening, sir. This is First Sergeant Wallace. I'm with the DoD rapid mobilization team. It is my duty to inform you that the Joint Red Cell Number Eighteen Delta has been activated, sir, and you're on the roster. We have escorts that should be at your home any moment..."

"They're already here."

"Very good, sir. We're extremely sorry for the short notice. You were an alternate, but someone got bumped. Please remember that your participation in a Joint Red Cell is confidential..."

The Red Cell. So that's what this was about.

"...If asked, you are to inform any friends and family made aware of your departure that you have been assigned a work trip. The escorts will take you to—"

"Wait. Hold on. You want me to leave now?"

"That's correct, sir." The man on the phone went on for a moment longer, providing details like what to bring—"just your ID"—and how long he'd be gone—"about two weeks." David had trouble concentrating. He was still in disbelief, frustrated and feeling guilty about leaving his wife like this.

Finally, "Mr. Manning? Hello? Sir, do you understand your orders?"

*Orders?* David hadn't heard that one in a while. It had been several years since David had been in the military. The last orders he'd had were for his honorable discharge.

Their newborn was crying in the kitchen. Lindsay, still frazzled, left to go check on the baby. Their Jack Russell terrier barked from his kennel, where David had stuffed him before answering the door. David could hear his three-year-old daughter asking her mother what was wrong.

"Nothing, honey. Nothing's wrong..." Lindsay said, looking worriedly at her husband.

David said into the phone, "Is there any wiggle room here? I mean, this is completely unexpected. And *two weeks*..."

"I'm afraid not, sir. This is an urgent matter of national security."

His sense of duty won out. "I understand, thank you." He hung up. Looking at the men in the doorway, he said, "Please give me one moment."

They looked at each other. One of them said, "We'll need to leave in two minutes, Mr. Manning."

David shook his head, exhaling in frustration. He walked over to his wife, who was cradling their youngest in her arms. The look on her face said it all. She had heard enough of the conversation to know that he was going to have to go away for a while. He had been traveling a lot for work lately, which was hard on a family with young kids.

"This is nuts," Lindsay whispered when they were in the kitchen. David could still feel the eyes of the government men in the doorway on him. "No notice? They don't want you to pack a bag? David...you work for In-Q-Tel, not...you know..."

All he could do was shrug. "I signed the retainer with the CIA last year. Technically, they can do this if they want to."

"Don't you need to contact your work?"

"The guy on the phone said it was taken care of."

David did his best to put on a good face, even though he was just as frustrated as his wife. He hugged Maddie, his three-year old, patted his newborn on the head, and then kissed his wife goodbye.

"Call us if you can."

"I will. Remember, this is a business trip." Their eyes met. Hers rolled.

A few minutes later he was in the backseat of a dark SUV, rolling through the streets of Vienna, Virginia, toward God knew where.

The night had started off well enough. David had picked up his favorite pizza from Joe's off Nutley Street. Lindsay had gushed about the new Mommy and Me class she was taking at the gym. Her only complaint being how much harder it was now that she had a double stroller. Maddie had spent the dinner chasing the family dog around the kitchen.

Now David was leaving on a trip with mysterious government men. One of them was scrolling through radio stations and momentarily paused when it landed on NPR. They were replaying a news story he had heard this morning. China was beginning to unload much of the American debt it owned. China's steel production had also slowed. US markets were getting jittery. They quoted the usual experts, who gave their opinions on whether catastrophe was waiting around the corner. Then the man in the front flipped the radio off.

Traffic was heavy. Rain began sprinkling the windshield, blurring the red taillights ahead. I-66 was moving, but slowly. They picked up the Dulles Toll Road a moment later.

"We going to the airport?" David asked.

No answer. Nice chaps.

He began to think about what was so urgent that a Red Cell needed to be activated like this. And why had they needed him, specifically? His job. It had to be his job. The military guy on the

phone had given David that line about someone dropping out...
but there weren't too many people with David's expertise.

David worked at In-Q-Tel—a venture capital firm unlike any
other. In-Q-Tel was a nonprofit firm in Arlington, Virginia, whose
sole purpose was to invest in and secure the most advanced information technology for use by the CIA and other US intelligence
agencies. His job was to identify and evaluate new technologies
that could be acquired and used by the government.

The people who had activated the Red Cell must want information on something he'd worked on. Some technology. But
David jumped from project to project every few months. He had
worked there for a number of years now. They could be after
information on any number of dozens of highly classified projects.
But the Red Cells were supposed to come up with ways that
terrorists or nation-states might attack the US. David wasn't really
an expert on that. He was just a technologist.

He'd spent his first few years out of the Navy working for In-Q-
Tel as a low-level tech researcher. His recent promotion meant
that he traveled more and got to work on the higher-priority
projects. But it was still research. David got all his information
about terrorists and spies from books, TV, and the occasional NPR
story.

David thought about his family. He remembered telling
Lindsay that he loved her when he'd left for work that morning.
He had kissed her on the cheek as she nursed their youngest
daughter, Taylor. Lindsay's eyes had been half-closed as she sat in
the rocking chair, but she had smiled. David traveled often now.
Lindsay held the house together. She practically raised the kids
herself. She was the perfect companion. He owed her everything,
and loved her more every day, if that was possible.

He didn't know why, but he thought of his mother. David tried
to think of the last time he'd visited his mother. It had been a year
earlier, in the large waterfront home his parents had owned near

Annapolis, Maryland. He tried to remember the last thing he had said to her but couldn't. It was probably about his work. She was always telling him he worked too hard and too long, and that the government couldn't keep pushing people like that. That Mrs. Green's son from church had a government job and he was home every day at 4 p.m. and never had to travel.

He hoped he hadn't been condescending in his response. She only said those things because she cared for him. If she were still around, he would have spent more time with her...

A Navy wife for more than thirty-five years, she had been tough as nails and dedicated to her three children. She had practically raised them on her own with their father gone so much. David wished she had still been around when Taylor was born. It would have been nice to let her see one more crying grandchild. A slice of heaven for a dying grandmother. But hardship and sacrifice were a way of life in a military family like the Mannings.

David was jolted back to the present as the SUV slowed and turned onto a road near Dulles Airport. Large airliners took off and landed in the rain, their engines roaring.

The SUV came to a halt outside a security gate on the outskirts of Dulles Airport. A few dark hangars stood on the other side of the fence. The gate opened and the SUV lurched forward, stopping next to a Gulfstream G-V.

David's door opened and he felt a rush of cool air. The men gestured for him to follow, and together they marched up the steep staircase that rose into the cabin of the aircraft, the loud sound of the jet engines starting up as he entered.

They indicated for him to sit down and then walked back outside, leaving David alone in the jet. Through the cockpit door, he could see the pilots performing their preflight checks.

Another SUV pulled up outside and three people got out. David couldn't make them out through the rain on the window, but one of them walked over to David's escorts, who had just stepped out of the aircraft.

A voice said, "We ready to go?"

"Yes, sir. We'll be airborne in five."

"Roger. Thanks, gents, that will be all." David's escorts departed.

The three new arrivals walked up the stairway and entered. They were a mass of wet, dark jackets. One was a woman, David realized. Another was a large brute of a man who had the same ogreish look of David's escorts. The last man was talking to one of the pilots, who had just come back into the cabin to shut the door. A ground crewman outside had taken away the rolling stairs.

The jet engine noise faded, and then a hiss as the cabin door closed.

A rush of relief and maddening curiosity flooded him. The person who had been talking to the pilots was Tom Connolly, one of the senior managers at David's work. David didn't work directly for him, but they had been in meetings together. *What the hell was he doing here?*

Tom saw David looking at him. "Hang in there, David. We'll explain everything in a moment. Once we take off. Sorry about the short notice on activation. It's not ideal."

They all lurched a bit as the aircraft began taxiing.

David relaxed a little, looking around. He was sitting in the spacious cabin of a world-class private jet. It was huge—and almost empty. There were ten luxurious seats, including the cream leather couch where David now sat.

Tom wore a wrinkled suit and a tired face. The woman was short and round. She looked to be in her early forties, with fading highlights in her hair and a very odd smile on her face considering the situation. It was a sheepish look, like she was hoping David wasn't going to be mad at her.

"What the hell is going on, Tom? Why are you here?" David asked, looking back and forth between them.

As he spoke, he heard the engines come to life. They were all pushed backward as the aircraft took off and rotated upwards into the night sky.

Tom leaned over and yelled above the noise of the engines. "I'm sorry, Dave! This was the best way to do this! We had to act fast!"

David's ears popped as the aircraft gained altitude, and his body slid in the turns. He repositioned himself to sit upright. The loud noise from the jet's takeoff had subsided, and the four of them sat staring each other down in the large cabin.

Tom said, "Are you alright?"

David nodded. He kept his guard up. He didn't know Tom too well, but he knew his reputation. *Jerk* was the single most-used description. He was supposed to be one of those guys who thought he was smarter than everyone else in the room, regardless of his expertise on the subject at hand, and he tended to treat people like they were idiots. In an organization full of smart people, he was not loved. David had worked with him a handful of times, and each time Tom had used that condescending tone, like the engineers and analysts were wasting his time.

Tom said, "You hungry? Thirsty?"

"Is there a bathroom in here?"

Tom snorted. "Sure. It's down in the back. I'll explain everything when you get back. Go."

David got up and hobbled past the woman to the back of the plane, with Tom's assistant—the big guy— eying him.

"Leave the door open," said the henchman.

David urinated and washed his hands, then splashed some water on his face. He headed back to sit in the seat across from Tom. His body sank into the plush leather chair.

Tom was on the white phone connected to his seat. He had a grim look.

The woman held out her hand and said, "Hi, I'm Brooke Walters." She gave him a polite smile.

"David Manning," he said.

Tom spoke over them on the phone. He said, "So it's confirmed? He's gone? Okay. Understood. Yes, we're airborne. Walters and one from In-Q-Tel. No. We had to go with someone else. Manning. Yes, I'll explain later. Yes. That's everyone on the list. Yes. Yes. Okay. I'll talk to you then." He hung up the phone and looked over at David, letting out a deep sigh.

David closed his eyes and took a few deep breaths, trying to calm himself. He then looked directly at Tom and asked, "Tom, what just happened?"

Tom tilted his head and stared back at him. David could smell stale tobacco on his breath. There was an opened pack of Marlboro reds on the table.

Tom said, "We had to make a last-minute addition to our team —you. Sorry about that. It had to be done."

The woman seemed to shrink into her seat.

David said, "*I realize that.* Why? What was so important that a Red Cell had to be activated on such short notice? And what do you have to do with it?"

Tom stared up at him, his face shifting into a tired frown. He glanced at the big guy and said, "Can you give us a minute?"

The henchman nodded, went to the back of the plane, and sat down. Tom waited until he was out of earshot before speaking. He took out a folder and read through some of the papers.

"Says here you're an Annapolis guy. Just like your dad. And your brother and sister went there too. That's quite the Naval Academy legacy, huh?"

"What is that you're reading from?"

"Your file."

"My file?"

"So your dad was an admiral."

"*Is* an admiral. Could you please tell me what this is all about?"

Tom raised his eyebrows and said, "And your brother was a SEAL...and now he works for... oh, I hadn't seen this yet. He works for us?"

David frowned. "No. He doesn't work for In-Q-Tel."

The woman laughed. Tom looked up from the file and smiled.

Tom said, "In-Q-Tel. *Right*. Dave, let's get a few things straight. I am not employed by In-Q-Tel. Not really. It's a more of a part-time deal for me. My real employer is the same organization that indirectly pays the bills at In-Q-Tel. The Central Intelligence Agency. I specialize in counterespionage."

David frowned. "What are you talking about?"

Tom ignored him. "This situation all started a few weeks ago. We've uncovered some very disturbing bits of information. I'd heard rumors, of course, but until you hear it from a reliable source, you tend to discount those as conspiracy theories. Rumors like that...just seem too crazy to believe."

Tom was lost in thought for a moment and then looked David directly in the eye. "A penetration of that scope...and at those high levels. It's unthinkable." He sighed. "But it looks like it's happened. And the same source that tipped us off on that told us something much worse." He looked down at the file again. "Now, we've got a long flight ahead of us. I promise I'll answer your questions. But I only recently found out I'd be taking you on this little vacation, so humor me for a few minutes while I peruse your biography."

David clenched and unclenched his jaw, trying to be patient.

He said, "Tom. Look...if this is about some national security breach on a project or something, I'll cooperate with whatever you need. But I still don't understand how taking me from my home on zero notice could possibly be necessary. And what do I have to do with whatever is going on?"

Tom ignored him. "Your sister's a Navy pilot, huh? Hmm. Some family. And you...failed out of flight school. Huh. I guess you were the black sheep? That must have been one hell of a conversation with old Dad." Tom looked up briefly. Enough time to see the flash of anger in David's eyes.

"It was a medical disqualification. Bad eyesight."

Tom waved off the rebuttal. David decided that the jerk personality wasn't a CIA cover. That part was genuine.

He said, "So then you got a job with In-Q-Tel as an analyst in 2008 and have been with the company ever since. Your current project is ARES, correct?"

David looked at the woman and then back at Tom.

Tom saw his hesitation. "Relax, she's cleared. She's NSA."

David looked at her in surprise. She smiled cheerfully.

The air phone next to Tom rang. He answered, "Connolly here, go."

David turned to Brooke and whispered, "Okay, can *you* tell me what's going on?"

She said, "Sure can. First, I just want to say how sorry I am about how they took you. I had nothing to do with that. I just found out about all of this yesterday—"

Tom hung up the phone and got up, walking to the front of the plane. Brooke and David watched as he opened the door to the cockpit, spoke to the pilots, then walked back and sat down. The plane banked to the right and David felt his stomach flutter. Whatever Tom had said, it seemed like the pilots had made some course corrections.

David said, "Changing our destination?"

Tom said, "We didn't really have a destination prior to takeoff. The pilots had to file in flight. We're good now. We'll be in California in six hours."

Had they really just taken off without knowing where they were going? What kind of mess was David in?

David said, "Alright. I'm all ears."

Tom's voice was gruff. He said, "We lost someone. Actually, I just confirmed that on the phone a few minutes ago. He had been missing for about a week. But now it seems they've identified the body. An agent stationed in China. He was the one who sent us the warning a few weeks ago. Stumbled onto something big. Bigger than any of us imagined. Turns out all those rumors had some legs."

David let out a sigh. "I'm sorry about the agent. What rumors?"

Tom said, "Dave, how closely have you been following the news about China's economy?"

David said, "I mean, I've seen the news. It's tanking, right? Our stock market is getting hit pretty bad too."

"Right. Their stock market is in decline. But more important is that China's unemployment is starting to rise. And their median income is starting to drop. What you probably haven't seen on the news is that there have been several workers' strikes. And some protests. The government over there is putting the kibosh on that for now. They're good at censorship. But sooner or later, *60 Minutes* or CNN will pick it up."

"I'm still not following how this gets me on this airplane..."

Tom replied, "Because, David, we have reason to believe that China is planning to invade the United States."

\* \* \*

David now understood the urgency.

Tom continued. "There are leaders in their government that have set plans in motion. Our agent was there to investigate some inner circle that was supposed to deal with the 'economic problem.' We thought it was going to be more censorship, or maybe some sort of monetary policy that pisses off the Fed. Were we ever wrong."

David just sat there, numb and confused. A moment ago he had been worried about being summoned away on a work trip on no notice and then put on a jet going to God knew where. Now he was being told that World War III was going to start. He still didn't see how this involved him, but the magnitude of the situation gave him the patience to listen without asking.

"This inner circle of Chinese leaders came up with a solution, alright. Now here's what you need to know. Why you're here. There's a fire on the horizon. A few of my colleagues and I are trying to fight this fire. We're either going to prevent it or have to put it out when it reaches us. Either way, you're going to be part of a group that will contribute. I'm taking you to a place where you'll be able to help us prepare our defense. We were going to use someone else, but there was a conflict at the last minute. Plus, there is a good chance I'm being watched. We all had to jump through hoops to get on this plane unseen. No one could know that you would be going on this trip. No one can know that this trip exists. For these reasons, I had to bring you here tonight without notifying you ahead of time. To keep it secret. And *that* is about as simple as I can make it."

David stared back at Tom, guarding his emotions. He didn't know what to feel. Anger. Distrust. His sense of duty was making its way into his mix of feelings. A million things ran through his head, but one was at the top.

David said, "What about my family, Tom?"

"I'll make sure they know you're okay. You won't be communicating with them for a while."

"My wife is going to kill me. I didn't—"

"Alright, hold on. Now you listen to me, David. Listen very carefully. The reason you're here is more important than getting put in the doghouse by your wife. Get that through your head up front. This is top-level national security shit. I need you to understand that. I need you to put your country first, and to quit bitching about the way it had to start. I said I'm sorry. But honestly, I don't really give a shit about the inconvenience it caused. To be quite honest, I've got bigger things to worry about. The bottom line is, we needed you and we had to do it this way."

David fell silent as his face flushed. They sat, not speaking, for a moment. The only sound was the thrum of the engines. Brooke stared, interested in the drama but trying not to appear so.

Finally, David asked, "Where are we headed? California?"

Tom smiled in a way that made David uneasy. "At first. Yes. After that, I wish I could tell you, pal."

David studied Tom for a few seconds before saying, "How long will I be gone?"

"A couple weeks. Four at the most."

David rolled his eyes.

"Don't look so upset, buddy—like I said, I'll give your wife a call for you. I'll cover for you. You won't be able to call her yourself. I can tell you that after we land, you'll get on another jet with other members of your team. I won't be going. Got other fish to fry. *I* don't even know where *that* flight is headed. Due to the sensitive nature of this mission, we've kept a lot of info compartmentalized. But when you arrive, they'll give you a brief, which will help explain everything. Just know that this is a vital project that will immensely help our nation's security. And there is a specific need for someone with your background."

"What background is that?"

"You'll be perfect. Your knowledge of the Navy should even help. But mostly...your knowledge of ARES."

"What does this have to do with ARES?"

ARES was the code name for a cyberweapon that David had researched a little over two months ago. The NSA was enormously interested, and David had been sent out to evaluate and secure the technology for the US government.

"You'll find out when you get there. Plan to discuss it. You know it better than anyone besides those MIT kids who created it. From my understanding, many of the people who will be going will have different pieces of the puzzle. The group that has put this little shindig together knows enough to realize the danger, but we need to get you all in a room together to really make sense of it. And that can't be done easily; too many possible eavesdroppers to worry about. Hence the remote location."

David glanced out the window. He could see the setting sun painting the tops of the clouds orange on the western horizon. He sipped his coffee and tried to make sense of it all. He wasn't sure what to believe and couldn't think straight. He was still too worked up from what had just happened. He was worried about his wife and how she would react to his being gone for four weeks without any phone calls.

"You'll call my wife soon?"

Tom nodded. "Scout's honor."

"Tom, I gotta be honest with you—this is all a little too insane. Is there anything else you can tell me about what I'll be doing?"

Tom said, "I've seen some of the evidence. The threat is real. One CIA agent already sacrificed his life to get the word out. And lately, finding people we can trust has proven quite challenging."

David said, "What do you mean?"

Tom shifted his gaze between Brooke and David. "There are...*breaches*...in several key parts of our government."

"What?" said Brooke. Apparently David wasn't the only one learning new things. "What agencies are affected?"

"Sleeper agents have been activated in several organizations, I'm afraid. Hence the secrecy and unorthodox methodology we're using. Trust me, if we could do this in the D.C. area, we would."

"The NSA? Are there spies in the NSA?"

Tom said, "I'm sorry. I can't elaborate. Protocol—you understand. You'll get read in when you arrive at your location. Hell, even deciding on a secure location was tough. But here is what I *can* tell you. You guys are going to come up with plans that could help stop this war. There's a woman there running things. She's very high up in the intel world. She's excellent, and right at the heart of all of this. Give her whatever she asks for. You have full authority to talk about any of the things you've worked on in the past. That's why you were chosen."

David was processing, shaking his head. "Why would China go to war with the United States?"

Tom replied, "Can't say for sure. The Chinese didn't bother to tell me."

Brooke finally spoke up. "Why does any country go to war? National security, land, economics, religion, politics."

Tom said, "Times are a-changing in China. My personal opinion? Decisions to start a war always come down to what's in the best interests of the powerful few. The people in charge get scared that they'll lose their throne. So they act. Powerful people like the ones we've been looking into don't have the same inhibitions we little folk do. For them, every option is on the table. Even war."

"So what will I be doing when we get to wherever we're going?"

Tom said, "The Red Cell has been activated to help plan out scenarios—how they might attack us—so that we can be ready. That's really as much as I can tell you. Probably more than I should."

David nodded. "I see." He wasn't totally sure that he did. But he was starting to.

Tom asked, "Dave, can I count on you? I know this sounds cheesy, but your country needs you. I mean it."

He hated it when people called him Dave. "Yeah, Tom...of course. Sorry I was giving you a hard time."

Tom shrugged and looked at his watch. "I need to get some sleep. It's been a long few days. You hungry?"

Tom motioned the big guy that he could come back and sit down near them. Big Guy brought a cooler over and passed out submarine sandwiches and sodas. David took a turkey-and-ham sub and a diet cola. He took one bite of the sandwich and left the rest. He wasn't hungry. The bumpy plane didn't help. This still didn't feel right. But if all of this was true, then of course he was going to do everything he could to help his country.

*China.* More than a billion people. The only military in the world that compared to the United States. It was the doomsday scenario his instructors had talked about back at the Naval Academy. David had once heard that if it ever came to war with China, every response plan the United States had involved using tactical nuclear weapons. It was simple math. There were just too many Chinese.

If this was really happening, would the Navy call him back up? He had only been an active-duty officer for a few months. About as long as it had taken the medical staff at Navy flight school to figure out that his eyes had gone bad. However, once you're commissioned, you're commissioned for life, right? So was he going to be sitting on a boat a year from now, facing an onslaught of Chinese anti-ship missiles racing toward him? It was too incredible to seem real, and too distant to inspire the fear that seemed appropriate.

David still didn't like Tom, but if what he said was true, then this time in history could be pivotal. Like the days before Pearl Harbor. Or perhaps like the days before Germany invaded Poland. Much of the world was just going about its everyday routine, unaware of the massive conflict that was about to erupt. Over sixty million people had died in World War II. Could a war of that scale really be on the horizon?

David turned and looked at the other two men, both of whom

were now sleeping in their fully reclined seats. He wasn't sure that he could sleep himself.

Brooke came around and sat in the empty seat across from him. She smiled and raised her eyebrows like she wanted to talk.

She said, "How are you doing?"

"Well, I just got taken from my home and now I'm being flown God knows where on some sort of secret CIA plane to help save the country from World War Three. I'm good. How are you?"

"It's good to have a sense of humor about it."

"I suppose."

Brooke was a talker. She saw that David was receptive to conversation, and the floodgates opened. She said, "I just found out about twenty-four hours ago. My boss made me meet him off the grounds of Fort Meade. He introduced me to Tom and gave me the quick and dirty.

"I can't believe it either. I work in signals intelligence. To be completely honest, I spy on the Chinese for a living. Used to be on the Iran team. Now I'm on China. I work in cyberoperations. We hack into their computers. They hack into ours. It's like the Cold War all over again, but over the Internet. But just like the Cold War, there are rules. Over the past couple of weeks, though, I've noticed a few things that were very unusual. Some of the rules were being broken."

"What do you mean?"

"Well, like this CIA guy they killed. Tom didn't tell you what he was looking for. It was part of an op that I was working. Have you ever heard of the CCDI?"

"No."

"It's the Central Commission for Discipline Inspection. A Chinese organization that's supposed to root out corruption in their government. A few months ago, it got a new boss. A guy by the name of Jinshan. Cheng Jinshan. Heard of him?"

"Uh, no."

She laughed. "Sorry, of course you haven't. Sometimes I forget that everyone doesn't spend all day studying obscure Chinese businessmen and politicians. Well, this guy Jinshan is well connected. He's a very successful entrepreneur, but was also rumored to be tapped into the Chinese cyberwarfare units with some of his Internet companies. We knew he was working closely with the government agency that heads up their Internet censorship program."

David said, "How's he involved in all of this?"

"Turns out, he's more than tapped into the government's cyberwarfare. He practically *runs* China's cyberwarfare program. This guy has been interwoven into their operations from the beginning. Anyway, Jinshan is now put in charge of the CCDI, a position that's almost always given to a politician. But this time the Chinese president himself picks Jinshan, a businessman."

"This is for cyberwarfare?"

"No. Stay with me. Jinshan has his hands in everything. He owns a lot of companies. At least one of them does the majority of the real technically challenging work for China's offensive hacking programs. When you hear about cyberattacks on the news that originate in China? It's probably run by one of this guy's teams. But his newest job is in an organization that has nothing to do with cyber. That is the CCDI. The CCDI is *supposed* to get rid of crooked politicians. And trust me, China, like everywhere else, has plenty of them."

David said, "Supposed to. But that's not what Jinshan is doing?"

"We think the Chinese president has been using Jinshan and the CCDI to whittle away at the government's leadership and shape it the way he wants. It's Tyrant 101: clean house of all who could oppose you."

"So what did you guys do?"

"Well, naturally we at the NSA started paying much closer

attention to him. I was looking into Jinshan's secured files and computers—"

"Is that legal?"

She looked annoyed. "Are you a lawyer?"

"No."

"Good. Well, neither am I, so let's not worry about legality, shall we? Anyway, it turns out he really is a much bigger fish than we thought. Like I said, he had his hands in everything. He rubs elbows with their highest-ranking military brass and has played golf with several members of their Politburo. Some people think he might even be responsible for getting the current Chinese president into office. So we started an operation to monitor him more closely. The CIA agent who was killed was our man on the ground. But I had no idea what he'd uncovered until yesterday, when Tom read me in."

David said, "So what does Jinshan have to do with a Chinese attack on the US?"

"I don't know exactly. I just know that our ground asset had started getting close to people in the CCDI. He began to realize that the whole point of that organization, which is supposed to be about stopping corruption, was now to fill key government leadership roles with people who were handpicked by Jinshan.

"I told you that before Jinshan got tapped for the CCDI leadership role, we didn't have too much on him. Well, that isn't true for the people he was picking to fill different political leadership roles. They're stacking the deck with politicians who are or have been closely aligned to the military and intelligence services. It's like they're militarizing all government posts over there.

"The CIA agent was supposed to get into some secure hard drive that would give us more info on their strategy and endgame. That's where he must have gotten the info Tom shared earlier. Someone must have been onto him, though..."

"How is this not making world news?"

"Think about what else Jinshan controls—the information. The Chinese media is owned by the government. What he doesn't want made public doesn't get made public. And honestly, nothing worthy of the big global news agencies has happened yet. But if you connect the dots, there are major shifts in leadership taking place."

"Who else at the NSA knows about what Tom told us?"

"About the attack plans? Not many that I know of. My boss was working with Tom and some others in the CIA. But at the NSA, it was just my boss and me. We compartmentalize information like crazy. Thank goodness we do. If there really are sleepers in the NSA, we wouldn't want this to get out. We wouldn't want them to know that we know. With any luck, we might still be able to get out ahead of this thing."

Brooke and David talked for another hour. She was a local Maryland girl, had gone to UMBC and excelled in mathematics and computer science. She had interned at the NSA while in college and worked there for the past fifteen years.

Eventually, David politely hinted that he needed a nap. He got the impression that she would talk the entire flight if he let her. But they ended their conversation, and David found himself alone, looking out the oval window into the vast evening sky.

David kept thinking about his family. He was worried about the short term and how his wife would cope with being alone with the kids for so long. And he was worried about the long term—about how their lives might change if America really was thrust into a war of this scale. David's family would be affected more than most.

When your father was an admiral, it was expected that each child would serve, go to sea, and give up the comforts of civilian life. The other two siblings were certainly fulfilling this obligation. His sister, Victoria, was a rising-star helicopter pilot living in Jacksonville, Florida. Their brother, Chase, had been a SEAL. Now he did overseas security work for the State Department...at least, that's what David had thought. What had Tom meant by saying he works for *us*? David was the only one who hadn't turned military service into a career.

Aside from the occasional holiday, David hadn't seen much of his father or siblings over the past decade. Being in the military after 9/11 meant a lifestyle of long and frequent deployments. As the commander of the Navy's newest carrier strike group, this was likely Admiral Manning's last time at sea.

David realized that the last time he had seen the three of them was at his mother's funeral. She'd died a little over a year ago now. It was a cruel irony that a woman who had loved others so deeply would die of heart failure at the young age of sixty-one. David had thought about her every day since then, and it had taken over a month for those thoughts to stop drawing tears.

Now his father and the three siblings were scattered around the world, each one serving their country in his or her own way. Was a coming global war really about to envelop David's family? A few hours ago, that thought would have seemed preposterous.

It was all just too hard to believe. What was the saying? The simplest explanation was usually correct. The problem in this situation was that there didn't appear to be any simple explanations.

Talking to Brooke had helped. After the first five minutes of speaking to her, David had instantly liked and trusted her. She was smart. If he had learned anything from his days at the Naval Academy, it was to follow smart people. It almost never failed. Almost.

David saw a pen and paper on the table and decided to write his wife a note. He wrote down what he thought he would be allowed to say. Mostly he just wanted to let her know that he was okay. Then he leaned back into the cold plastic of the window and shut his eyes. Sleep was not quick to come. The window pressed up against his forehead, and his mind began to drift to thoughts of what a war with China would really be like, and what kind of world his daughters might grow up in.

David awoke to a firm shake of his shoulder. It was the big guy in tactical gear.

"We're here. Time to go."

He looked up, dazed and still sleepy. "Okay. Where is here?"

"Let's go," replied Big Guy.

The plane was shut down. David hadn't intended on sleeping, but eventually the fatigue had gotten to him. He had slept through the landing. He started walking down the cabin of the plane, feeling guilty that he wasn't immediately going to call his wife, when he remembered the note. He grabbed it off the table, got up and walked out the open door of the plane.

An empty twilight sky cast grey and purple hues over a silent runway. There was an identical aircraft parked next to the one David had just arrived on. Other than that, the airport was deserted. The faint runway lights were the only man-made illumination.

Tom walked around the nose of the plane and handed David a large black duffel bag. "Here. It's clothes and toiletries. Not your own, but they should fit. You'll get your phone and wallet back when you return. Sorry about the inconvenience."

David realized that there were voices coming from the other plane. He ducked under the fuselage to see people getting on the other jet.

"Who are they?" David asked.

"A few of the other consultants. That's what we're calling you guys. Consultants. You'll meet them on the plane," said Tom.

"We've got to go. Like I said, I'll tell your wife you're okay, and don't worry about work. It'll be there when you get back."

He grinned, but the wrinkles stopped at his eyes. David didn't have a good feeling about this.

David handed him the note and said, "Here. Please deliver this to my wife."

Tom looked down at the paper. He nodded and said, "Of course. Sure thing."

"Mr. Manning?" called a voice. David looked over and saw a guy in a silly-looking airline uniform, his cap half-cocked to the side.

"That's me."

"Right this way, sir."

Tom waved and said, "Good luck. Remember, this may be one of the most important things you ever do. So do your best and don't screw it up."

David frowned at that. *Hell of a pep talk.* He walked over to the other plane, still unsure whether this was the best decision. David took a deep breath and walked up the ladder and into the aircraft.

* * *

A few minutes later, Tom and his assistant stood on the flight line and watched as David's jet disappeared to the west. Tom closed his eyes and took a long drag from his cigarette. *No turning back now.*

The man in tactical gear said, "Are you really going to call his wife?"

Tom glared at him without answering. Then he said, "Come on. Let's get in the plane. We've got work to do." He flicked the smoldering cigarette onto the tarmac and headed up the stairs of the jet.

# 2

*Our historic dominance...is diminishing...China is going to rise, we all know that. [But] how are they behaving? That is really the question.*
    —Admiral Samuel J. Locklear III, US Navy, Commander of the US Pacific Command, January 2014

The plane ride was long and uncomfortable. David's face was covered with day-old stubble, and his eyes were slightly bloodshot from the lack of sleep. He also needed a shower. Badly. While the seats on the jet had the same luxury cushions as the first aircraft, there is nothing in the world that can make a nine-hour plane ride comfortable.

As soon as they had gotten in the aircraft, a male "flight attendant," who David was pretty sure held no formal position with an airline, had given them each twenty-page briefs to read. He'd also provided them food and drinks. Other than that, the man didn't speak for the duration of the trip.

David rather liked the two other passengers he met on the plane. Each of them was going to participate in the same capacity as David. Brooke and he found that they were the best informed of the group. All the other two knew was that their Red Cell had been activated due to national security.

Bill Stanley was a defense contractor who lived in Nevada. He had retired from the Air Force more than a decade ago and had a wife and two grown boys. He worked on drones and "a few jets that you wouldn't believe existed if I told you." David learned that Bill commuted to work every day on a US Air Force Boeing 767. He would drive to Las Vegas's McCarran International Airport, then fly to what was once known as Area 51. They joked about UFOs and aliens, then realized that nothing was very funny now that World War III might be on the horizon. Bill spent most of his time working on the long-range satellite communications to and from high-tech US military aircraft and drones.

Henry Glickstein was a self-proclaimed "maker" and telecommunications guru who had worked for several of the big tech companies. The entire time they spoke, he never stopped smiling or walking around the plane's cabin inspecting every element. He had designed data farms and overseen the layout of fiber-optic networks for a living and gave David the impression that he was a workaholic; an engineer who couldn't stop trying to solve whatever problem lay in front of him. He was a jokester, but a competent and driven one. It was like his mind was moving so fast that he had to throw in a few one-liners every so often so he didn't get bored.

All of them, including David, had been on one of the government's highly classified Red Cell rosters, paid an annual retainer in case their expertise was needed. Normally Red Cells were planned months in advance, and attendees given plenty of warning. Not this time.

The others were astonished to hear David's story of being approached at his home and given no notice prior. Their own invitations had not been quite so abrupt. As had occurred with Brooke, a single person in their chain of command had contacted the two men just twenty-four hours earlier. Those in their chain of command had been spoken to by the CIA's Red Cell organizers. A legitimate cover—a business trip—had been formulated, and off they went. They had been told not to discuss it with anyone, and to pack for several weeks.

They each felt a sense of duty to participate in what was deemed a crucial project. The two men hadn't known about the connection to a possible Chinese invasion until David and Brooke told them. They were floored. Most of the plane ride was spent talking about different scenarios for why China would do something like this.

The more David thought about it, the more he realized how hard it was going to be for Americans to believe something like this could really happen. Americans were comfortable. Human beings were reactive, not proactive, when they were comfortable. It was hard to get people to prepare for a hurricane if they hadn't been hit in recent years. And that's exactly what this was: an approaching storm of monumental proportions. A world war hadn't happened in David's lifetime. Would people prepare for the storm? Or would they watch the news reports from their couches in disbelief, waiting for a resolution?

The briefs the flight attendant handed out gave them little new information. They were to be consultants to the US government in a Red Cell. According to the document, Red Cells were used by the CIA to "think outside the box about a full range of relevant analytic issues." *Whatever that meant.* Each consultant was to provide the team with insights and critical knowledge from their individual area of expertise. When the group finished reading, they had more questions than answers. The second half of the flight was once again used for sleeping.

Unlike the first plane, the shades on this plane's windows were sealed shut. Security protocol, the flight attendant had told them. It wasn't until they landed and opened the doors that they saw natural light again. It was late afternoon at their destination. David wondered how many time zones they had passed through. The door to the jet opened and revealed bright blue skies and an inrush of thick, tropical air.

The group's tired eyes were wide as they looked around at their landing spot. There was ocean everywhere. It reminded David of one of those old World War II island air bases built in the middle of the Pacific. It was tiny, as islands went—or air bases, for that matter. They could only see about half of the island before it curved around into the sea. The runway looked like it barely fit, surrounded by black sandy beaches and turquoise waters on three sides. On the other side of the runway was a set of four concrete structures that were separated from tropical rainforest by a tall barbed-wire fence. The dense green vegetation rose higher and higher up along a towering jungle-covered mountain.

Today was arrival day for several groups of consultants. Another jet taxied back out to the runway. It looked identical to the aircraft they had come in on. David watched that jet's group of passengers carrying their bags up the sandy path to the buildings. The flight attendant directed his group to do the same.

David and his new companions grabbed their things and followed suit. When they reached the buildings, they were shown to their quarters by an Air Force major in his summer blues.

"Name?" he asked as David approached.

"David Manning."

"Manning. Yup. Room 214. Up the stairs. Here's your key. Throw your stuff in your room. Please meet at the Classroom in one hour. It's the big building up on the hill with the large glass windows that overlook the runway."

"Got it. Thanks." David wanted to ask the major a million questions, but the others were checking in, so he decided to wait. It sounded like they were to get an in-brief in another hour.

An hour later, David sat admiring the swaying palms and clear blue sea through the panoramic windows of the large amphitheater-style classroom. He had showered and shaved using items from the duffel bag Tom had provided. It felt good, but he was still exhausted from the trip.

He thought about his wife and daughters. Lindsay was probably in tears. God, he hoped she would forgive him for this. If this was all really happening, he didn't see how he had a choice. David wondered why he kept thinking like that. As if this might not be real. Was it the magnitude of a war with China? Or was it something else that caused him to feel uncomfortable?

The setting sun created a painting of bright oranges and deep purples over the water. However, none of them knew exactly *which* body of water it was. David thought it had to be the South Pacific based on the time of flight and climate. But if that was true, why take them here, so far away?

The room was filled with curious men and women from a variety of places. Some wore power suits. Some had crew cuts and wore military fatigues. Still others had on skinny jeans with fitted tees. David gathered from several informal introductions that their backgrounds were as diverse as their looks suggested. There were computer programmers and scientists, engineers and psychologists, military officers and policy analysts. All were well educated and incredibly bright. David counted twenty of them in all. Like Henry and Bill, each had been told that their purpose there had something to do with a very important national security project. But that was all they had been told before flying to the island. It seemed that Tom was the one recruiter who had spilled the beans. David's friends from his plane had already started to spread the word that this was about China, creating quite a bit of excitement.

David overheard a conversation between two men who were sitting nearby.

"You think we're near Diego Garcia? No way, man. We're right next to Guam."

"What makes you say that?"

"Time of flight. Plus I heard we have a CIA black site on one of the islands near Guam. This has got to be it."

"Well why bring us all the way out here?"

"You think they care about us? This location has to do with them. They probably bring in their Asia experts here from China, Japan, and Korea. Just a short flight for the station chiefs and operations officers. Convenient to their location."

The chatter hushed as a tall and very attractive Asian woman walked to the center of the classroom's lowered stage. She wore black slacks and a sleeveless silk shirt. She looked out at the members of the audience and they looked back at her, silenced.

She said, "Ladies and gentlemen, welcome to the Red Cell. There are two reasons that you are here. First, to piece together what we collectively know about a planned Chinese attack on the United States."

The statement drew a mix of shock and disbelief. A few shouted questions, but the woman held out her hands for silence.

She continued, "I know this is hard for most of you to believe. But I assure you it is real. I ask that you hold all of your questions until the end. I believe I will cover a lot of them right now, and we will be providing a lot of amplifying details into the night. But I say again, we have reason to believe that China is planning to attack the United States in some type of large-scale military operation within the next twelve to eighteen months."

Shouts erupted from the room and, again, the woman held out her palms until people quieted down. David found her calm and confidence remarkable. "We'll answer all questions in due time. The second reason you're all here is to actually *develop plans for China to attack the United States*. I know this sounds ludicrous at first, but hear me out. That's the main objective of a Red Cell.

Because we don't know exactly what the enemy *will* do, we want to be prepared for what they *could* do. Over the next few weeks, you will have no communication with the outside world. You will work from early in the morning until late at night. And it will be crucially important work."

She walked off the stage as she spoke. She stepped up the tiered levels of the classroom, careful to make eye contact with everyone in the room.

"We want you to collaborate and innovate. Do what you do best—find solutions to challenging problems. Each of you has been chosen because you are one of the top minds in your field. This is a highly selective program. You each have been hand-picked for a certain relevant skill set. You should be proud of the service that you will perform for your country, although it will not be something that you can ever put on a resume."

David watched as she marched back down the stairs and stood on the lower stage. She had perfect posture, tanned skin, and great muscle tone. She was very tall. He figured she must be five foot eleven. And she spoke with a captivating charisma that made it hard to take his eyes off her.

"Many of you had top-secret clearances with our government or the military prior to arriving. Those of you who did not have been rushed an interim clearance. Normally that can take a year or more. But this was an exceptional case...and we've done our homework. Everyone has been quickly but fully vetted. When I'm done here, you will all file into the next room to sign some admin papers, including a nondisclosure agreement. Nothing that goes on here will ever be made public. These sessions are classified at the highest level."

She stood completely still. Every pause seemed to signify the importance of what she was saying.

"Secrecy is not our only priority. We want the work here to be of the very best quality. It must be. You have authority from the highest levels of our government to share any and all knowledge gained from your prior work experience in order to ensure that we take every possible consideration into account on this project. You will all be free to discuss anything with each other, regardless of classification level, to achieve our ultimate goal of protecting the United States."

David noticed some of the people sitting in the seats around the classroom raise their heads a little higher. They were proud to have been chosen for something that was deemed so important. A few squirmed at the idea of sharing classified information in an unfamiliar setting.

"My name," the woman said, "is Lena Chou. I'm normally one of the CIA's clandestine operations officers. Here on this island, however, I represent a joint task force that includes, among others, the NSA, CIA, FBI, Homeland Security, all branches of the military, and several other agencies...even DARPA. That's right, the geeks that invented the Internet."

Lena gave a bright smile that lit up the room. There were nervous chuckles in the audience.

"I will be the supervisor of this Red Cell for the next three weeks. I've done this twice before. In past Red Cells, we've used people like you from very creative and diverse fields to help build mock attack scenarios. We've even used authors of techno thrillers to help us create fictional terrorist attack plots. While we don't have any authors here this time, we are trying something new. Natesh Chaudry is the CEO of a consulting firm located in Silicon Valley. Natesh, would you like to say anything?"

A young man who couldn't have been past his late twenties stood up from his seat in the back row. He wore stylish jeans and a collared Lacoste shirt.

He said, "Hello, guys, I'm Natesh. I'm glad to meet all of you. I just arrived here today like you. Also like you, I didn't know where I was going or what exactly this was about. Lena gave me a little bit of a preview about thirty minutes ago. Needless to say, I'm still in shock. Probably like a lot of you. But I'm glad that I'm getting the opportunity to contribute to something so important."

David thought this young man looked like he was out of his league. He seemed nervous. David didn't blame him. Still, he spoke with an easygoing tone that made him instantly trustworthy.

Natesh continued, "Like Lena said, my team and I work in California with a variety of companies. We help some of the top firms in the world increase their level of innovation in new products and services. Normally I bring members of my team with me. Due to the sensitive nature of this project, it's just me here this time.

"To put it simply, I'm an idea guy. I've built my company by helping other companies create winning ideas. I've been brought in to act as a moderator during the sessions. I plan to break us up into teams for much of the time, and I'll float between stations. Sometimes, if the conversation goes to one of my areas of expertise, I'll offer insights.

"Honestly, while I don't have much expertise in the invasion department"—Natesh was half-laughing in disbelief as he said that—"I'm a strategist at my core. I think you'll find that I can help connect some of your insights in ways that will make our overarching ideas more powerful."

The classroom smiled with a tense politeness. David could tell from their expressions that people were just beginning to wrap their minds around what was going on.

Natesh said, "Please use your area of expertise where it's helpful, but be flexible and open to new ideas. Try not to say 'that won't work' too much. Use the people around you to find out new ways that it *can* work. Think about the links from one activity to another. Try to help figure out all the possible connections and solutions. I'll help out with this more as we go. Thanks, and I look forward to working with you all."

Lena said, "Thank you, Natesh. Today, we'll go over what we, as representatives of our country, know to be true right now. Our big-picture goal for week one is to identify potential vulnerabilities. The goal of week two is to plan out how to best take action to capitalize on those vulnerabilities."

A deep voice from the back of the room spoke up. "Are we going to be planning the actual defenses too?"

Lena looked up and cocked her head. She spoke with the effortless rhythm of someone who had done a thousand public speaking events. "Could you please state your name and your background?"

The man cleared his throat. "Sure. Sorry. My name is Bill Stanley. I'm a defense contractor. I work on satellite connections to drones and reconnaissance aircraft. And I'm retired Air Force."

Lena said, "Excellent. Mr. Stanley, welcome to the island and thank you for your service. To answer your question, we want you to help build out a potential Chinese attack plan with your knowledge of what the expected American response would look like. We want you to plan around that as if you are really trying to win the war for the Chinese. Some of you have actually worked on counterterrorism plans. Some of you have worked on plans to counter 'what-if' scenarios...like if North Korea invaded the South or if China invaded Taiwan. But, ladies and gentlemen, this is going to be different."

She clicked a remote control in her hand and a large flat-screen monitor in the front of the room went from a black screen to a map of the Pacific Rim.

"The short answer to Mr. Stanley's question is no. We are not here to plan our nation's defense. Some of you might have good ideas about this and could even be considered experts...but that isn't why you're here. We want you to play the bad guy. If we brought you into this project to plan the defense also, you'd be thinking of problems at the same time you would be thinking of solutions, and you wouldn't be as good at creating attack plans. At least, that's what our psychologists have told us." She gave a nod to the grey-haired man in the second row, who nodded back. Apparently, he was a psychologist.

She clicked on the remote and the screen changed to a black map of the United States with a bunch of different-sized blue dots scattered throughout.

"Anyone know what this is?" she asked.

"Those look like where our bases are," Bill responded.

"That's right." She clicked on the button again and images of ships, tanks, soldiers, and aircraft popped up next to each of the bases, with numbers next to them. "And what's this?"

"That's our order of battle," someone said from the back.

"Correct," Lena said. "Does everyone know what that means?"

There were a lot of heads shaking no. "An order of battle is essentially how many of each type of weapon or fighting asset we have. Let's look at a few statistics."

She clicked again and a grid popped up.

Ships
    US: 473
    China: 520

Tanks
    US: 8,325
    China: 9,150

Aircraft

US: 13,680
China: 2,788


"What are your takeaways here?" Lena asked.

David watched from the back of the class. He remained quiet, never one to like speaking up in a classroom setting.

A young man in jeans sitting in the front row said, "It looks to me like we'd kick China's butt in a fight because our air superiority would probably blow everything else up before China could do any damage."

Lena said, "Okay. Now let's look at a different set of numbers."


Military Personnel
    US: 2.3 Million
    China: 4.5 Million


Personnel Fit for Military Service
    US: 120 Million
    China: 618 Million


Labor Force Strength
    US: 155 Million
    China: 798 Million


"Thoughts?" Lena asked.

Someone whistled. David knew it was a mismatch. Everyone knew how big China was. But if it really came to a land war...those numbers were a bit scary.

Natesh said, "That's a lot of manpower. And a lot of production capability when compared to the US."

One of the uniformed military officers said, "Okay, Lena, this is great. But it's not like China can drive right over and attack us rifleman against rifleman. That's just not the way warfare works anymore. The militaries would clash in the air and across the Pacific before it ever came to that. And I know for a fact that we have a pretty serious technological advantage over most of the Chinese platforms."

"So if China was to attack us, do you think that our military would be able to hold them off?"

The man shifted in his seat and said, "I mean...I would guess... yeah. I think so, probably."

Lena said, "Okay. We as a group are going to get very smart very quickly on some of the data that might help us answer this question. Many of you're asking yourselves right now, can China beat us? But we don't want you to think of it like that. We want you to think of it like this. How can China beat us? Assume that they can. Uncover the path they must take. Only then can we really prepare our defense. It's thinking like this that has kept us safe from another 9/11 for so many years. Now, you each will get familiar with China's capabilities and use your collective expertise to identify America's weaknesses. There will be a different set of experts who will create the defensive response plan based on our learnings. That will be weeks after we're finished, and most of you will not be involved. For us, these next few weeks are about figuring out the most effective strategies and tactics that China could use to make war on the US. Does that make sense?"

"Yes, ma'am," said the military officer.

Lena continued, "After September eleventh, we created a Red Cell designed to prevent another major terrorist attack. Typically, the opposing force in a military exercise is red and the allied force is blue. A cell, for those of you who are unfamiliar, is the unit where plans are made. Hence, the Red Cell is used to create the enemy's plans. After September eleventh, we used this organization to help us think outside the box and hypothesize what our enemies might do. At that time, it was terrorist attacks that we were focused on. It helped us tremendously in identifying what defensive mechanisms needed to be strengthened, and what targets had no adequate defense in place."

She stood looking at the group. The audience was captivated.

"Each of you was carefully selected for having a great combination of experience in fields that will likely be very important to these plans. But you've also been selected for another very important reason. You can be trusted. Or more accurately, most of you have bosses that can be trusted. Each of you was handpicked by the person who sent you here. This group has not been compromised. We put this operation together as a way to prepare now while another op is underway to root out Chinese spies that have infiltrated us. More on that momentarily. The consultants in this Red Cell need to figure out what we think we could be up against. What plans are already in motion? Some of you know bits and pieces that will inform this. What do we think the Chinese could do? The rest will be hypothesis. What should their targets be and how would they attack them? Each of us knows something that will likely prove crucial. It's up to us to work efficiently so that we're well prepared for what's to come."

As David listened to Lena speak, his doubts began to recede. It was all starting to make sense. Didn't In-Q-Tel constantly worry about the Chinese hacking their systems? There were cyberattacks going on back and forth between the East and West every day. It was a modern cold war. She was an excellent speaker. The more he listened to her, the more a war with China seemed realistic. Either that or Lena was a remarkable liar.

Lena said, "We'll begin sharing out tonight after dinner. We want to know what *you* all think the biggest weaknesses in our defense are. When you look at 9/11 and at Pearl Harbor, our nation was not prepared. We did not see it coming because we had been conditioned not to look in the right places. Attacks like those are what we're here to prevent. We're here to think of all the different ways a foreign power might try to do serious harm to our nation. Some of you have extensive knowledge of things like nuclear power plants and the electrical grid. Some of you understand very different things, like how the US populace might respond to propaganda or psychological operations."

The classroom collectively raised their eyebrows at that one.

"Oh yes...that's right. We won't just be looking at a onetime kinetic attack. This isn't a hit-and-run that we're planning for. We'll also be looking at ways that China might be able to invade us and successfully occupy our nation. That will be week three. What would they do? How would they go about it? Shock and awe? Win hearts and minds? We will conduct psychological operations planning. We don't want the defense team that looks at our work to just build a big moat with nothing behind it. You must think of what China should do to control the castle once inside the walls. Only then will our defense planners be able to cover our castle grounds with *spikes*."

There was commotion in the room.

"Many of you doubt our reasons for concern. You may believe that China could be planning an attack. But you're saying to yourself, *everyone* knows that the US is the mightiest country in the world, with the greatest military in the world. I ask you to please hold those assumptions in check while we're here. We have a duty to our country to suspend disbelief and to think of new and different ways that China could overcome our advantages. We must identify all of our nation's vulnerabilities and commit ourselves to this mindset of offensive planning against the United States. This is how we will truly help our defensive planners—by giving them an effective blueprint for a Chinese invasion."

There were nods of understanding in the audience. In David's office life, most meetings involved tables of people with laptops open and cell phones out. He was struck by the level of undivided attention that Lena commanded when she spoke. Granted, there were no computers or phones in anyone's possession. But it was more than that. Between her charisma and confidence, she controlled the eyes of everyone in the room. Aside from her speech, the only sound was the thrum of the air conditioning coming through the floor vents.

She said, "This threat requires urgent action and new ideas. We can't use the same lessons learned in the sessions that were held a decade ago, when we were trying to protect against another September eleventh, because we're no longer trying to protect against terrorists, but against the country with the largest economy and military on the planet."

The room became quiet. David could sense that reality was setting in for the others in the classroom.

"A few weeks ago, we lost contact with one of our assets in Shanghai. Before that happened, he sent me a message that revealed two important things. The most important was what we've already discussed. China is planning to attack the United States. Very few in the Chinese leadership are aware of this plan. They're dedicated to keeping it secret. But rest assured, the decision makers that matter are very aware. The second big item that our Chinese asset revealed is the reason you all are here, instead of a team from the Pentagon doing this *in* the Pentagon. We as a country have been infiltrated by the Chinese intelligence community. Badly. And they've been actively deepening this penetration. The Chinese have spies feeding them information from inside just about every key government organization. Sleepers have been activated. New operatives have been inserted. They're making moves to get ready for a war."

David heard rumbles from around the room.

"There's a bit of a cat-and-mouse game going on right now. There's just a small team assigned to this project. We're keeping this operation quiet, even from our own agencies, while we figure out whom we can trust. At the same time, we know that we have to plan our defense. While we know that the Chinese are planning the attack and we know some of their objectives, we don't know exactly *how* they intend to do it. We know a little, but not nearly enough. That's where you come in. This isn't just a regular consulting project. We want you to be ruthless and calculating as you think of what they might do. We'll provide you with what we've uncovered as their probable objectives. But before our man was killed...and, yes, he was killed..."

A few people gasped. Most stared at Lena in shock. She spoke with an unemotional detachment. They were hanging on every word.

"...we were unable to get any of their detailed plans. We've begun a very thorough mole hunt in the government and military right now. We need to use the next few months to root out every Chinese spy that has infiltrated us. Only then can we share this information with the people who will need to know. What we don't want to do is tip our hand and bring on war without preparation. We're afraid that if we start disseminating this information and some of their spies find out, the Chinese might move up their timetable before we can prepare. Also, in that scenario, they would then be attacking with their spies in place. That *can't* happen."

She looked around the room.

"I know this is shocking. I know it may seem unbelievable if you're just now hearing it. But I assure you it is very real. Our world may soon change drastically. We may be in a war like our generation has never known. So I ask that you each do your part to the best of your ability. Work hard. Make the best decisions you can. Help to prepare our country for the worst. Good luck. Now, let's get to work."

The group sat stunned. Slowly, people started to stand up and move down the aisles and towards the back door of the room, where the administrative papers waited. The Air Force major was there, helping everyone get their paperwork done. The crowd resumed speculation on what the future had in store with a renewed fervor.

David found himself waiting in line to sign his nondisclosure agreement and collect a security badge. That struck him as a bit silly. If this island really was in the middle of nowhere, wouldn't Lena and whoever else was running this show already know exactly who was here? The badges seemed more for show than anything. *But show for whom?*

"Thank you for participating today, Mr. Manning."

David hadn't seen Lena walk up behind him. Closer up, she was even more attractive. Her dark brown eyes stared intently into his.

"Of course. I'm glad to help."

"I'm very interested to hear more about ARES. We'll look forward to a full briefing from you later. I'm fascinated to hear about its capabilities. And to know more about these men that have created the program."

David was surprised she knew about it. But if that was why Tom had sent him, it made sense that she would.

He said, "ARES. Yeah. Well, I don't know if you would even call them men. The three of them were in their early twenties. Boys, I'd say."

She shook her head. "Remarkable. But I guess many of our strongest tech companies were started by exuberant youths. It takes a fiery intellect to really change the world. Like young Natesh there."

She nodded toward Natesh, who was out of earshot across the room.

David said, "It sounds like we'll need that brain power to help us, in light of the plot you've uncovered. Hopefully we can harness that power for the good guys."

Lena said, "David, that's why we brought you all here, to harness that intellectual power. And I promise you we'll do exactly that."

She nodded a farewell, turned, and walked out the door.

David watched her go and heard an uneasy voice in his head begin to whisper. It was the same voice he'd heard when Tom had been speaking to him on the plane. Lena and Tom had both said all the right things. But the whisper was still there. The whisper was what his father used to call it when David was a boy. His father's sage advice never failed to keep David out of trouble: *When the whisper tells you not to follow the pack, hear the whisper like a scream.*

## 3

---

*The supreme art of war is to subdue the enemy without fighting.*
—Sun Tzu

Natesh sat on his bed, his moist palms pressed against white cotton bedsheets. He was always the most nervous on the first day. That was when all those intelligent and accomplished eyes began to judge him. In the first thirty minutes, Natesh found, the vast majority of his spectators made their decision as to the worth of his service. So like any good salesman, he had to nail it during that initial moment of truth. And he did it, time after time.

That was how he had made his millions. Not through his intellectual prowess. Smart people were a dime a dozen. Natesh made his millions by selling himself. He delivered both a high-quality exhibition and intellectual output for his clients. But he had to give them a convincing show for their money.

He always got nervous, but today's nervousness went beyond anything he had felt before. He needed to keep calm. Just stick to the script. He must forget that the final product here wasn't a product at all, but bloodshed. He tried to console himself with the fact that if he did his job well, there would be less of it.

Natesh had his routine. The stories changed depending on the exact project, but the basic formula stayed constant. Introductions came first. Then he would tell a story to both captivate and serve as inspiration for a strategy. For this project, Natesh decided that he would tell his story about a professional pickpocket from New York City. That one usually went over well. Natesh would follow that up with comparisons between the competitors. Normally his competitors were two major conglomerates. Today, they were two superpowers. From there, Natesh would get to the meat of the conversation. He would go over project objectives and begin brainstorming about ways to create competitive advantage. MBAs usually ate it up. He wasn't so sure about this audience.

It was highly likely that the activities they created in this particular project would involve killing on a mass scale. It would be unlike anything Natesh had worked on before. He hoped that his gift for analysis and strategic thinking would transcend the line between corporate battle and actual battle. Certainly the man who had picked him for this assignment thought so.

But oftentimes, with the gift of genius comes the curse of thinking deeply. Life's harsh realities were magnified by this lens. Natesh thought about how people on the Manhattan Project had felt, knowing that they were designing death. There was the utilitarian justification that was used by so many after the bombs were dropped on Japan. A far larger number would supposedly have been lost in a hostile invasion of the Japanese mainland. Was this war planning analogous to that? They were designing a most efficient plan for war. Natesh hoped that the greatest good would rise from the smoke.

Three sharp knocks sounded on his door.

He opened it to find Lena staring at him.

Natesh's parents were both Indian. While he would never admit as much in an American society dominated by political correctness, he preferred women that were from a similar ethnic background to his own. Lena, however, was captivatingly beautiful. Her looks seriously called into question any previous preference Natesh had. Her dark brown eyes had a fire that showed intelligence, confidence, and—what was it? There was some other quality there. Passion? No. Ruthless commitment. She looked like she had never failed at anything in her life, and like she had expected as much. With full lips and a well-proportioned, athletic body, she looked like she could have been a model for one of those women's fitness magazines. Natesh wondered if it was her looks that made his blood pressure rise when she was around. No, it was her ruthlessness.

"Good morning, Lena. We have another twenty minutes before—"

"Let's talk in my office. Please follow me."

She turned and walked down the barracks hallway. Natesh grabbed his key and presentation notes off his nightstand and hustled to catch up. He was glad that he had gotten ready early. They walked out of the barracks and down a hundred-foot stretch of gravel that brought them to the smallest building on the island base. Everyone assumed that this was a base, although Lena was likely the only one who knew for sure. An arc of tropical trees shaded the path.

Natesh's feet crunched through the stones and seashells as he walked. The morning sun cast a beautiful light over the beaches beyond the runway. He wanted to stop and admire the monstrous green mountain at the heart of the island, but Lena trudged onward at a quick pace. A trickle of sweat slid down his forehead as he hobbled after her.

They reached the concrete structure with satellite dishes and a group of antennae on top. Razor wire lined the roof. Metal bars caged in each of the narrow windows, making it look like a small-town jail. Lena's fingers danced over the digital keypad as she typed in the code to the single steel door. Natesh heard a faint beep and then a click as the door unlatched.

As they entered, Lena said, "This is the Communications building. You'll be spending some time in here over the next few weeks." She sealed the door behind them.

Inside was a small room with two computer monitors and two swivel chairs. Rays of bright yellowish morning light came in from the high-up rectangular windows, illuminating one wall. She motioned for him to sit, and he took a seat in one of the chairs. She remained standing.

Lena stared at him, her eyes filled with that ever-present intensity. He had seen that look from many a successful entrepreneur in Silicon Valley. Athletes called it the eye of the tiger. Natesh thought this metaphor fit. Lena was every bit the predator.

Her voice was flat. "So...are you all set?"

Natesh could feel the sweat between the tips of his fingers and his palms. "Yes. All set." He tried to sound calm.

She saw through the lie. "You're worried?"

Natesh said, "It's just a lot to process, that's all."

"Yes." She nodded.

"I'm fine. I've done this sort of thing many times. I'll be fine."

Disapproval flickered in her eyes, then calm. Her voice was soft as she said, "Natesh. We've watched you for some time now. You're quite capable. I know that you've never done anything like *this* before. But to be frank, no one has. Stick to your routine. Get in a rhythm, and be the conduit for others to provide the information."

He nodded. "Sure. Sure. As you say. I will be good. Thanks."

"I'm here to help."

She motioned around toward the computer monitors. "Major Combs and you will be the only ones with access to this room, besides me, of course. Take this paper. On it is your code that will open the outer door to this building. Memorize it. You won't be able to take it with you. You'll be able to go on these computers and get information from the outside world. These computers are on a censored and monitored network. You won't be able to access the whole Internet. If there are any sites that you need or information that you aren't able to get, the email system only goes to one person. He is my colleague who will be able to do external research for you. In order to make things simple and secure, we're going to have you and the major serve as the information-gathering middlemen. If there is external data that the consultants need to access as you're making your plans, you two will come here to get it. Understood?"

Natesh nodded. "Yes." He looked around the room. The computers were bulkier than what he was used to. Military grade, he imagined. There was another steel door at the far side of the room. It had a keypad next to it, just like the one on the outside of the building.

Natesh asked, "Does my code work on that door?"

"No," replied Lena.

"What's back there?"

"My living quarters."

"You think you'll need a digital lock on your living quarters?"

She said, "We had better head to class."

They rose and walked outside, Lena shutting the door as they left. Once again they walked next to each other on the gravel path. This time they headed to the second largest of the buildings, the Classroom.

The Classroom sat atop a small hill that overlooked the runway on one side. A pristine beach of dark sand lay just outside its walls on the other. Breaking waves intermingled with the sounds of island gulls hovering overhead.

It was almost 8 a.m. Natesh just had to get through this presentation. Then he would have the momentum to get through this first day. Then he would get through the first week. And then...

well, there was a lot of change ahead. Natesh tried not to think of how important his part might be.

As if she could hear his thoughts, Lena said, "Just breathe. We briefed them yesterday on the big picture. They understand what's at stake here. Remember that. Everyone here wants to help defend the United States. You're a talented man. And you're performing a great service." She put her hand on the muscle between his neck and shoulder, giving it a gentle squeeze. "I know you're absorbing a lot right now. We all are. But you need to relax, Natesh. All of this will work out."

They stood outside the double glass doors of the Classroom building.

"Thanks," he replied. There was nothing like a few choice words from an attractive woman to prop up the ego of a doubting man. What was more, Lena seemed to have a gift for handling people.

Moments later, Natesh stood on the auditorium stage, studying the faces in his audience. His nerves calmed as he shifted into business mode. About half of the seats were filled. The other Red Cell participants were funneling in. Most people sipped steaming coffee from Styrofoam cups.

The loud drone of aircraft engines caused most people to look out the expansive windows. A large multiengine propeller plane rolled down the runway. Every other day, that plane was supposed to be bringing in supplies from who knew where. Lena and the Major had told them about it last night during their indoctrination. This was the first drop-off.

They had been told about all of the buildings on the island. They were told where to go to get food and to wash their clothes. There was very little infrastructure. Only a handful of Asian maids and cooks lived in back of the cafeteria. None spoke English, not that it mattered. The major had warned against speaking with them. They were cleared to work here, but no conversations were to go on within earshot of any of them.

There were strict security rules to follow. Lena had explained the rules clearly. Don't go outside the boundaries of the base fence. It circled the runway and the buildings, but split the island in half, with nothing but mountainous jungle on the other side. Don't communicate off the island. Natesh wasn't sure how anyone could have pulled that off anyway. It wasn't like they had a satellite phone. Lena told them that if anyone had any problems, medical or otherwise, they were to see her as soon as possible. No one had raised any concerns.

Natesh watched the runway scene through the window as men in protective eyewear and helmets jumped down from a retractable ramp on the rear of the aircraft. The men rolled off crates near one of the taxiways and then immediately hopped back on board. Within minutes, the plane had taken off. As soon as it had, the Asian stewards that cooked their food and made up their rooms each day scurried out to the crates and brought them back to the cafeteria building. What was this place?

Everyone was seated. Natesh walked over and stood up in front of the podium. He looked at his watch. 8:01 a.m.

"Good morning. I hope you all have been able to sleep better than I have."

He got a few tired smiles in reply.

"Well...at least we all know why we're here. Let's do the best we possibly can at this. The better job we do of planning out possible Chinese attack strategies and tactics, the better our nation will be able to prepare."

"Amen," someone said in the back. There were several nods of approval at that. Most of the group had progressed from the frantic denials and arguments of last night into a patriotic eagerness to contribute.

"So..." He looked at everyone in the room and saw Lena in the back, standing by the window. She gave him an encouraging smile and a polite nod, as if to prod him along.

Natesh cleared his throat. He said, "Let's look at the facts. We started to examine some of the numbers yesterday. On everyone's desk is an official report that compares China and the US. It's a threat assessment conducted jointly by the CIA and the Pentagon last year that essentially does what we're going to do today. It's a SWOT analysis. For those of you that aren't familiar, SWOT stands for Strengths, Weaknesses, Opportunities, and Threats. But what took the CIA and the Pentagon over six months to conclude, I can sum up in two sentences. One: China is really big. And two: the United States has a military technology advantage. Let me ask you all a question. If you all have ten men and I have just one...but my one has a gun whereas your ten men have swords...how would you attack me?"

"I'd rush you," said a young man in the front row.

"Alright. So, rushing the man with a gun, that would be an example of a tactic we could use. We, if we were the Chinese, could gather as many troops as possible and start ramping up production of military assets. We could start massing troops on US beachheads and overcome the American military with overwhelming force. But I can tell you from my experience in business strategy that this may not be the best tactic to use if it's not accompanied by other strong initiatives. Our strategy must also take into account our long-term goals. Our strategy will help us to identify the best tactical options. We can then make a series of tactical choices with our end goal in mind."

Natesh looked out at his audience. Several of the military men had looks of skepticism on their faces. They saw a young Indian man trying to teach them about military strategy. That was fine with Natesh. Let them think what they wanted. He clenched his jaw a few times and focused on Lena, standing in the back of the room. She gave him a thumbs-up. She really was a nice coach.

Natesh's voice grew stronger. "What can China do better than the United States? And when you think about this, I want you all to keep thinking about the stated objectives that our spy uncovered. We went over them last night. Objective One: Capture and Permanently Occupy the United States. What are the implications of this? How does that limit China's tactical choices?"

Brooke said, "If China wants long-term control over US territory, then they would likely want to do minimal damage. You don't want to dent up a car before you steal it. That means they'd use non-nuclear tactics to preserve infrastructure."

David raised his hand. "If they want to be in the US long-term, that also means that they have to plan to win hearts and minds. Kind of like what we tried to do in Iraq."

Natesh pointed at them both. "Exactly. Now you're thinking about this the right way. What advantages does China have that they could leverage?"

People started to shout out ideas. The energy of a high-participation classroom took hold. In a strange way, people were into this. He let the group conversation keep going for a while. He wanted everyone to get comfortable contributing and talking openly. There was a good discussion of several different ways China could capitalize on their size and resources.

After about twenty minutes, Natesh looked at his watch and said, "Okay. We're doing great. Let's recap. We talked about Chinese advantages: size, first-mover advantage, surprise, industrial capacity, and quantity of certain assets. We discussed how the US is more technologically advanced with most weapons. I heard someone mention that this could be an interesting route to explore as an opportunity for China instead of a weakness. In the business world, this is a valuable way to unlock competitive advantage. If we really can turn a perceived strength into a weakness, that should be a major part of our focus. Let's flag that one and come back to it. Okay, so pulling these first few ideas all together: Firstly, how does China execute a surprise attack that allows them to maximize first-mover advantage, take out America's technological advantage, and leverage the numerical advantage of their troops? Secondly, how does China keep hold of the United States territory long-term without destroying needed infrastructure or creating a resistance movement? Does everyone agree that these were a few of our initial killer questions?"

People gave cordial yet uneasy nods. It was hard to feel patriotic about planning your nation's invasion.

"Okay, let's take a five-minute break."

The group got up and scattered to bathrooms and stocked refrigerators. Natesh uncapped a plastic water bottle and took a swig as he went back to the podium. Bill and David were there waiting for him.

David said, "Hey, nice job so far."

"Thank you, David. I appreciate the participation."

Bill said, "Yep, I think this group should do a fine job at this. I just wish I'd known it was going to take this long."

"Oh? You got somewhere to be?" David said.

Bill looked uncomfortable, like he hadn't meant to share. "Well. The truth is, Allison's been sick."

David looked at Natesh and then back to Bill. "Oh. Hey, I'm sorry to hear that."

Bill said, "Ah, it's alright. It's been going on for a few years now, on and off. I agreed with my boss that I would go on this trip just a few days ago, before we knew her results. But just a few hours before I left, we found out. I told her I would cancel the trip, but she said the chemo wouldn't start until I got back."

Natesh looked down at the floor. He was still in his twenties. He'd never known anyone with cancer. But he knew what it was like to lose a family member. "Bill, I'm so sorry. Please let me know if there's anything I can do."

Bill looked up as if he'd snapped out of a spell. "Oh, ah, thanks there, Natesh. Naw, you don't worry about it. Sorry to bring it up. It's just been on my mind. Let's just get back to work and get this done right." David and Bill walked up the stairs of the stadium-seating classroom as Natesh rechecked his notes.

After everyone sat back down, he began, "I wasn't always a California guy. I went to high school in the Big Apple. I remember one field trip we took when I was seventeen. We went to see this professional pickpocket, if you can believe it. This guy had learned the trade from his family but he didn't want to be a criminal himself. So he decided to teach seminars and do shows about being a pickpocket. He would call people up on stage and say, 'Hi, my name is so and so, and in less than three minutes, I'm going to take your wallet.' And the thing is...he would do just that. It was unbelievable to see. And the audience members who were up there on the stage would have no idea it had happened until after the fact."

Natesh was getting comfortable now. He walked down from the stage and up the stairs, the way Lena had yesterday when they had all arrived. There she was, still in the back of the class. She wasn't looking at him now. Natesh saw her watching people and then writing notes in her book.

"This fellow was a professional pickpocket. But not the kind that made a living taking people's money. This was a man who had learned how to do all of those things on the street, but now lived an honest life by performing for audiences and showing people how it was done. He was incredible. I saw him take a man's wallet, then his cell phone, and even his wristwatch without him knowing it. But that wasn't all. He actually took the man's eyeglasses off his face. The man's *eyeglasses*. I know it's hard to believe, and I wouldn't believe it if I hadn't seen it myself."

Natesh gave a wide grin. "It was incredible. My friends, I've worked on strategy for a number of years. I realize that I'm younger than the majority of you here. But in studying our situation for the past day and comparing it to various past scenarios in the private sector, I think this may be one of the potential routes we can take. We need to identify how we can take America's glasses right off its face."

Bill said, "You want the Chinese to become pickpockets?"

Still smiling, Natesh responded, "Precisely that. You see, the pickpocket told us all how he was able to do what he did. He told us how much practice it had taken him to perfect the sleight-of-hand moves to take the various articles from people without them realizing it. But that was less than half the trick. It all has to do with cognitive science. Our brains can only process so much information at once. So if they get too much information all at the same time, they're forced to prioritize. Through the power of suggestion, the pickpocket directs their attention to various other things. The mind must prioritize information. The pickpocket simply helps suggest a priority order that's advantageous to his agenda. If he wants to take your wallet, he calls attention to your wristwatch. While you're looking at your wristwatch on your left hand, he'll talk to you, pat you on the shoulder with one hand, and take your wallet with the other. He moves in close so there is less time to react. Before you know it, there are just too many activities happening at once to process them all efficiently."

David said, "So you think China should launch a bunch of distractions?"

Natesh said, "Again, we're here to plan the attack. I think that the people we have in this room can help us to identify and plan enough high-priority decoy events that the United States won't see the eyeglasses taken off their face."

Brooke raised her hand and said, "Natesh, I appreciate a good story. But having worked in signals intelligence collections, we do a pretty good job of monitoring China. How do you propose that—"

"I'm not saying that you don't, Brooke. But I think we need to come up with ideas for how to create a distraction that would effectively require the majority of the United States' time and resources to be dedicated to it. Better yet, let's think of a few distractions. Tie them together. But don't tie them to China. So when the United States has its eye on its wallet and cell phone, the glasses become overlooked."

"And how do you do that?" asked Brooke.

"Start a separate war. Make the US go to war with another country so they're spread thin and absorbed in it," said David. "That's what I'd do."

Henry said, "Okay, what country can we pick a fight with that would cause us to mobilize the most military assets? How about Canada? I hate those guys and their polite manners."

"Iran? North Korea? Russia?" said Brooke. Others chimed in with their own opinions. The group chatted about it and remained reasonable in their arguments for each nation.

"It's gotta be Iran," said Major Combs. "If the US went to war with Russia or North Korea, we'd be in a better location to fight back against China. I wouldn't want that if I was them."

"That's true. You'd want the United States to be distracted and also in a bad position to respond," said someone from the front of the room.

"So how do we start a war with Iran? One that doesn't get the US pissed off at China for starting it?" asked David.

Natesh said, "Okay. Here's the way we'll do this. You all have plastic buckets with sticky notes and markers near your desks. If you don't, share with the people next to you. Write down a few ways that you think we could plausibly start an Iranian-US war. Again, we are China for this exercise. How can China encourage the start of a US-Iranian war without implicating themselves? Think about your own areas of expertise and use that if it applies. Everyone write it down on your piece of paper. Write down a few ideas if you have them. Then bring them up to these whiteboards behind me and stick them there. Brooke, would you mind helping me? We'll bucket these ideas into categories once they're all up here. Okay, you've all got ten minutes."

Soon the whiteboards at the front of the classroom were filled. Brooke wrote down different categories with her dry erase marker and stuck the notes in straight columns under each one. Natesh thought to himself how familiar this scene felt. It was the same exercise he had done a million times for corporate America. In the past, Natesh had filled whiteboards with things like consumer insights, software advantages, hardware designs attributes, and countless other service- or product-oriented lists. He looked at the rainbows of sticky notes on the board and thought to himself how innocent it looked. And how within a year, one of these ideas might very well come to fruition and begin soaking the world in blood.

The session lasted all day. During lunchtime, the group ate sandwiches at their desks and went over Chinese military capabilities and strategy. The afternoon was a share session. Various members of the team provided amplifying information from their respective fields. Brooke disclosed what she knew about the operation in Shanghai. An expert on Asian Pacific politics and military gave his opinion on the Chinese military buildup over the past decade. Henry said that several of the telecom companies he worked with had reportedly been hacked in the past few months. Word on the street was that the Chinese were testing their security.

By 5 p.m., the constant talking had exhausted Natesh. The lead idea was becoming clear. The best Chinese attack would be to overcome America's strengths by somehow negating their technological advantages. But the group still bickered back and forth on how that could be done.

Bill was red-faced. He said, "Look, you've still got five thousand reasons why the Chinese couldn't attack us. And each one of them has a nuclear tip. Uncle Sam's got submarines ready to fire off their missiles at a moment's notice, and they can't possibly have all of those boomers located. There are US Air Force bombers and missile silos that are still playing the same Cold War game: deterrence. It doesn't matter that China doesn't want to launch nukes on us. If they try to attack us on land, *we* will launch nukes on them and obliterate their attacking force. Even our current liberal-ass president would use a nuclear weapon if someone were attacking his house. Excuse my politics."

A few people grinned. Most ignored the jab.

"He's right," said Brooke. "Not only that, but American communications and navigation technology is best-in-class. We have more technologically advanced ships, aircraft, and weapons that can do real damage at long range."

"It's called hyperwar," said one of the military officers. "Speed is the key factor. We can talk about China head-faking with a war in Iran till we're blue in the face, but the fact of the matter is, if America really wanted to, we could mobilize a global attack that would destroy a majority of Chinese military assets within twenty-four hours."

Natesh rubbed his eyes. "But I thought we had discussed this. These technologies rely on a few key activities to take place, correct? So if those activities are removed, there goes the advantage. This—"

Another of the military officers in the front row said, "Natesh, look...military strategy isn't like in the business world. We aren't talking about apps on your smartphone. We're talking about complex, interwoven technologies like the navigation systems in an F-18 and the GPS smart bombs it carries. We have technologies like the secure data link that connects all of our armed forces so that they can combine each other's sensor data and look at one enhanced battle picture. There isn't one silver bullet that could take out all these technological advantages and eliminate the nuclear threat. I appreciate that we're all here trying to prevent a war. China's nothing to scoff at, certainly. But we've been talking about different ways to do it all day, and I just don't see how this threat can go beyond just that—a threat."

There were nods of agreement in the audience as others backed up the idea of American superiority. Brooke said, "There's just no way for China to overcome the technology advantage and nuclear response of the United States."

Lena hadn't said a word all day. She stood tall in the back of the room. The light from the windows contrasted against her silhouette. But now her voice was firm.

"Actually, there *is*…"

**4**

_Tricks, traps, ambushes and other efforts resulting in the surprise of one party by another have been commonplace in Chinese warfare from as far back as we have records._

    —Military historian David A. Graff

The class sat in stunned silence, waiting for Lena to finish.

"What do you mean?" asked Bill.

Lena said, "The Chinese have a way to wipe out America's satellites. It's a new and very powerful cyberweapon, developed in America. We don't know how or when they got it, but our latest intelligence confirms that they are in possession and testing it out."

The blood drained from David's face as he realized why he had been chosen to come to this island. "They have ARES?" he asked, knowing the answer.

"Yes," replied Lena.

Brooke asked, "What's ARES?"

David said, "It's a cyberweapon, like she said. The place I work...we keep an eye out for different types of information technology that might be useful to our intelligence agencies. About a year ago, some students at MIT created a type of worm that could bypass all known security in several key communications channels. It was designed to work on data farms and the vast majority of military and communications satellites. When coupled with other programs that the Defense Department already had, the applications became devastatingly potent. It could potentially take satellites offline, hijack their signals, or even crash them into the earth's atmosphere. In data-server farms, which much of the cloud-based world is now reliant upon, the theory is that it could cut power long enough for the servers to overheat and become seriously damaged. The MIT students used a lot of the same code that the NSA's STUXNET used to sabotage Iranian nuclear centrifuges a few years ago. But this worm was several orders of magnitude more advanced than that. What these kids came up with was unreal."

"And the Chinese have this?" said Henry.

Lena nodded. "We believe so."

"Awesome. Glad my taxes are being put to good use." Henry looked up at the ceiling, thinking. "So, let's say there are between fifteen hundred and two thousand active satellites right now. Most are communications satellites. About a third are military satellites. Those numbers include foreign ones. There are another two to three thousand inactive satellites just floating in orbit. I would think that the most efficient means of F-ing us over would be to program all of the active ones to crash."

The classroom was quiet.

Bill said, "Can they really do that?"

Brooke said, "Well, it wouldn't be easy. There are a lot of protections. But ultimately it comes down to two things—do you have the hacking capability, and do you have the hardware capability? Russia and China would likely be the only nations that could do something like that. And they'd only be able to do it for a short period of time as far as I know. I'm probably not supposed to admit this, but China actually took control of two of our satellites back in 2008—a Landsat 7 and a Terra AM-1. They had control for twelve minutes. People got fired. But it's hard to do. It takes an incredible amount of energy to power the dish on the ground. Probably around five to ten million watts."

Someone asked, "How much is that?"

Henry said, "About the output for a really big TV antenna, or a small African nation. It's a lot of power, and that's just for one satellite. But we aren't talking brute force here. This ARES, if I understand correctly, wouldn't just help them grab a satellite with a high-powered dish on the ground. Am I right?"

David nodded. "Yes. You are. It's a game changer because the worm gets past the security systems and takes it over with a cyber-attack. You no longer need brute strength to hack into a satellite. They effectively steal our username and password and then replace it so we can't regain control. And they aren't just limited to one satellite at a time. They can scattershot multiple vehicles. If they developed the hardware that the US Air Force and NSA have, they could theoretically take over all of our satellites in under twelve hours."

Henry said, "Sweet. So just to be clear, total worst scenario imaginable. That's all you need to say. Total worst scenario imaginable. Awesome."

"There goes the US military's communications and navigation advantage."

"Christ..." said the military officer in the front row. "But wouldn't people find out? I mean, who monitors this stuff?"

Brooke said, "Of course we'd find out. There are lots of agencies that monitor it. NORAD. The NSA. Langley. The National Reconnaissance Office in Chantilly, Virginia. The point is, we wouldn't be able to do anything about it."

Natesh said, "But China would probably wait until the right time to do this. What do you military guys call it? When you make sure you hit the enemy with everything you have at the same time?"

Major Combs said, "Simultaneous time on top."

David began to feel dizzy as he saw where all of this was leading.

Natesh asked, "What would the damage be? What would it look like if China took out all our satellites?"

Henry said, "It would put a strain on us at first, but the underwater and land-based fiber-optic cables handle the vast majority of our data transfers. You might notice it on some international phone calls. Obviously satellite TV and satellite phones would be down. Eventually, though, it would get worse..."

"What about the loss of GPS? What would that do?" Natesh asked.

Bill said, "That would hurt a lot. There is just such a dependence on GPS today. Between that and the loss of weather satellites over the oceans, I wouldn't be surprised to see global air traffic grind to a halt on day one. Ships and aircraft would have to navigate the old-fashioned way, and that means slower and burning more fuel. Say goodbye to drones, too. The US Air Force minted more drone pilots this year than regular pilots. If they were to take out satellites, we wouldn't be able to use drones nearly as well. Probably not at all over long range."

Brooke said, "I think that would have a much bigger impact on the military's ability to fight war than most people realize. Almost all of our weapons and weapons-delivery platforms rely on GPS navigation to precisely track and hit their targets. If you took out the entire global satellite network, that would be a huge technological equalizer."

Henry said, "I get the military thing. But there is a bigger-picture impact here. All those GPS satellites help us synchronize our global clocks. Timing between everything from traffic lights to water treatment to railroad schedules would start getting clogged up. Web searches would be affected and the Internet could drastically slow down. Think about the financial markets. All those hypertraders moving shares in the blink of an eye? Now people around the world aren't on the same clock anymore. The information isn't getting spread around evenly. In this day and age, that's a *huge* deal. Now, how many of you are on your mobile phones all day long? If they hit the data farms, those phones are going to be much less useful. If the Chinese can really do this, that weapon is designed to start the apocalypse. If someone crashed all our satellites and cloud storage, there would be a complete network collapse. There would be a huge stock market crash, followed by a huge food shortage, followed by rampant riots in the street and a total breakdown in society. I swear to God, I'm not exaggerating here. How many of you have kids? What would you do for the last loaf of bread if your kid was starving and you didn't think there was another bread truck coming? Take this weapon seriously. And consider stocking up on bread, water, and *Seinfeld* DVDs."

Bill said, "But hold on here. First, that still doesn't solve the nuclear deterrence factor."

David said, "Actually...to be honest, especially if they disrupted communications enough, I just don't think we would go through with it."

"Go through with what?"

David said, "A nuclear counterattack."

"Even if they cripple our nation?"

"Well...yes, even then. Because a nuclear reaction wouldn't be proportional."

Bill said, "Well, what about a good old-fashioned conventional military response? I mean, bullets don't need satellites, right?"

David said, "Think about it this way—if they shut down all our satellites like that, our government decision makers would be deaf, dumb, and blind. If they started a military attack, and let's say they jammed long-range radio communication...I'm not saying that we wouldn't respond with a counterattack against China if we had a clear picture of what was going on, but it takes a very long time for the US government to gather enough political support to attack a foreign country when we *do* have clear evidence. If all of a sudden, we just didn't have any communications with our armed forces—if no one had electricity or phone lines—do you see our politicians having the confidence in the information they were getting to launch a World War Three–style military retaliation on China? I mean, until twenty-four hours ago, *I* would have told you that you were crazy to suggest any of this. I would have said, 'Hell no, China won't attack us.' Think of all the trade they'd be giving up. It would be economic suicide. No one would believe it. Our technology has enabled hyperwar. But the decision-making process hasn't gotten any faster. And this isn't 1983. Our leaders haven't been conditioned to expect a global nuclear war the way they were back in the eighties. If an attack happened then, we all knew who it was. The Soviets. The Evil Empire. But China isn't really seen as an enemy today. Their cyberwar against us is mostly covert. Their military buildup is second-page news. People get cheap iPhones and low prices at Walmart, and trade with China is at an all-time high. I just don't see a quick response—nuclear or conventional—as realistic if the picture isn't clear. And that's what this weapon does very well—it clouds the picture."

No one said anything for a moment. People absorbed David's thoughts. Some were no doubt struggling with the question of whether nuclear deterrence was good or bad.

Brooke cleared her throat and said, "Well, this conversation turned out to be scary. But I still have a question about the premise of this war plan. Let's suppose that our politicians have neither the information nor the balls to launch a quick response back at an attacking superpower. I will try not to insert my hatred of all liberal politics here. Now, I'm more disturbed by the threat of a cyberattack on our satellites than anyone. I mean, I rely on cyberoperations every day to do my job in Fort Meade. But I fail to see why we still have reason to believe that this is a real threat. Why is a cyberattack on these satellites a game changer? Can one of you Air Force guys please help me out here? Aren't there already missiles that can shoot down satellites? And there are other ways to disrupt data centers, right? Why is this ARES such a big deal? What is new about this weapon compared to what they could have already done?"

David said, "Well, they can now control more satellites in a shorter time."

Brooke shook her head and said, "No. That's not enough of a leap for me. My point is, they could have done the same things through different means. Maybe it would be slower, but... what am I missing here?"

Most of the classroom looked at Lena, but she didn't say anything back. Instead, the answer came from Henry.

He said to Lena, "Ohhhh. I see what's going on here."

Everyone stared, waiting for him to continue.

Henry said, "The worm has already been uploaded, hasn't it? There is some sort of countdown in place."

Eyes shot back to Lena. She nodded.

David then said, "That was it, wasn't it? That's how you knew they're really going to attack. That's what this new intelligence was that your dead agent uncovered."

"Part of it. Yes," she said.

Some of them put it together and some didn't. Someone whistled. A few swore. Up until now, David had still had his doubts. He hadn't truly believed that China was going to attack the United States. Sure, there may have been intelligence that indicated they were thinking about it. But in his heart, David had believed that somehow this was all going to go away. Cooler heads would prevail. The Red Cell would just become some crazy what-if scenario planning session. David had harbored these thoughts since Tom had first told him about the project. But the evidence was now falling into place. The reasons for secrecy. The signs of war. Suddenly this all became very real.

He gazed outside, thinking about the implications of a war of this scale. He could see tropical thunderheads on the horizon, each with a white mist streaming down to the distant ocean. Storms approaching. Fitting.

Someone said, "What's the countdown matter for?"

David sighed and said, "It means that they're going to follow through. The satellite-killer is a first-strike weapon. And the countdown means they've already pulled the trigger. It's true that they probably have missiles that could do this. They've had them for years, actually. But if there is a countdown, then that means that they have a plan in motion. And everything that we're doing here matters a whole lot more."

"Well, when does the countdown stop?" Henry asked.

Everyone in the room locked their eyes on Lena. She looked as if she wasn't sure whether she should answer.

Finally, she said, "To be honest, we don't know."

One of the people a row down from David asked, "How do they know there is a countdown but not know when the program will activate?"

For a second, David thought he saw Bill look uneasy, like he wanted to say something important. But then Brooke said, "With worms, you can program them to have infinite countdowns. So this program can count down, look for a signal from an outside source, and then reset or execute depending on what inputs it receives. Imagine that this worm is an alarm clock that looks for a signal each day at seven a.m. If it receives the signal it's looking for, it will start beeping. If not, it will reset for another period of time. That's probably what is going on here. It happens a lot in cyberwarfare. We can detect when something is active, but not know exactly when it will execute."

David thought he saw Lena glance at Bill. Then she said, "Brooke is exactly correct. In this case, the countdown keeps resetting after not receiving an activation signal. That's my understanding. So we know it's there, waiting to be activated, but we don't know when it will occur. Given the periodicity of the resets, our best estimate is in twelve to eighteen months."

* * *

David woke up to the green-glowing beep of his watch alarm. He had collapsed on his bed at 5:30 p.m., intending just to shut his eyes for thirty minutes. But the fatigue of his jet lag and the all-day sessions had drained him. While just about everyone else had filed into the cafeteria as soon as the afternoon team meetings ended, David took a nap. It was now 7:15 p.m. and David would have to hightail it to make it to dinner before the cafeteria closed.

He threw on a tee shirt, khaki shorts, and a pair of Reebok sneakers and then rushed over to the cafeteria. He walked into the meal hall to the clatter of metal dishware being cleaned in the back. Bill was the lone diner. David walked through the buffet line, scooping heaping piles of mashed potatoes, green beans, and what looked like pot roast onto his plate. He grabbed a few bottles of water and a banana and walked over to the table where the other man sat.

"Mind if I join you?" David asked.

"Sure, sure." Bill was in midchew. He took a gulp from his cup and said, "Helluva day, huh?"

Bill ran his hand through his thick fluorescent-white hair. He was dressed in a collared shirt that was tucked into a pair of light blue jeans. Black sneakers completed the outfit. David thought that he looked like he could have been a grandpa.

"Where are you from again, Bill?" David asked.

"West Texas. But I've lived in Nevada for the past few years. And honestly, before that I was Air Force, so I've lived all over. Yourself?"

"Virginia. Right outside D.C. I'm a Navy brat myself."

"I've been there. Nice area. Lousy traffic."

David nodded as he finished a bite of the overcooked roast. "Yup."

A few moments passed. Small talk didn't seem to be either man's forte.

Finally Bill spoke. "This all just makes you reevaluate your life, you know?"

David spoke through chews. "Yeah. The end of the world will do that."

"I'm not saying I regret anything. My wife always says to our kids that regrets ain't worth fussing over. Because there's better things ahead than behind."

"Sounds like a smart lady. Wonder how she ended up with you?"

"Hah. Yeah." Bill looked sad at her mention.

David said, "I hope my family is alright. My dad, sister, and brother are all active-duty Navy. I would imagine their jobs just got a lot more dangerous."

Bill raised his eyebrows and took a drink. "I'm sure they'll be okay. With any luck, we'll come out of this all right. I remember the Bay of Pigs when I was a little kid. It seemed like the world was about to end then, too. We used to practice getting under our desks at school in case the Russians nuked us. Imagine that. And that all blew over. Hopefully this will too." While his words were meant to comfort, he didn't sound like he believed them.

"My mother passed a year ago. Heart failure." David didn't know why he said it. It just came out.

"I'm so sorry," said Bill.

"Thanks. It hit us pretty hard. So after my mother died, my father, sister, and brother were all home together for a short while. It was the first time I'd seen Chase in two years. Crazy. He was always deploying with the SEALs."

"He was a SEAL? Impressive."

"Oh yes. Everyone's always impressed with Chase. So he came home, took a month off from his work, and we got to hang out a bunch. Now, I've never been the athlete that my brother and sister were. But the day after Chase flew in for the funeral, he asked me to go on a run with him. He goes on these super-long runs. We drove down to D.C. and ran around the Theodore Roosevelt Island and finished on the Washington & Old Dominion Trail. Very scenic. Very long run. I hadn't run more than two miles since I graduated Annapolis. My mother used to love taking long walks around that area. She always said that her kids got her athletic genes. Heart disease. Unbelievable. It's a cruel, ironic world if you ask me. Anyway, my brother insists that I go with him on this run. We go for five miles along the trail and I swear that something changed inside me. It was therapeutic. It sounds funny, but that run was like a way to say goodbye to my mother. Maybe she was with us? Well, I've been running almost every day since. I actually did my first triathlon two months ago and I'm training for another. I got a taste of a runner's high that day and I keep going back for more."

"That's sounds like a healthy hobby. What's the problem?"

"You talked about all this China stuff making you reevaluate your life. My mom's death did it for me. Part of my conclusion was that I needed to reconnect with my family more. I missed my brother and sister. I've been doing pretty well keeping up with them through email more. I've even flown down to Jacksonville to hang out with my sister. My dad is almost impossible to get time with. He might as well be the president the way the Navy treats him. Still, with all this talk of war, I'm just worried. I don't want to lose any of them…" David's voice trailed off.

Bill put his hand on his shoulder and looked him in the eye. "David, better things are coming. I'll pray for it. You mark it down, and I'll pray for it."

The entrance door opened and Natesh walked in. He waved at the two men and received polite acknowledgments in return. A moment later he plopped down like a sandbag across the table.

"You look pretty beat, young man," said Bill.

Natesh raised his eyebrows and said, "My friend…you cannot imagine. I'm exhausted. This project is quite intense." He drank his plastic cup of ice water until the cubes slid down to his mouth. He bit an ice cube and began crunching it in his teeth.

Bill asked, "What did you all think of the last part of the meeting today?"

Natesh said, "You mean Lena's revelation? It was compelling. What did you think?"

David said, "I was pretty shocked. I work on classified technology for a living. I've seen a lot of real cutting-edge stuff. If they have ARES, that's bad news."

"It sure is," Bill agreed. "There's that silver bullet we were talking about all day."

David nodded. "Imagine our ships, our troops in combat, and our aircraft without any navigation or smart weapons. A great deal of our communication—arguably the most important parts—would be wiped out. We'd be back to Vietnam-era technology. And the thing is, our military is pretty reliant on the tech we have. I mean, when was the last time you wrote a letter? Has your cursive handwriting gotten any worse since you were in grade school? No need to practice with email, right? The same will go for war fighting. No need to practice using a compass all the time if you have GPS. And if the other guys are practicing, advantage them."

Natesh said, "Or worse, if the Chinese retain their technology. I believe they just launched their own GPS system. I'm sure it would be quite possible to crash our satellites and leave theirs intact."

David looked at each of them. That little voice in his head was talking to him again. Something just didn't sit right about all this. Natesh and Bill both seemed like good trustworthy men. He wanted to ask them if they believed everything they'd heard over the past twenty-four hours. Instead, he just kept silent.

Natesh said, "Lena and the major will be taking us through some more of the Chinese military capabilities and limitations this evening. We should probably leave in another few minutes."

"Sure thing. Don't want to be late for the CIA lady," said David.

Bill said, "So...Lena said we could go to her if we had any issues, right?"

Natesh said, "Yes, that's what she said. She said she can get us anything that we need while we're here."

Bill's voice sounded pained, like he was trying to figure out what to do. "That's my issue. Look, I just don't know if I can afford to be here."

David was pretty sure that he was referring to his wife's illness.

Natesh said, "I'm...I'm not really sure what to say. I know this is probably obvious the way you're feeling. But, I assume you're worried about your wife?"

Bill let out a deep sigh. "Yep. I realize this is important. But I got a lot of important things on my plate right about now. Before the world goes to hell, I'd rather spend that time with my wife. No offense to you fine gentlemen."

David ate the last bite of his green beans and wiped his mouth with a napkin. He thought about the position Bill was in and where they were in the world. The guy needed to get off this island.

Natesh said, "Why don't you go talk to Lena tonight after our end-of-day meeting is over? Let her know what you're thinking so she can hear you out. She seems like a reasonable woman. I wouldn't be surprised if she let you just fly back home. Perhaps you can just sign a paper. We're volunteers, right?"

David thought about his own abrupt "activation" less than forty-eight hours ago and wondered if they were volunteers or not. If Bill's wife was dying, he had to get home.

David said, "I agree. Go talk to her."

A flash of lightning out the cafeteria window caught their attention. A few moments later, they heard the distant rumble of thunder fill the sky.

Bill said, "Maybe I will. Maybe she can help me out. Yeah, you're probably right." He smiled.

It was after 11 p.m. when Lena and Bill walked back from the Classroom to the Communications building. The group meeting educating everyone on Chinese military and defense capabilities went for almost three hours. When the meeting ended, people were happy to get back to the barracks. Raindrops began to fall as the outskirts of a thundercloud grazed the island.

Bill had approached Lena immediately after the night meeting in the classroom. She was very understanding and suggested they go sit down and discuss it further. Bill had a good feeling. Women were just better that way. They understood the importance of family. Maybe that was because they bore children. Bill remembered one of his macho-man, hard-ass commanding officers back in the Air Force who had denied his leave chit during Desert Shield. That had forced Bill to miss the birth of his second child. That guy was a jerk. But Lena seemed much more understanding.

They reached the Comms building, and Lena went to type her code into the digital keypad next to the door. She looked over at

Bill and then typed with her body positioned so that he couldn't see. The keypad beeped and there was a click as the door unlocked. She opened it and they went into a room that reminded Bill of an airport control tower. He could hear the rain start coming down in sheets just as they entered. Bill wiped away the rainwater from his hair as he looked over the room. There were several TV screens, all of them off. Three black swivel chairs were placed in front of computer monitors. There was a second door on the far wall that looked like it connected to the rest of the structure. It too had a digital keypad.

Lena motioned for Bill to sit. He took one of the swivel chairs and looked around the room. He wondered where she slept. Must have been behind that door. The computers looked new. When had they built this place? The technology to open and close these doors was pretty sophisticated. Bill saw Lena sit down across from him and cross her legs. She looked relaxed. She really was a nice woman.

Bill told her what was on his mind. He told her about his wife's cancer and her history of it. They had a few neighbors that could look after her, but it wasn't the physical stuff that he was worried about. Bill poured his heart out before he even knew that he had. All this talk of war and strategy and China had distracted him plenty good, but the thoughts of his wife came tumbling back and they were wrapped in emotion. He hoped the display would be enough.

Lena listened. She was an intense woman, Bill noticed. The kind that leaned forward in her chair at all times. Like she had to be ready to pounce. It was awful funny seeing a woman sit like that. Reminded him of a fighter pilot or something.

When he was done talking he felt embarrassed but was glad to get it off his chest. Bill let Lena know that he felt an obligation to help out, but had a bigger responsibility back home. Lena seemed like she got it. Family had to come first. She said all the right things when he was done, smiling. She understood. He saw that in her eyes. Now she would tell him what he needed to hear.

Bill said, "I mean...Lena, I understand how important this all is. But there must be some other person that can take my place. Maybe someone else at my office. My director will be able to help with that, just like he helped get me here. I presume you already know him, since he sent me here."

She was sitting close to him, leaning in and following every word like she really cared.

Lena said, "Bill, of course. Whatever you need. When would you like to leave?"

He let out a sigh of relief. "Oh, thank you. Thank you so much. I hate to be a burden. I'd be happy to participate. Maybe I could help out remotely? Through the Internet? I just...I need to get back to her."

Lena nodded and gave the warmest of smiles. She reached over and squeezed his shoulder. "Anything at all. We can arrange for a plane first thing in the morning if you like?"

"Oh, thank you so much. I...it's just. I feel bad even asking. But I don't want to waste any time. And I don't know how much we've got...me and my wife."

"Actually, Bill, it's funny you phrase it like that."

Bill frowned. "Come again? I'm afraid I don't follow."

Lena's demeanor changed. Her smile was a little less warm. Her eyes a bit less glowing. "How much time *have* we got, Bill?"

Bill shook his head. "What do you mean?"

"Bill, do you have *something else* you would like to share with me?"

Bill paused. He looked at her and frowned.

"Bill. Come now. Remember, I worked with your boss to get you here. I already have a good idea of what everyone knows. But we brought you here to confirm. I expected to hear you speak up today when they brought up the countdown."

Bill let out a deep breath and looked at the floor. How could she know this? His manager didn't even know *everything*.

He said, "I didn't want to bring it up. I wasn't sure if it was exactly what we were talking about."

"You found a countdown embedded in satellites that you use to connect to Air Force drones halfway around the world. A countdown that was put there by a foreign entity. And you weren't sure if it was *relevant*? I'm sure that you've been quite absorbed by what's going on at home. But please...what do you know about the countdown?"

Bill looked at her. If he had told everyone what he knew, he never would have gotten out of there. It was a hell of a selfish thing to do, keeping something like that to himself. But he had to see his wife. If the world really was coming to an end that soon...

"Six months," he finally said.

She didn't blink. She even looked like she already knew. Which was impossible. His manager, the one who had sent him there, only knew that they had found a sequenced countdown. But as far as he knew, Bill was still working out the code.

"We found the code in one of our satellites a week ago. One that we use to relay GPS data to Predator drones. Then we checked a few other satellites. It was in all of them. Whoever put it there knew what they were doing. But we thought it was just a computer virus. Until today I had no idea what it could be for. Honest. You're right, though. We were pretty sure that some foreign agency did it. We knew it was a countdown. At first, we thought the countdown was just going to keep resetting like you guys were talking about earlier. But then when my boss was gone, I figured out the timing. It was coded, but I ran it through a decryption program. Then I did the math. Six months. If this is the same cyberweapon that David was talking about, that's how long we have until this war starts. And that's why I have to get back to my wife. I need to be with her, Lena."

Lena said, "What did the others here say about this when you told them?"

"Who? What others?"

"The other consultants here on the island. What did they say about this?"

Bill was embarrassed. He said quietly, "I haven't told anyone else. Hell, my boss doesn't even know all that. I was going to let him know about the timing next week. He was out for a few days when I figured it out. Then Burns, my director, contacted me about this project. But he didn't know yet either. Come to think of it, how did you—"

Bill never saw it coming.

Lena twisted her torso around, drove her arm forward, and snapped the bottom of her palm into Bill's solar plexus with an impossibly strong force. A shot of agonizing pain and a rapid loss of the ability to breathe left Bill crumpled on the floor.

Bill tried to gasp for breath but his stomach muscles were cramped too badly. He vaguely understood that Lena was twisting his large body so that he lay flat on his back, the concrete floor cold on his neck.

He started to wheeze and she slammed her open palm into his nose, the back of his head beating against the hard stone. Then came a momentary flash of black and white stars and a ringing in his ears. Bill's vision was a blur of dark computer screens and concrete flooring. The rain poured down loud on the roof. A clap of thunder sounded outside.

Lena was rolling him and tying his hands and feet with something tight. He just needed a minute to rest. She had to *stop*. His head hurt so much. Bill didn't understand what was going on. Lena seemed like a sweet girl. She had smiled and listened to his story. He didn't understand why she'd hit him. Bill felt a trickle of blood rolling down the back of his head, where it had hit the concrete. The cut must have been bad.

Lena stood over him and hissed, "Are you familiar with the blood choke? Your Marines call it that. I just adore the label."

She pressed one foot into his chest, eyeing him like he was a prize deer she had just bagged. Her eyes were filled with a terrifying eagerness.

Bill lay on the ground, weak and not comprehending what was happening. He tried to get up but his head hurt, and Lena easily pressed his chest back down to the floor. His energy was gone and his head ached. Her hands crept over his neck. Bill instinctively tried to protect himself, but his hands and legs were tied up.

He watched as she crouched down over him, moving with the grace of a true predator. Her face got close enough that he could feel her breath. He couldn't understand what was happening. The look in her eyes terrified him. *Why was she doing this?*

Lena whispered, "It's alright. Just relax. Shhhh. Here's what will happen. I'm going to squeeze your carotid arteries and stop the blood flow to your brain. It's an extremely efficient technique. Much faster than cutting off the oxygen supply via your windpipe. You'll then go unconscious, and I'll have to decide what to do with you. I may kill you. I'm not quite ready to make that call. I need to think on it. But with any luck, you'll wake up good as new under close supervision. Now, it's time to sleep."

His eyes bulged with fear. Her fingers tightened around his neck. She squeezed hard enough that it hurt. He felt the blood pressure around his face and neck begin to rise. He squirmed with all his might, but she was incredibly strong and had too much leverage. Bill's vision grew dark. It felt like she was choking him, but he could still breathe...he could still fight...he could...

\* \* \*

Lena rose and walked to the phone, lifting the handle to her ear. She spoke in Mandarin. "Contact the destroyer *Lanzhou*. Tell them that they must send their alert helicopter. It must land on the north end of the runway at one a.m. Be prepared to take a passenger in restraints. Call me if there are any problems. Once he is on the ship, await my further instruction. Keep him under observation. Do not let him speak with anyone."

She looked at Bill's limp body on the floor. Before hanging up the phone, she said, "Also—send a message to Mr. Jinshan. Inform him that I may need to move up our timetable. I have my doubts that the *voluntary* extraction of information will last a full three weeks."

**5**
———

*I am not afraid of an army of lions led by a sheep; I am afraid of an army of sheep led by a lion.*
    —Alexander the Great

### Present Day

David's internal clock was all messed up. His nap earlier hadn't helped. He tried to sleep but couldn't. He checked his watch. It was almost 1 a.m. A cool sea breeze drifted in from the screened window. A bright half-moon lit up the sliver of sea that was visible from his room. The thunderstorms had passed.

He wanted nothing more than to be able to shut his eyes, fall asleep and then wake up and realize that this had all been just a bad dream. Like in the movies. David could open his eyes and see his wife lying next to him. His girls quietly sleeping down the hall. There would be no CIA operative named Lena, no Red Cell preparing for a future war with China. In his perfectly safe alternate reality, David would have never met Natesh or the major or any of the consultants on this island.

David sighed. He had too much energy to sleep. And he still

had remnants of jet lag from the flight halfway around the world yesterday. Screw it. He was going to take a walk outside.

He threw on his clothes and sneakers and headed down the concrete stairs and outside the barracks. Outside he could hear loud bird songs coming from the jungle-covered mountain. A few large moths fluttered around the light positioned above the barracks door.

David walked along the sandy path towards the beach. He had nothing better to do. Why not? The runway was in between the shore and where he was now. It was a beautiful night. He loved the way the air looked and felt so clear after a storm came through. It was like they sucked up all the haze and humidity and left nothing but pure crisp air behind.

David walked past the Communications building and heard a rumble in the distance. At first he thought it was the buzzing of an air-conditioning unit or some generator attached to one of the buildings. Then the rumble grew into a reverberation. He recognized that noise. The reverberations got louder and changed pitch. A helicopter. And it was getting closer, by the sound of it. Why would it be coming here in the middle of the night? An uneasy feeling grew inside him.

David stood on the gravel path and tried to look into the black sky above the ocean for any sign of an aircraft. Nothing. It was like looking into a black hole.

A set of dim blue lights flickered on at the end of the runway. He could just barely see them, but it was enough for him to notice. Had someone turned them on for the helicopter to land? David heard the sound of a door opening directly behind him, coming from the Communications building.

He hid. He didn't know why he was doing it, but every instinct in his body pushed him behind a group of tall palms and bushes. He then spread himself flat on the ground and held his breath. The moon was out, but he was in the shadows.

The sounds of the rotors grew and David finally spotted the helo as it passed in front of the moon. Its lights were off. Usually helicopters only did that when they didn't want to be seen. It was probably military.

David didn't even hear her. Lena walked right by him, only a few feet in front of his hiding spot. She was alone, wearing some sort of helmet with a clear visor over her face, and walking straight toward the runway. A moment later the helicopter touched down, blowing sand and small shells into the air with its rotor wash. Someone from the helicopter ran out to Lena and then followed her back into the Communications building.

They emerged only seconds later, carrying a large man slouched over their shoulders. It looked like the man was completely limp: either unconscious or worse. If David could have pressed himself completely underground, he would have. Something felt terribly off about this. It was hard for David to see clearly in the darkness. The sound of the rotors made it impossible to hear much more. He held his breath and lay completely still as they passed the bush.

Then he saw the man's face. It was Bill, the man David had eaten dinner with just several hours earlier. Bill was supposed to have told Lena that he wanted to be sent home to see his sick wife. The moonlight illuminated his thick mess of white hair. They were dragging him to the helicopter. *Holy shit*. Was he alive?

Lena and the man from the helicopter slowly carried Bill under the spinning rotors and into the cabin of the aircraft. She then left the helicopter and walked back up toward David. His blood chilled. It looked like she was heading right toward his bush. Each step took her closer and closer. The sound of the helicopter was still loud. If he yelled, no one in the building would hear him.

Just as David thought that Lena had spotted him, she stopped and turned toward the runway. The helicopter lifted off and dipped its nose, accelerating and climbing into the night. David could just barely make out the outline of the aircraft, but he was pretty sure that it wasn't a Seahawk, like the one his sister in the Navy flew. This helicopter looked different. It was smaller and had an enclosed tail. Like the Maryland State Police helicopters that he saw around DC. Or maybe a Coast Guard helicopter. Could that be a Coast Guard helo? No way. Not this far from home. So who was it? And what the hell was Lena doing dropping off an unconscious Bill into the backseat?

With the helicopter out of sight, Lena walked back towards the Communications building. David couldn't see the entrance from his hiding spot, but he lay in the bushes for a full ten minutes to be sure she was inside.

What did this mean? What was going on? Had Bill gone to her and tried to get off the island? Was this their way of moving him? Had they killed him? David was less sure of who he could trust now than at any time since his Red Cell activation. He definitely could not trust Lena. Was this Red Cell even legit? Should he try to get off the island or get word out somehow? He had no idea how he could do that.

David finally got up and quickly dusted some of the sand off his clothes. He walked as quietly as he could back to the barracks, looking at the Communications building as he went by to make sure Lena didn't pop out. There were no windows that he could see through, but there were glass slits at the top of the building through which light was emanating.

He arrived at the barracks and opened the door as slowly as possible. He did not want to be seen.

He heard the crunch of someone walking on the gravel coming from the path behind him.

David's heart raced as he slipped inside and closed the door. He didn't know if he had been spotted, but it sounded like someone was following him. He tiptoed up the stairs onto the second floor. Coverless halogen bulbs lit the hallway. The brightness ruined his night vision and forced him to squint. He fumbled for his room key as he got to his door.

Footsteps echoed from the concrete stairway David had just walked up. He was almost inside.

"Hello, David," Lena said. She walked towards him.

There was nothing he could do about the look on his face. That look of instant shock and fear at seeing the one person he hoped not to. He then gave the best impersonation of nonchalance he could muster.

"Hello. What are you doing up here?" He didn't know what else to say.

She was all business. "I would ask you the same thing, David. Why are you up so late outside your room? Were you outside?"

"Um, yes. I thought I heard...a helicopter."

"Did you?"

"Yeah. It woke me up. I just went to the door on the ground floor to see if I could see it."

"And did you? See it?"

"Nah. It was too dark. Do you know what it was doing here? The helicopter?" His fingers hovered around the metal door handle.

"Did you go outside?"

"No. I just looked from the door. Why? Is that okay? I don't want to break any rules."

She cocked her head and said, "The helicopter was taking Bill back to his family. His wife is sick. He wanted to get home and see her. I helped him to do so. The helicopter was the best way. I can't say more. Security. You understand."

"Oh, sure. Sorry. Well, that's great that you were able to help him. I'm feeling pretty tired. I should get to bed. This jet lag is playing havoc with my circadian rhythm. Thanks, Lena. See you tomorrow."

Lena took a step toward him and he instinctively cringed.

She said, "David, it looks like your outfit may have gotten a bit sandy. Better brush off." She swiped particles of dark island sand off his shirt. He was covered in a thin layer of the stuff from lying on the ground outside. Her face was inches away, and her emotionless eyes peered into his own. He felt his palms sweating. In another place and time, it might have been a come-on. But here, it was chilling.

He whispered, "Thanks. Goodnight."

With that, he turned and entered his room, shutting the door behind him. He stood on the other side of the door sweating, and listening for her footsteps. He heard nothing. Was she just standing there too, listening for his movements? If he stayed still, that would be suspicious. He winced as he locked his door, about thirty seconds later than seemed appropriate. A dead bolt had never sounded so loud. He then turned out his lights and got into bed. He could hear noises coming from outside for the next few minutes. It sounded like Lena was going into Bill's room and rummaging around. Probably packing up his things. A few minutes after that, there was silence.

His thoughts drifted back to his family. Right now he wanted nothing more than to get home to his wife and children. For the past two days David had trusted the people that brought him here. He had been convinced of their noble purpose.

Until now. Now, he had no idea what to believe.

There was no way he would get any sleep tonight. He wasn't sure what tomorrow would bring. Were they prisoners here? Who could he trust? Had Lena killed Bill? Even if he wasn't dead, had Bill been removed unconscious just for asking to leave? Was secrecy so important that the CIA would imprison them all? A worse thought: was Lena even CIA? He had never seen the face of the man who'd helped her carry Bill. It had been concealed by his helmet and mask. But that helicopter didn't look like any he had seen in the Navy. Was she even American? David was only certain about one thing: *he must figure out how to get off this island alive.*

* * *

*14 Years Earlier, Washington, D.C.*

Lena sat in her car and looked at her watch. He should be here any minute. She tried not to be nervous. She told herself that there could be many reasons why he would make contact with her. She was almost finished with her undergraduate degree. And she had performed a few small tasks around the D.C. area. Mostly surveillance or eavesdropping—things that she had learned from her initial training on how to be an intelligence operative. By all accounts she had performed admirably. Was he here to give her praise? Perhaps this meeting was a simple checkup? Or to discuss future duties? Still, she knew this man's reputation. Mr. Cheng Jinshan was a very important businessman, and a legendary puppeteer for his network of spies. This visit would not be for a trivial reason.

She parked at the corner of Thirty-Sixth Street and Prospect. At exactly noon she got out of her car and walked to The Tombs, a swanky Georgetown bar across the street. The inside was dark and empty. It was a weekday and most people wouldn't arrive until happy hour. A bartender was at the far side of the room, wiping down the glossy tables.

Lena scanned to see if Jinshan was already here.

The bartender spotted her. "You ready to order?" he asked.

"No. Just—"

"Two Dewars on the rocks. We'll sit by the fireplace." The hardened voice from behind froze her. She was sixteen when she had last heard that voice. The day that he had recruited her. She tried not to think about that day of tears.

She turned and held out her hand. "Hello, sir."

"Hello, Lena." He studied her for a moment and then walked on, disregarding her outstretched hand.

They sat at a long wooden table tucked beside a large brick fireplace. The flames blazed and crackled. A dozen crew paddles formed a semicircle on the stones above the fire.

The bartender brought two heavy glasses of light brown liquid and went back to cleaning.

"Do you drink?" the man asked, taking a sip.

She gave a weak smile. "A little. Not like the others at my school. I have more important things to do with my time." She felt like this was half evaluation, half job interview.

"I see," was his only reply.

They sat for a few moments. The silence made her uncomfortable. She tried to think of something appropriate to say but nothing came to mind.

"You've done well here," he said finally.

"Thank you."

"Your grades and athletic performance have been exemplary. Your linguistic skills are superb. Also...your *extracurricular* performance has been noted." She was pretty sure that he didn't mean school clubs. Her small contributions to the spy trade were likely what he was referring to.

"Thank you." She nodded, pursing her lips. She was humble. Compliments made her uneasy.

"Still...we've watched you closely, Lena. You've had specific guidelines on how you can interact with others here."

The tone of his voice told her that he was going somewhere with this. Her heart stopped. She had been careful. They couldn't possibly know about *him*. It had only been a few months. Maybe she had slipped up on something else. Filed a report wrong, possibly? But the pit forming in her stomach told her otherwise. She took a sip from her glass.

"And we've observed a few...*deviations*."

Her face reddened. They knew. She had hoped to God that it wasn't about this. She hadn't meant for it to happen. He was on the track team with her. They had both been at a hotel and had spent some time alone. He was a quiet boy. She liked the attention. She knew that it was against the rules. Just like she had years ago. When she was sixteen.

"You've taken a lover."

She looked at her feet. The taste of whiskey heated her throat.

"It's alright, Lena. I'm not judging you. You are human, after all. But still, we need to know that you will be able to abide by our strict guidelines in any environment. This program isn't for everyone. We need deeply committed personnel. You are still in training here. It may not always seem like it. But you are. And you need to keep a minimalist lifestyle. That means no relationships of this nature. You must sacrifice, lest you grow sluggish. Or worse, *compromised*. We don't want relationships to inhibit future placement. And we don't want to ever put you in a position where you could slip and say something to the wrong person."

She looked at him. For a split second, she thought of denying it. She could deceive him. Say that it was nothing. But with Jinshan, she could not risk it. Never lie to Jinshan. That's what she had been told by the others. She must take responsibility and hope for the best. "Of course, sir. Of course. It's my fault. I just— I'm sorry. I'll break it off at once. I will do better. I'm sorry. Please—"

"No, no. Lena, this isn't about a relationship." He took a deep gulp from his glass and laid it on the table, ice clinking the edges. "It's about trust."

"You can trust me, sir." She saw all of her hard work slipping away. It was a terrifying prospect. She had spent years training to be here. She didn't want to go back to what could await her if she failed out of the program.

"We have invested a lot of time and energy into you. As I have stated, your performance has been very high quality. I personally have followed your development, and I see great things in store for you, Lena. But I *have* to know that I can trust you."

"Yes, yes. Of course. I am so sorry. Please." She shook her head. She hoped that she had not jeopardized her career.

"Lena, I am here for two reasons. First, to tell you that I have selected you for a special program. I want you to follow a particular career track. One that many don't even know exists. If you do this, you will be working on our most covert and most important assignments. You'll receive a lot more specialized training. And your contribution to your country will be of the utmost importance. In future assignments, you'll report directly to me."

Her heart skipped a beat. He was going to let her continue. She could keep moving up. She would retain her honor. Lena nodded vigorously, trying to hold back her emotions.

"The second thing I am here to tell you is that I need you to perform one final act in this segment of your training. I need you to demonstrate your loyalty...your dedication...and your ability to put the mission above all else in your life. If you can do this, I will know that I can trust you. And we can move forward as I described."

"Of course. Anything. Please just let me know—"

He leaned forward and whispered, "You will kill your boyfriend."

Her world stopped.

He spoke but she barely heard him. "Please understand: this is not because I think you told him anything about your role with us. I believe you when you say that you have kept your secrets. No, Lena, this order is a way for me to know that you are capable of this kind of thing. If I select you for this special assignment, your future career will require a level of emotional detachment from your professional endeavors that few possess. Some could refer to this quality as heartless, ruthless, cold, calculating. Call it what you will. Lena, you must be all of these things if you are to be a weapon. I don't need you to be just a listener. I have many listeners. I need you to be, at times, an assassin. You have been trained in many techniques. Now you will put them into action. Show me that you can effectively perform this task."

She felt sick. The look on his face—it was as if he felt nothing at asking her this. What kind of man could ask this? She threw out the thought as quickly as it entered her mind. He had given her a second chance in life. Her family was proud of her for serving her country. She would never see them again, but she had retained her honor.

He continued, "Make it look like an accident. This will ensure that you aren't questioned. Play the part of the devastated girl-friend. You will graduate from college in a few months. Begin to cut ties with any other friends you had while here. We'll set you up with your next job. I have big things planned, Lena. And I want you to be a part of those plans."

She thought of last night. Of skin on skin. Of the way he had made her feel. But it wasn't who she was. She must remember that. Love and lust were fleeting. Duty and honor were immortal. She breathed in deeply, and then let out a slow release of air through her nose. Lena forced all of her emotion out of her body.

She looked back at the man sitting across from her. His single-breasted suit was exquisite. Gold cufflinks and an expensive watch. He spent much of his time in boardrooms and private jets, and looked the part. Jinshan was not here on business, however. Just how he became connected to the clandestine operations arm of her nation's government was still a mystery to her. But she knew that he held a position of great authority within it. She also knew of his loyalty to those he took under his wing…and of his reputation for being brutal to those that crossed him.

This wasn't a choice. It was a hurdle. Like so many she had jumped. Lena looked to ensure the barkeep was out of earshot and whispered, "Of course, sir. I will do this without hesitation. I will prove to you my loyalty to my country. My loyalty to China."

The next morning, a bleary-eyed and nervous David walked into the classroom. He arrived ten minutes before the first session was supposed to begin. Lena stood up on her usual perch, at the top level of stadium seating. He tried not to look at her. He was positive she was looking at him.

In the front of the class, Natesh divided the group into teams as they entered. Each team was assigned a leader, and each leader received a single sheet of paper with instructions for the session. Natesh was going on about how the smaller teams would put out better work faster. Now that they were starting their second full day of work on the island, Natesh was driving them to move quicker and more efficiently. David's team was to focus on disrupting communications.

Before they broke up, Lena announced to the room, "I need to say something. Just so all of you are aware, Bill Stanley has been removed."

David thought that was an interesting way to put it.

Natesh asked, "What do you mean?"

Lena said, "Apparently, his wife is very sick. Last night he came to me after our meeting. He asked to be removed from the sessions and returned home. We reiterated the importance of secrecy and flew him off the island immediately." She looked at David as she spoke. Like she was trying to observe any reaction he might have. He didn't blink.

On the inside, however, he wanted to scream out to everyone that she was lying. At least, he thought she was. But he couldn't prove it. And yelling out that he had seen Bill being dragged unconscious into a suspicious-looking helicopter might not be his best move. Not if he wanted to see his wife and family again.

Norman Shepherd spoke first. He was a burly former Marine from Long Island. David thought he had said that he worked for Maersk Line now.

Norman said, "So you just flew him off? Just like that? Man, tonight I'm gonna come say I need a trip to Vegas. Think that would be all right? I knew I heard a helo flying nearby last night. Friggin' thing sounded like it was right outside my window."

Natesh said, "Alright, thanks, Lena. Glad that Bill is taken care of."

Lena nodded and said, "Me too. And please, if anyone else has any personal situations that need attending to, please don't hesitate to bring them to my attention."

Natesh said, "Okay, everyone, please go to your assigned team rooms. We'll meet back here after lunch. Remember, if you need Major Combs or me to look up anything for you today, write it down and give it to me before you break for lunch at eleven thirty. We'll get it back to you by the afternoon."

The class rose and funneled out the door into separate meeting rooms. David followed.

He couldn't believe that everyone just accepted Bill's departure. But then again, why wouldn't they? They were each here performing a service to their country. Lena had done nothing that would cause anyone to take her at less than face value. If anything, she had positioned herself as the helpful caretaker, able to solve any and all of their problems. She would get you towels for your rooms, organize the American defense for World War III, and whisk you off the island at a moment's notice if you asked nicely. The problem was, you might be unconscious or dead when you were whisked. But she was attractive and charismatic and had established credibility. She dished out this lie so effortlessly, and her audience eagerly scarfed it up. David wondered: if she was lying about Bill, *what else was a lie?*

He needed to keep on his mask. Whether Lena suspected him or not, he couldn't let his guard down around her.

He now questioned the entire premise for gathering the Red Cell on this island. David had been working out the two most likely scenarios in his head. One, Lena was CIA, just like she said. It was possible that she had rendered Bill unconscious because secrecy was just that important. An extreme measure, but not with nefarious intent. Hell, if it was just about secrecy, maybe Bill really *was* home with his wife right now. Maybe Lena had given him a tranquilizer that he had taken voluntarily. He ran it through his head. *Okay, Bill. You can go see your wife, but we need to put you under until you get there. We don't want you to see anyone or anything. Security, you understand.* That *could* be what happened to Bill. This was the best-case scenario.

But an unlikely one. It was the helicopter that bothered him. That helo didn't look like any US Navy helicopter he had ever seen, even in the dim light.

The second scenario was what really concerned David. In this scenario, one unsettling question led to another. What if Lena wasn't CIA? What if she wasn't American? Then some foreign entity, likely China itself, was using the members of the Red Cell to gather classified information.

Why would any government take a risk like that? Was there really a countdown until China shut off all US satellites? Was there really an invasion plan? If the answer was yes, perhaps that was a big enough reason to justify kidnapping so many Americans from their soil.

What were Lena and crew going to do with David and the consultants when they were done with them? What would they do to them if they found out this was all staged? David couldn't conceive of a way that any of the consultants would get home safely in this situation. Any intelligence organization that would do this would want to hide it—permanently. Whether that meant killing them or keeping them prisoner likely had to do with their future utility.

Lena was definitely involved in whatever was really going on. But who else knew? David needed to figure out how deep this went. And while he did that, he needed to pretend that everything was just fine. Until he knew who the good guys were, it was too risky to look suspicious.

David walked out of the classroom, careful not to look up at Lena. But he just knew that she was looking right at him.

* * *

He walked down the hallway. Cheap tile floors and concrete walls. Fluorescent lights. It reminded David of an old elementary school. Everything was simple, functional, and clean. He walked to the third door on the left. Inside was a small meeting room, where Natesh sat at the lone white plastic table.

Natesh smiled and said, "Hello, David."

"Morning." He nodded back. Even common courtesies felt forced after what he had seen last night. David gritted his teeth and sat down. It took everything he had in him to hold it together.

Three others entered the room. Brooke, the woman who worked at the NSA. Henry Glickstein, the telecom expert who rarely stopped joking around. David had met those two on the plane ride to the island. A young woman that David hadn't met walked in behind them. The woman had short blond hair that was dark at the roots. She looked intense and proud. Like someone who ran the rat race each day and tried to win.

She put out her hand to David and Natesh, saying, "Hello, guys, my name is Tess McDonald."

They exchanged greetings.

Natesh asked, "And what do you do for a living, Tess?"

"I'm a consultant. I work out of Boston."

Henry said, "Isn't everyone a consultant nowadays? I mean, the guy at Blockbuster Video is a consultant. I consulted with him on movie recommendations."

Tess raised her eyebrows, not sure how to take Henry's humor. She said, "I've done a lot of DOD projects. I specialize in East Asian Affairs—policy and political analysis. And I've worked on a lot of the DoD's weapons acquisitions programs. I'm pretty familiar with what weapons technology we have and what our capabilities are. If you tell me what you want blown up, I can tell you the right bullet. And I can name most of the members of the Central Politburo of the Communist Party of China. My two specialties seemed to be a good fit for this group. That's why I'm here, I believe." Her tone was polite, but all business. Like she was working with a client.

Natesh said, "Excellent. Well, we're very glad to have you with us, Tess."

The five group members stared at each other momentarily, then Natesh said, "Okay, let's get to work. This morning our group is going to get more detailed on how to disrupt the US communications networks. What do we think China would need to do? I agree with yesterday's hypothesis that taking out electricity would be important. How could we do it?"

The group began offering ideas, just shouting them out.

David didn't know what to do. He no longer believed in their reason for being here. He wasn't fully committed. He didn't want to say anything that could be helpful to a potential enemy nation, if that was a real possibility. After what he had seen last night, he couldn't speak freely and keep a good conscience. He decided to keep quiet. It turned out to be pretty easy. The others were all talkers.

Henry cleared his throat and said, "Okay, where did we leave off yesterday? I don't know how you would do it, but I would try to cut the transoceanic fiber-optic cables that connect the United States with the rest of the world. If I were going to lay siege to a house, I'd cut the phone lines. I think the same works for a nation at war."

Brooke asked, "Could you use some type of depth charge, like in the old war movies?"

Tess said, "Actually, the Navy doesn't really use depth charges anymore. You had to practically hit the sub with the canister for it to work. During the Cold War, the US and the Soviets developed *nuclear* depth charges. But I'm pretty sure they've gotten rid of all of those. It wasn't the best situation to be in for the attacking force, for obvious reasons."

Henry raised his eyebrows. "Well, if that's the best way to get the job done, we should still recommend nuking the cables. I didn't really want to be the first one to start talking about nukes, but if cutting the Internet and phone lines across the oceans means using nukes, let's include that as a possible way to do it. Leave everything on the table until we find a better way. Anyone have any other methods?"

Brooke said, "You could get one of those deep submergence vehicles and place explosives on it. It would probably take more time and precision. But then again, you wouldn't have to worry about setting off a nuclear bomb underneath your boat. I would imagine that most sailors wouldn't like that, huh?"

Henry said, "I believe those were the obvious reasons Tess mentioned. But, if that's the best way, let's look at it."

Natesh said, "Okay, so we've got a submarine laying explosive charges on the cables and/or someone dropping nuclear depth charges. Either way, we recommend destroying the cables, right?"

Henry nodded. "It would be a very effective way to wreck Internet and phone communications that lead into and out of the United States."

Natesh said, "How many underwater cables are there?"

Henry raised his eyebrows, thinking. He said, "I mean...there are a *lot* of them. There must be over a dozen locations on both coasts. On the East Coast of the US, the major land entry point locations are near New York and Miami, and in New Jersey. California has a ton of landing zones. A lot of these cables are actually private. Most people think that the Internet is all open. But a lot of the big tech companies and telecoms have cables that just ferry their private data back and forth. It makes it more efficient. All those cables are spread out far from each other as they cross the ocean floor—diversification."

"Why?" asked Brooke.

"Safety. That way if there is some catastrophe like an earthquake, the other cables will pick up the load. That makes for a more logistically challenging operation. But eventually, they all end up pretty close to each other when they get to the coast. If you want to ruin as much bandwidth as possible, it would make sense to do it closer to shore, where there is less distance to cover by the attacking asset. There would be a smaller area to deploy your explosives to if you did it right off the coast of the US. But then you have to think about the cables that connect Mexico and Canada with the US also. I mean, ideally you would destroy those as well. But even if you don't, the bandwidth mismatch that you would have created by destroying the submarine cables would crush the flow rate."

Natesh said, "Okay, that makes sense to me. Let's just get all this stuff down on our sticky notes, post them up on the board, and we'll come back to it. Now, what about inside the US? How would you go about disrupting the communication there?"

Henry said, "I'd cut power sources and damage all the major

highway intersections. If you cut the electrical grid in enough places, there will be some real issues. Generators for major buildings would go through their fuel supply pretty quickly." He got up and went over to the mini fridge in the corner of the room and opened it up. "Anyone want a bottled water?"

A few people nodded and he tossed bottles to them.

"Why would you hit the highways?" asked Tess.

Natesh spoke. "Snail mail?"

Henry said, "Yeah. Snail mail, and even word of mouth. If phones and Internet are taken out, that's going to have everyone shifting to TV and radio to get their information old-school style, with antennas. I'm not sure most people even still have antennas. But I would imagine that China would also try to target the media centers."

Natesh said, "Try to remember, for this exercise, *we* are China. What would *you* do?"

David didn't like the sound of that.

Henry said, "Maybe take out phones, TV, and radio with a cyberattack prior to cutting power? That's how I'd do it. Anyway, people will eventually get their information through word of mouth. If we make traveling long distances hard to do, that will mean that we can control the information better. We could keep parts of the country in the dark longer while we're invading."

Tess said, "We should shut down air travel too."

Brooke said, "Is that communication? Wouldn't that be more something that the Defense teams should handle? Or...I don't know..."

Natesh said, "Let's just keep it as a priority. Just write it down. Any ideas on how you would disrupt air travel?"

Brooke said, "What happened that time in Chicago? The time that they shut down all flights for a few days because air traffic control was burned down and sabotaged by an employee. Could we shut down air traffic by taking out all of those air traffic control centers?"

Henry thought and said, "Yeah. Yeah, actually that would probably work pretty well. Some aircraft would still be able to fly with their visual flight rules. But most commercial traffic flies on instruments. That means they'll need those air traffic control centers. That's a good idea. Although really, if we do two-thirds of these things we're talking about, the whole country will be in mass chaos anyway. Taking out the satellites and data centers will go a long way, I think. But cutting the hard lines and central hubs like the air traffic control centers—that would seriously inhibit our ability to adapt after the satellites go down. Think everyone in a city driving without any of their GPS or stoplights working. Total gridlock. That's what we're talking about."

David kept getting flashbacks to the night before. He could see Bill being carried along the sandy path to the runway and dumped into a helicopter. The more ideas people came up with on how to disrupt America's communications, the more David thought that there was no good reason for what he'd seen last night. If Lena wasn't CIA—if she wasn't an American—then all this planning was for another country. David was starting to feel ill. He wanted to scream. Instead, he just kept listening to the plans.

Plans.

*He* didn't yet have a plan. His father had told David and his siblings a million times as they were growing up that one must *always* have a plan. After David's brother Chase had been shot in Afghanistan—it was a graze, but it had still earned him a Purple Heart—his father had amended his advice, comically, to "always have a *good* plan." David needed a good plan, and fast. If every group was coming up with plans to invade America like this, David didn't want to think about what would happen if the plans were actually put into motion.

Others must have felt his unease. Brooke said, "David, are you okay? You've been pretty quiet."

"Yeah. Sorry. Just a little tired. Probably just jet lag."

Natesh said, "Feel free to take a break. We've got a few weeks. You can afford to pace yourself, my friend."

David didn't want anyone to think anything unusual of him. He said, "I'm alright. Thanks." He still felt ill.

The group kept going. It went on that way for the next hour. Natesh drawing out ideas from the group. David doing his best to be a poor participant. The mood was a mix of gloom and excitement. People were coming to terms with the sheer magnitude of the threat. But oddly, the group seemed to enjoy the task of planning out the war. It was an interesting intellectual exercise for people who had studied such things.

After the first hour, they took a bio break. Everyone got up, stretched their legs, and went out into the hallway towards the restrooms. Other groups were out there, chatting it up. It was weirdly like high school. The consultants in the Red Cell were like kids in between class. Some were socializing. Others were talking about what each of the other groups was doing.

David and Brooke returned to the meeting room first. The others were still down the hall, conversing.

Brooke said, "How is your family?"

He looked at her blankly.

"Oh. Right. No phones. Sorry. Do you think they're okay? I'm sure they're okay. I'm sure Tom talked to your wife. I'm sure they're fine." She seemed to be a nervous talker. "How many kids did you say you had?"

"I have two girls—both young," he said, smiling politely. He thought about his girls for a moment and the smile faded. "If any of this stuff we're discussing were really to happen..."

Brooke pressed her lips together and gave him a sympathetic look. She shook her head. "I know. Even the things that we've talked about just now. I can't imagine a world going through any of that. My grandfather was in World War Two. I've read a lot of books about that time. The whole world was transformed overnight. Car factories became war machine factories. There were tens of millions dying. The atrocities that people took part in around the world. I mean, can you imagine that happening in a civil society today?"

"Depends what you mean by a civil society, I guess."

"What do you mean?"

"I mean I'm sure that plenty of Germans involved in the Holocaust atrocities were civil before they were put into that situation. Civil can mean a lot of things. They may have been polite or kind or clean or wealthy or proper. But when the war was on and they got in a uniform and were put in a group and told to pull a switch, they did it. War and groupthink can be a hell of a thing..."

She looked appalled. "Well, I would never—"

David said, "I'm sure you wouldn't, Brooke. Not with what you know now and the way you've likely been raised. All I'm saying is that people, if put into the right set of circumstances, can do things that they never would have imagined. I mean, if you look at other events of World War Two, even our country, which I think always tries to act with the noblest of intentions, did some things —the fire bombings, the nuclear weapons—that seem unthinkable when you read about them today. I'm still having a hard time believing the premise of this project. I keep thinking that this is just going to turn out to be a paper exercise. I guess I'm half hoping that will be the case. Because these things that we're talking about. These *plans*. It's like World War Two all over again. But this time our country would be the battlefield."

Brooke said, "You keep taking this to a pretty dark place. I guess that sitting here in these air-conditioned meeting rooms, it's hard for me to fully think of this as a real probability. Maybe that's it. Maybe—like you said—I just don't really believe that any of this stuff could really happen. You think it could really get that bad? I mean, if the Chinese really did invade?"

David wanted to talk to her about what he'd seen last night, but thought better of it. Instead, he said, "A few years ago, I remember hearing this reporter talk about her time in Rwanda. She went and interviewed a bunch of people that were involved in the genocide there. She spoke with people on both sides. The Hutus and the Tutsis. Before the violence broke out, many of them were neighbors—friends, even. She talked to this one guy. This was years after all the people were killed there. Anyway, this guy was a godfather to one of the children he killed. He said he couldn't explain why he did it. He didn't know what had come over him."

Brooke looked at him and covered her mouth.

He said, "It was like a craziness took over that country. I think that's what war must be like when it comes to your home. People become animals. They don't reason. Don't think. Just act on impulses. A lot of times, they're evil impulses. I think war is like a disease. When it spreads to a new land, it infects that place and the people who live there."

Brooke said, "And what about what we're doing here? Planning how China would attack us—do you think we're contributing to the spread of this disease? Or helping to prevent it?"

David said, "I think there's such a thing as a just war. I certainly think that the United States has always tried to fight for the right reasons, and with honor. I know for a fact that we train our military to question the morality of their orders, and to always fight for the side of justice. But Brooke, between you and me, I'm not sure that what we're doing here is rooted in those moral values."

Brooke said, "What do you mean?"

They heard the others coming closer to the door.

David's face flushed. He wasn't sure what to say. He clumsily patted her shoulder and said, "Hey—I'm not ready to talk about it yet. But I'll tell you later. Trust me. Let's just keep this between us for now, okay?"

She looked at him and furrowed her eyebrows in confusion. Then she nodded and whispered, "Of course."

The others filed into the room. Brooke turned away and looked lost in thought. In his head, David made a note to himself that he would put Brooke in the "trustworthy" column. He had seen enough of her. He wasn't sure when he would get the chance, but he needed to let her know what had happened to Bill and enroll her in his plan. Now he just needed a plan.

**6**

---

*The two most powerful warriors are patience and time.*
  —Leo Tolstoy

David Manning awoke at 5 a.m. One week. He had been on the island for a full week. During that time he had lain low. He didn't contribute much. Only when he absolutely had to in order not to seem suspicious. They remained separated in teams for the whole week. He had only heard rumors about what the other teams were working on. Major Combs decided that the best thing for everyone was to keep the information compartmentalized for security purposes. Natesh objected but was overruled by Lena. People still talked, though. The consultants were mostly cut from the same cloth. Ex-military and government action officers and midlevel managers. They were used to having so many rules that it was impossible to obey all of them and still get the job done. So naturally, during meals or breaks, they talked.

That was how David began hearing about the other plans. The Pacific war plans. The US invasion plans. The pre-war psychological operations. It was very comprehensive. Still an early-stage outline, with many details to be worked out. But the consultants that formed the Red Cell were both very sharp and extremely knowledgeable. With each new bit of the plans that David became privy to, he grew more and more worried about who was really getting this information.

David had never hurt anyone before. He'd joined the military, if only for a brief time, to defend and protect. He didn't know if he had it in him to hurt someone. But the more he thought about what had happened to Bill, the more he thought that his life was in danger. The more he heard about the war plans, the more he worried about the future well-being of his family.

Stress took its toll. He barely ate during meals. He couldn't sleep. He couldn't remember the last time he had prayed before he came to this island, but now David prayed each night in the silence of his room. Still, he knew something was missing that de-stressed him at home.

The night before, he had decided to use the sneakers they had given him in his duffel bag and go running. He needed a good long sweat. It would help keep him from getting sluggish, and from going insane with worry.

With no other obvious place to work out, he ran around the six-thousand-foot runway. The air was humid and there was a light breeze. The only sounds he could hear were his footsteps on the pavement and the rhythmic crashing of waves on the shore. At dawn, he witnessed one of the most beautiful sunrises he had ever seen. As he ran, he also got a view of most of the island's base.

Sweat dripped from his forehead and into his eyes. He wiped it away with his forearm. His stride was long, his breathing measured. The sun peeked out over the horizon. He was almost done with the run and was feeling good.

The runway was like his own personal track. David finished another runway length and turned to cross the far end line of the runway. He was facing the waves as he crossed to the other side of the pavement. He would turn right once more and then have a final runway length to go before he arrived back at the side of the base where the buildings were located. He was a mile away from Lena, the classroom, and everyone that was part of the Red Cell.

Just before he made his turn, something caught his eye near the water.

The fence.

The barbed-wire fence ran around the base and runway like a giant squared-off horseshoe, with the two ends descending into the ocean over a mile apart. The runway and all the buildings lay inside the fence. It rose up a good ten or fifteen feet in the air and was covered by sharp steel razor wire. All around the fence, the jungle bush had been cut away and the ground scorched. That resulted in a clear path to walk next to the fence for about eight feet on either side. Beyond that man-made clearing of dirt, ash, and metal, a dark jungle rose up in thick green masses. There were several acres of rainforest on the inside of the fence, the base side, which the makers had not bothered to clear. The result was a half-mile corridor that rose at a shallow grade from the base to the apex, three-quarters of a mile away and curved around from the far end of the runway to the other side of the island. If David had wanted to, he imagined that he could run right along that narrow path and come out near his buildings. But that wasn't what struck him about the fence.

What was odd about the fence was that it existed at all.

He had read a book recently about a town with a wall around it. It was a science fiction book, and the entire town was surrounded by an electrified fence and tall pines. The author quoted a poem by Robert Frost. David was reminded of this poem now. There were only two reasons to build a wall. To keep something out—or to keep something in.

They were surrounded by ocean in all directions. Gravel, scorched earth, and concrete had cleared away the plants that could threaten to overgrow the base structures and runway. So then why would you need a barbed-wire fence on an island? *Unless there was something else on that island that you didn't want people to see...*

The barbed-wire fence went straight out into the sea and sank lower and lower until about fifty feet out it was lapped over by greenish-blue salt water. A man could, if so inclined, swim out fifty-one feet, and go right around it.

David suddenly found the need to restart his swim training in addition to his morning runs. But not today. The sun was up, and he had to get back in time for class to start. Tomorrow he would get up earlier. He needed to go when it was dark, like it had been for the first twenty minutes of his run.

He reached the far corner of the runway, turned ninety degrees, and continued on the final leg of his run, back towards the buildings. He could feel his heart pumping. The idea that he was going to break the rules and possibly find a new clue excited him. He wouldn't just sit on his hands and wait for Lena and whoever the other organizers were to decide his fate. He would take action. He would take control. He began to feel better about himself and his situation.

Then he saw her.

A second pair of feet joined the rhythmic pattern of David's steps on the runway. He looked up, wiping sweat from his brow. Lena. She was running in the reverse direction on the opposite side of the runway. She wore a tight black athletic shirt and tiny grey running shorts. Her long dark hair was up in a ponytail, weighed down by the same sweat that glistened off her skin. Her leg muscles rippled with each stride. She ran like an Olympic distance runner, effortlessly keeping a pace that, to David, looked more like a sprint. But something told him that for her, it wasn't. David was a little glad that she was on the opposite side of the runway. He liked running alone, and he didn't want to get passed by a woman. Especially one that might one day try to kill him.

Lena waved at him. No smile. A guarded, half-amused look. Like she knew something that he didn't. Like she was trying to figure out whether he was a threat. He gave her an awkward head nod, and it took everything in his power not to look after her as she passed. The patter of her footsteps faded into the ever-present sound of crashing waves along the shore.

A few minutes later, David's jog turned into a walk as he approached the cluster of buildings at his end of the runway. Gravel and sand crunched beneath his feet as he walked down the narrow path past the buildings and onto the beach near his barracks. The sun was fully above the horizon now. David stretched his muscles and waited for his breathing to slow. Sweat dripped from his forehead to his nose and onto the dark sand below.

He wondered why the sand here had such a dark grey-black color. He didn't think the island's lone mountain looked volcanic. Maybe one of the scientists in the group would know.

A few moments went by as he stretched and tried to meditate. He controlled his breathing and did his best to let go of the stress that filled him. The magnificent view helped. Even with everything that was going on, he could still take comfort in the solace of an empty tropical beach after a long morning run.

"Mind if I join you?"

He hadn't heard her approach. Could she really have run all the way to the end of the runway and back that quickly?

"Good morning, Lena."

"I didn't know you were a runner. How far did you go?" she asked.

He checked his watch. "Fifty minutes."

He was still breathing hard. Try as he might, he could not think of a single uncontroversial thing to say to her.

She sat down next to him in the sand, extending one of her legs and leaning toward her foot.

She said, "Beautiful morning to run, don't you think?"

"Yes. It is."

"I used to run a lot more than I do lately. Work has kept me busy."

He didn't reply.

She said, "But I couldn't resist a good beach run. I ran track in college. Middle distance. You?"

He said, "In college? I was on the sailing team."

"I see. What kind of boats? The little single-seaters? Or the larger ones?"

David said, "They were forty-four-footers."

"Ah. I see. And you would travel far from the shore on those?"

David looked at her, puzzled. Why the chitchat? Where was she going with this? "Um, yes. Of course."

Her eyes were cool. She said, "David, I'm going to give you some advice. Please imagine that this island is like one of your boats from your college days. It is a vessel, sailing away from the shore. It has just sailed into a squall. Everyone on board is part of a team, right? Everyone on board has a specific job to do. If the team doesn't work well together, it could be very dangerous for the others. And it is quite possible for *anyone* on board to fall off and be consumed by the sea."

He looked at her in silence.

She said, "But if everyone does what he or she is supposed to do, your boat will return safe and sound. *Clear?*"

He nodded. "Yes. I follow." His face was involuntarily turning red.

"Splendid." She held a stoic gaze.

He looked around and then at his wristwatch. He cleared his throat and said, "Well...I better head back. I'll see you later."

She smiled and said, "I look forward to it." She stared straight into his eyes as she spoke. Then she continued to stretch.

He didn't say anything else, just got up and left.

Lena watched him walk away, thinking of another run by the water she'd taken years ago.

\* \* \*

Thirty minutes later David was showered and dressed in a pair of khakis and a polo shirt. He saw Natesh walking toward the cafeteria and paired up with him.

"Good morning, David. You heading to eat?"

"Hi, Natesh. I am."

Natesh looked at the sweat on David's forehead. "You look like you just got done working out."

"Oh. Yes. I ran this morning. Sometimes it takes a while for my heart to stop pumping. Especially in this heat. Let's get in the air conditioning of this cafeteria. That should help."

They began walking along the gravel pathway toward the dining hall. David smelled sausage and cafeteria food in the air.

Moments later they joined Henry Glickstein at a cafeteria table. Glickstein seemed to be one of the few people on the island who were enjoying themselves. Everyone else was complaining about the lack of Internet or TV. They missed their families and the creature comforts of home. But here was Glickstein, joking and trying to get people to join a late-night poker game he had started. These classes were ending at 10 or 11 p.m. David didn't really want to play cards after a day of meetings. And he wasn't in the mood for joking, with what he had seen. He just wanted to sleep. And escape. Still, Henry seemed like a good guy. At least he wasn't trying to kill anyone.

Henry said, "Yeah, so not everyone's got money to pay right now, but we're keeping a very detailed set of IOUs to make sure that everyone knows how much they owe me when we get back to the States."

David smiled. This was a small but welcome distraction from worrying about Lena and her plans.

Natesh said, "Oh, no, thank you. I don't think I would be so good. I actually don't know how to play."

Henry said, "Are you kidding? Usually those are the best kind of poker players! And *definitely* the kind of people I enjoy playing with the most. If you're afraid of gambling your own money away, I'll spot you twenty dollars with only fifty percent interest. So even before I take your money, you'll already owe me. It'll be great. It's like I tell the kids that I sell cigarettes to...*first one's always on the house*."

David said, "Who had the deck of cards?"

Henry said, "Actually, we had to make them with pen and scrap paper from the classroom. Most of the hearts and face cards have dog-ears from that cheating swindler Brooke. Don't trust her. I think she may be part Canadian. Anyway, you guys should come. It'll be great. We'll plan World War Three by day and then blow off steam and play cards at night. We have room for two more. What do you say?"

Natesh laughed and held up his hands. "I give up. I'll come for a few minutes. It may be a good release."

David was going to decline, but then thought better of it. If he spent a little extra time with a few of the people here, he could possibly gain insight into who he could trust. And a closed-door card game might be a good pretense for gathering together a few allies.

David said, "Sure. I'll be there."

Henry said, "Wonderful. So, Natesh, what's on the meeting agenda today?"

"Well, I think we're at the next stage of planning. Today we should be starting to prioritize targets, align on methodology, and link up activities among different teams."

"How do we do that?" David asked.

Natesh said, "Sure. So let's say one of the objectives of our team was to shut down the Internet, for instance. We had discussed cutting submarine cables going across the Atlantic and Pacific, as well as cutting power sources inside the United States. I will try to mesh our objectives with those of the other teams. If multiple teams want to kill power sources, for example, we should focus our energy on that—no pun intended. Kill two birds with one stone, that type of thing. If we have a choice between cutting power and cutting the cables, we need to decide the priority. The point is that we want to maximize efficiency. Complete the highest-priority objectives with the least work and least complexity."

The cafeteria was alive with conversation. About fifteen of the consultants were in there, eating and talking. Behind the buffet line, two stewards cleaned dirty pots and pans. David saw Major Harold Combs, the Air Force officer who had checked everyone in on day one, enter through the cafeteria doors. He grabbed a hard plastic tray and filled his plate, then sat at the farthest table from David's. He sat alone, like he always did. Every few bites, the major would scan the room and look at the others like a warden looked at his prisoners.

Henry nodded. "Actually, that example brings up a question. What about after an attack? Would China really want to cut all the undersea cables that link it to the US if they're planning on occupying us? I would think not."

Natesh said, "That's something we need to talk over today. The Psychological Operations team and Comms team need to figure out some of the longer-term goals. I know Lena said that week three will be when we go over the occupation details, but I think we're all starting to realize that the choices we make at this stage in the project will affect the occupation results."

David drank from his plastic cup filled with orange liquid and crushed ice. *Efficient plans drawn up by some of our best experts.* This thing was spinning out of control. He needed to tell someone what he had seen and what he was thinking. He needed an ally. And he needed one soon.

Henry said to Natesh, "Along those lines, we're supposed to give you and the major any requests for external information, right? I will need you to get me some info from the Internet later. I'll write it down for you."

Natesh said, "Sure, no problem. What do you need?"

Henry said, "Exact maps of the undersea cables. I was going to do an options analysis of which locations to target. But I need those maps. Can you get them?"

Natesh said, "I think so. I will check before our afternoon break."

David tried to sound innocent. "Natesh—I'm just curious—I know you're somewhat of an expert with computers. Are the firewalls that they use in the Comms building really that good? I mean, it seems really inefficient for you to have to go through their censored search engine system. Could you just...I don't know... hack your way to the regular Internet and communicate that way?"

Natesh shot him a grin. "Well, I'm going to follow their protocol. A lot of the information we're asking for is classified, so the middlemen that we work through are obtaining it through special channels. But, yes, I believe their security to be somewhat rudimentary. I'm confident that if I really wanted to, I could find a workaround."

"Oh, sure. That makes sense. I was just curious," said David.

* * *

Natesh typed his code into the keypad of the Comms building and heard the beep, followed by the clicking sound of the door unlocking. He pulled the hefty metal door open, walked inside, and then pulled it shut behind him. It locked with a sharp, metallic clang.

Inside, rays of dusty sunlight reached like fingertips from the narrow slits high up on the concrete walls. There were two computer terminals. Major Combs sat at the first computer, typing away. Combs didn't bother to greet him. He barely looked up from his workstation. Natesh thought that was rude. But from what he'd seen of the major thus far, just about everything he did was antisocial. Natesh walked over to the empty computer station.

The major was housed with the rest of the group in the barracks, but he was treated differently by Lena. At each of the meals, Major Combs had eaten alone, even when others asked him to join their table. His behavior suggested that he didn't want to fraternize with any of the regular crew. It was like he thought that he was special in some way. He never smiled or spoke to the others unless it was to perform a specific duty. Unlike the other military members in the group, who had all switched over to more comfortable civilian attire at the first opportunity, the major insisted on wearing his regulation Air Force blues. It looked like he had even brought an iron to press them each night.

The gun was what Natesh really noticed. It was an Air Force-issued Beretta M9, the primary sidearm of the US military. A 9mm semiautomatic pistol, it held fifteen rounds in a detachable box magazine and had an effective firing range of fifty meters. And it was holstered snugly on Major Combs's belt. Natesh had seen several of the members of the group eyeing it uneasily. What he needed a gun for here was beyond Natesh. But apparently, Lena had asked him to wear it.

The major was the administrative officer of the Red Cell. He, like Natesh, had been given a few special responsibilities, including the use of the Comms room for Internet searches and closed-circuit email communication. So now Natesh typed on his computer, in a small concrete room, next to an armed and antisocial man.

Natesh decided to be friendly, regardless of his companion's behavior. He said, "Hello, Major. Good to see you. How has your day been?"

The major paused from his typing to peer at Natesh over his rimmed glasses. "Good day," he replied. He then resumed his intense keystrokes.

Natesh rolled his eyes and sat down at his console. Well, so much for that.

He looked at the computer. There were only two icons. One that said SEARCH and one that said EMAIL. Natesh had learned quickly that the SEARCH icon wasn't very useful. Whoever was in control of their Internet access had blocked such a large portion of the web that it was almost useless to attempt an organic search. Natesh was quite a talent when it came to computers. He had little doubt that if he wanted to, he could hack right past the firewalls. But he had been asked to play by their rules. Instead, Natesh pulled out his notepad that he had used during the day's meetings and began to type up an email.

*From: Natesh Chaudry*
    *To: Red Cell Support Center*
    *Subj: Day 7 Morning Information Request*

*I request the following information:*
    *-Geo-coordinates of all undersea fiber-optic cables that enter the US (would prefer a map)*
    *-Weapons capabilities of Chinese depth charges—are they able to destroy undersea cables? Do they have nuclear depth charges? Are there safety concerns for the deploying asset?*

*-Information on all large-scale TV and radio broadcast towers in US: frequency ranges, power sources, security, locations*

*-Information on converting shipping containers to personnel transports/lodging containers. Is it possible to convert large cargo ships into troop transports? Please send schematics of these ships and any examples of this being done in the past. Please also send schematics of shipping containers, and the names of companies in China that create these items.*

He hit SEND and shot the email off, expecting to get the information back within the hour. They were very prompt. He looked at his watch. Almost lunch. He would come back in the afternoon to get the information and then take it to the teams.

Natesh looked over at the major's screen. The major was reading an email reply that he had just received.

*From: Red Cell Support Center*
  *To: Major Harold Combs*
  *Subj: Weather Update*

*Weather conditions fair for next 24 hours. After 48 hours weather will deteriorate and reduce Site Support capability to Level 3 (remote). Tropical Cyclone #16 now at 50% probability of impacting Red Cell Site. Please notify Site Supervisor and confirm intentions.*

The email contained a map that showed a tropical system approaching their island. The funny thing about the map was that it had been sanitized. There was no land around them in any direction. So Natesh couldn't figure out where they were in the world based on looking at the map. These people were nuts about security.

Natesh said, "Are we expecting bad weather?"

Major Combs turned and sneered at Natesh. He said, "You should keep to your own screen."

Natesh cocked his head. "Hey, we're all on the same team. No need to get upset. What's the weather report? What are you reading?"

The major still looked angry, but he relented. "They've been talking about it since we got here. Some tropical storm they've been monitoring. They weren't sure if it was going to head this way but now it appears that it may. It looks like the worst of it should blow through the day after tomorrow. Might not get the airplane to resupply us that day. It shouldn't be a big deal."

Natesh said, "Aren't tropical storms a pretty big deal when you're on a small island?"

"Don't be a coward." The major turned back to his screen.

He said, "Intelligence isn't cowardice, *Harold*. Tell me, what else are you working on in here? I'm the moderator. I have a right to know. What information have you been looking up for the groups?"

The major glared at Natesh. Apparently he didn't like volunteering information. He also didn't like some twenty-something Indian-American kid pulling rank. The two stared at each other for a moment, neither budging.

The major said, "Fine. I've been doing a little work for the defense team. They've been getting into the weeds about warfare at sea. Ranges, sensor frequencies, depths, altitudes, limits, capabilities. The sorts of things that you civilians wouldn't understand. It's military stuff."

Natesh wasn't sure whether Major Combs didn't like him personally, didn't like civilians, or was just an ass in general. But he sure wasn't making a friend. Part of Natesh said to just leave it alone. He would get everything he needed later that day during the team debrief anyway. Another part of him was angered by the major blowing him off. He decided to press.

"What sort of stuff? What is the objective of your line of inquiry?"

The major rolled his eyes. He sighed but then said, "Well, in sea battle, the goal is to destroy your enemy's high-value unit. So in this case, the group that's working on the Pacific theater plan quickly migrated towards finding ways to kill the American carriers."

Natesh said, "And what was the conclusion? Did they come up with a preferred method?"

"Two, actually. One was old-fashioned, and one was what we're calling the 'Play Action' method."

Natesh said, "Go on. I need to know this, Major."

The major grinned. "Well, it's like this. The old-fashioned way to destroy a high-value unit at sea is by submarine. It's hard to stop and highly effective. The Chinese have *dozens* of submarines, and many are nuclear. That matters. Because nuclear submarines can go really far away. They aren't limited by having to refuel like their diesel cousins. They just need to resupply—food and stores. That's still no small task, if you're trying to stay hidden. The Chinese have very recently proven their ability to deploy their submarines over long distances. Really long distances. *Transoceanic* distances. That's very hard to do. But it greatly increases their value. If they can get those subs in torpedo range of our ports, it's theoretically possible that they could cripple our carrier fleet...and worse."

Natesh said, "What's worse than that? And don't we have carriers already overseas? Like in the Middle East?"

Major Combs said, "'Worse than that' can be a lot of things, once you have a vessel that carries missiles off the coast of the United States. And, yes, we do have carriers overseas. We in the military call that *deployed*. The US military has a very large amount of deployed assets at any given time. As a matter of fact, our most capable and battle-ready assets are usually deployed. So at any given time, because of the wars that we've been fighting and the high optempo our military is asked to keep up, what's left over at home is usually either in training or in maintenance. But the team has cooked up a plan to bypass them. That's the Play Action method. It's pretty brilliant, really. Lena offered a few of the ideas. The members of the team did the rest, connecting the dots."

"What ideas?"

"Play Action refers to faking out the American military. It's a football term. It's when you fake a running play and get the defense to react to that, but then throw a longer pass play. This is what the team decided on—getting the American military to commit to one type of defensive reaction and freezing them in place, then bypassing their assets and going for the main objective, where there is less protection in place."

"I don't follow." Natesh did follow. In fact, it was very similar to what he had discussed with the group on the first day. But the major seemed excited, and this was the best way to tease out more details of the plan.

The major was shaking his head, smiling. He obviously liked this a lot. Like it was a game to him.

Combs said, "We've already talked about some of this. The Chinese should create a staged war, right? United States versus Iran is what we decided on."

"They're sure they want to go with Iran?"

"They're sure. But which country we choose is not the point. The point is, the United States shifts a whole ton of assets to the Middle East—again—to fight Iran. There are a lot of things left to plan here, and we're still working out the details. And there would still be a decent-sized contingent of ships in the Pacific and allied military assets in places like Korea and Japan."

Natesh said, "I read the informational documents. Those bases are pretty sizable. And the US Pacific fleet has a very large amount of ships and submarines. I wouldn't think that a war with Iran would draw everything out of there."

"No, it wouldn't. But it would help. And that's when this ARES software goes off. It takes out GPS, and the Chinese, we presume, will launch a cyberattack on all our communications. Now the Play Action plan also calls for an EMP attack here."

"EMP?"

"Electromagnetic pulse. Are you familiar?"

"I am."

"Well, then, you know that it cripples electronics. It would leave the US Pacific fleet helpless. The Chinese will know it's coming, so they will have all their assets far enough away from the target zone that they'll be safe. After the EMPs are set off, the Chinese fleet will sail for the Eastern Pacific...and on to a variety of target locations. The Chinese subs would have static, defenseless targets where the EMPs are used."

Natesh said, "Could this really work? I'm a bit skeptical. Do the Chinese really have that capability?"

"Skeptical? Well, you keep being skeptical. The Chinese have been developing these weapons for decades."

"You sound like you admire them."

Combs shook his head in disgust. "Well, I admire that they take care of their military. Meanwhile we're ruining ours with budget cuts and mismanaged programs. Anyway—the Pacific Theater team gave me all the info they need me to look up. Just need a few specs on the exact Chinese EMP capabilities. Some of the Red Cell scientists are going to crunch the numbers later once I give them the data. The engineers said it would be relatively simple to build and program if they had the right information. And the military guys gave us almost all the details we needed on how our carrier groups defend against that sort of thing."

Natesh said, "Well, this is why we're here. Finding these vulnerabilities will help us plan the actual defense later, right?"

The major gave him a strange look, like that wasn't as important.

"Right," he said.

* * *

Brooke shuffled the deck like she was a Vegas dealer. When Henry found out that Norman Shepherd had a deck of cards, he invited him into the group. It was 10:30 p.m. and they were all sitting on the ugly carpet of her room. Last night Brooke had been playing alone with Henry, door open. She had been forced to listen to him talk the entire time about his collection of sports cars and ex-wives. She liked him just fine. He was funny. And while he was entertaining, and a decent poker player, she was happy to get a larger group involved.

Glickstein had recruited David, Natesh, and Norman. The evening meeting had just gotten out. They had agreed to play for one hour before they called it a night. With no Internet, no TV, and no phones, this was the best entertainment around. They were here for three weeks. At the pace they were going, everyone needed a little break.

Norman had used several rolls of Scotch tape, paper, and black marker to create makeshift chips. You couldn't shuffle them like Brooke liked to do when she went to the poker room just north of Fort Meade, but they served their purpose. She had a stack of the highest value chips in front of her. The rest of the group had not been so lucky.

Norman said, "Hey, Brooke, you should think about quitting the NSA and playing professional poker."

She smiled. "Nah. The NSA keeps me happy."

Glickstein said, "Yeah, happy reading my emails."

Norman asked, "Okay, since everyone here has a security clearance, I've always wanted to know. Do you guys really read everyone's emails? Do you really listen in on everyone's phone calls?"

She rolled her eyes and said, "Don't be silly. We don't read everyone's emails. Only Glickstein's."

Henry smirked knowingly. "I knew it."

Brooke was happy to notice that even David was relaxing, if only a little. He'd smiled more in the past ten minutes than he had all day in their team's meetings. She got the impression that he seriously didn't want to be here on the island. And something told her that it wasn't just because he missed his family. She was pretty good at reading people. He had made that one odd comment to her the other day, and then they'd never finished their conversation. What had he said? Something about not trusting the reason they were there. She made a mental note to ask him about that later.

Henry threw in two crumpled paper chips and said, "Raise twenty dollah."

"Fold."

"Fold."

"Call," said Natesh.

Brooke said, "Call," and threw in two chips.

The three players showed their cards. Natesh had them both beat with another full house. The group let out a mix of exclamations, swears, and laughter. It was good to let loose.

As Brooke shuffled, Henry said, "So, Natesh, have you been using your Internet access here to play online poker?"

Natesh said, "Ha-ha. No, my friend. The major and I are all business in there, I'm afraid."

Henry said, "So how's the major? That guy seems like a real asshole if you ask me. Pardon my French. I probably shouldn't talk bad about him. I don't really know him. But he never talks to anyone. And he always acts like he's above the rest of us. And why's he always carrying that gun around? What's he gonna do, shoot us if we get outta line?"

Norman said, "He's Air Force. I think he'd be more liable to brush your hair than shoot you."

Henry scoffed. He said, "But really—Natesh, what's his deal?"

Natesh shrugged. He said, "His deal? I don't know. He works with Lena pretty closely. I think she just wanted someone to act as security. Just in case."

Henry said, "Humph."

Brooke watched the exchange. She was used to having a lot of armed security where she worked. She wasn't too concerned. David's face was grey again. What was bothering him so much?

Norman said, "You guys hear about the Psychological Operations team's strategy to start a war with Iran? They looked at 9/11 and decided that the quickest way to get us to go to war with Iran would be to stage a terrorist attack on the United States that was so gruesome and emotionally charged that the public would demand retribution."

David said, "What was the plan?"

Norman just shook his head. "That one guy. Dr. Creighton. They're calling him Dr. Evil. The guy's kind of a freak. I'm not sure where they found him. So he came up with this idea involving a massive traffic jam on the Beltway around D.C."

Brooke said, "Uh...sorry, guys, but I hate to tell you. The Beltway *is* a traffic jam."

Norman said, "He basically designed a terrorist attack. His idea is to create a massive traffic jam and have several teams of terrorists with handguns just walk along the stopped traffic and shoot people in their cars. If you timed it well enough, he thought the casualties would get pretty high. And in the D.C. area, you're bound to get some high-profile targets, or their families, or coworkers of the decision makers. Dr. Evil also mentioned attacking *schools*."

Henry said, "Schools? What kind of sick plan is that?"

"Yeah. Schools. But not just any schools. Christian schools. The idea was that it would look like a religious thing. They said if you'd planned the Beltway attacks at the same times as the school attacks, you'd have virtually guaranteed a large-scale military response, just because of the national anger you would create. People would demand retribution, and look to the politicians to deliver."

Brooke said, "That's disgusting. I'm a little embarrassed that one of our groups even proposed that. I thought this was supposed to be about how China could attack us. Isn't that why we're here? Aren't we supposed to be focusing on military conflicts with the Chinese? How did one of the groups get to planning a school attack?"

Norman said, "Well, technically, this is what we were asked to do. They wanted us to come up with a way to get a lot of American assets out of the way, so to speak, so that China would have the least resistance possible."

Brooke looked at David. He had family in that area. He was glancing around at everyone nervously. He kept opening his mouth like he was going to speak, and then would stop and look down at the floor.

Finally, David said, "Guys…"

Natesh said, "Brooke, I know what you mean. But the task was to create China's most effective and efficient plan. They were looking for a way to remove American military obstacles."

David said, "*Guys.*"

Brooke said, "Still, that's disgusting. I don't know if I want to be part of talks like that."

Henry said, "Yeah, Bill was lucky he got to go home."

David said, "Guys, *I need to say something important.*"

Brooke and the others looked at David. He was looking at the floor. He was struggling with getting the words out.

Brooke said, "David, what is it?"

David looked up at her and said, "I don't think that Bill made it home."

Brooke frowned. "What are you talking about?"

"I saw something. The other night. When Bill left."

She could see that he was disturbed. This was the same troubled look he'd worn all day.

Norman said, "David, what's up? What did you see?"

He stayed silent. He turned and looked at the door. It was open just a crack. He got up and closed it, then returned to his spot on the floor. The others watched him with growing interest.

Natesh put his hand on David's shoulder and said, "David, you're among friends. Whatever is bothering you, you can trust us."

David said, "Sorry, I need to get this out, but I don't want anyone outside this room to hear."

Henry said, "No problem. We're in the trust tree here. Spill it. What's wrong?"

"It was when the helicopter came. The night Bill left. It was late. Middle of the night. I couldn't sleep. Jet lag or something. I don't know why I did it, but I decided to take a little walk outside. I guess I was still thinking about my family and needed to clear my head. I thought the walk would help..."

Brooke said, "And what did you see?"

"I saw Lena take Bill to the helicopter. It was dark, and something just didn't seem right. I guess I was having trust issues. When I heard the door to the Comms building open—I was standing nearby—I ducked into the bushes. I was hidden pretty well, I guess. Nobody saw me. Like I said, it was dark..."

Norman said, "You hid from her?"

David said, "Like I said, something just didn't feel right. Anyway, while I was hiding I saw her drag Bill out. He wasn't conscious."

"What!" Brooke put her hand over her mouth.

Henry held his hands out. "Shh. Let him finish."

David said, "I don't know if he was dead or what. But he wasn't walking under his own power. Lena met up with a guy from the helicopter and then took him up into her building…"

Norman got louder and used a stern voice. "*Wait.* Hold up. You're saying he was *unconscious*? What the—? Why didn't you say anything about this before?"

Henry's voice was soft. "Let him finish."

David said, "Sorry. I'm sorry for not letting you know sooner. But I'm afraid of what we're into here. I saw Lena walk down to the helicopter, then walk back up with a guy wearing a helmet and uniform—"

Norman said, "What color uniform?"

"I couldn't see. It was dark. But the two of them went into the building and then came out with Bill. Each of them had one of Bill's arms wrapped around their shoulders. They carried him like that—dragged him, really—down to the helicopter. Then Lena came back and the helo flew off. I waited a while before I moved. I didn't want to be seen. I wasn't sure what to think after witnessing that. I watched her go back into the Comms building. I waited ten minutes. I didn't want to take any chance and get seen. When I thought that the coast was clear, I walked as quickly as I could back up to my room. But she saw me…"

Brooke said, "*What?* What did she do?"

"She came into the barracks as I was opening the door to my room. She asked if I had gone outside and I said no. But I think she knew I was lying. She…she wiped some of the sand off my shirt and then left."

Henry covered his mouth with his fist, pressing his lips to his thumb. He looked lost in thought.

Brooke leaned forward, mouth open. She kept saying, "Why would she do that to Bill? Why would she do that to Bill?"

Natesh was the calmest of the group. He said, "David, are you sure there is not a reasonable explanation for any of this?"

The others looked at Natesh and then back at David.

David said, "I saw her again this morning. I was out running. On the runway."

Norman said, "You went running? Like—for exercise? After what you saw her do to Bill?"

David said, "Well, first off, I didn't actually see her do anything to Bill. But I've been going crazy keeping this to myself. And this may sound weird, but I'm kind of a workout nut. I needed to get my fix. I was like a stressed smoker who needed a cigarette."

Norman rolled his eyes and said, "Yeah, I knew guys like that in the Marines. Whatever, man. Just—*Jesus*, you know? This is a big deal. One—watch your back. And two—you should have told us. So what the hell happened when you saw her this morning?"

David said, "Nothing at first. She just ran right by me going the other direction. But then she came over to me when I was finished and stretching. It was a weird conversation. She told me to do my job and not—how did she put it? She told me not to make waves or something. She basically was telling me to shut up and keep quiet. Guys, I don't trust her at all. I was trying to think of a good reason for why I saw what I saw, but I can't think of one. I needed to tell someone. I'm starting to think..."

Brooke said, "Think what?"

Henry said, "You're starting to think that this operation isn't legit. Right?"

David nodded, "Right. I couldn't see that helicopter very well. But I come from a big Navy family. My sister's actually a helicopter pilot in the Navy. And I swear that thing didn't look or sound like one of ours."

Natesh said, "There has to be some reasonable explanation for all this."

They were whispering now. Brooke heard a few voices in the hallway outside her door. People walking back to their rooms.

Brooke said, "Okay, let's think about this logically. What are the facts?"

Henry said, "Well, Bill's gone. That's one fact."

David said, "Natesh, how long have you known Lena?"

Natesh said, "A week. Maybe ten days."

"Can you be sure that she is who she claims to be?"

The others studied Natesh. Maybe they were wondering if he wasn't in on it. Brooke thought that was highly unlikely. The guy was in his twenties. An entrepreneur. A business consultant. It wasn't the profile. *Right?*

Natesh said, "If we're going by the facts, then the answer is no. She approached me about ten days ago. First via phone. Then a onetime meeting at a rented office in the Bay Area."

Norman looked at David as he said, "So, David—you're saying you don't think she's really CIA?"

David said, "The way I see it, there could be two reasons why Bill would be taken away like that. One: Lena and this whole operation are legit. She's CIA but because of the level of secrecy of this operation, they kept Bill heavily sedated during transport. It was like putting a bag over his head so he wouldn't see anything. Two: Lena and this whole operation are not legitimate. In which case, all bets are off. And these plans that we're making got a whole lot scarier."

Norman said, "Holy shit. Holy shit..." He started looking around the room like he wanted to punch something.

Henry remained composed. It was a stark contrast to his normally humorous tone. He said, "I agree with your reasoning. I don't see too many possibilities beyond that. But let's go with scenario number two. Let's say Lena and this island are a big sham. What's the angle?"

Brooke was thinking. Her eyes went back and forth looking at the ceiling. She said, "Okay, look, I've been working on related operations for weeks. Fact: Jinshan and the Chinese invasion plot are real. David, you've worked on the cyberweapon that they supposedly have access to. ARES, right? We know that capability is real. Why would anyone bring us to this island if not to help plan the defense against a Chinese attack?"

David said, "But we're not planning the defense. We're planning the *attack*."

Brooke said, "So...Lena actually works for..."

Henry nodded. "Say it."

Brooke said, "...China."

Everyone was quiet.

Brooke said, "This has all been staged by China? But then we can't trust anything Lena has told us. So is ARES really in countdown?"

Henry said, "The question to ask is—are the Chinese really making plans to attack? If the answer to that is yes, what is this Red Cell all about? A way to gather extra information before the attack?"

Natesh said, "I'm not ready to conclude any of that yet...but I think it's prudent to evaluate all possibilities."

Henry said, "Look, I don't want to be racist or anything, but Lena is Asian. Probably Chinese ancestry. Maybe that's a little too obvious to make that connection, and I know we aren't supposed to profile anymore, but...I mean that's almost *too* obvious. All of the stewards are Asian, too. There's a highly freaking likely possibility that we're in the freaking Pacific, for God's sake. I mean, if we think of it like that, I start feeling like an idiot. They practically took us to the Sheraton in Beijing and asked us to fill out a Q&A on where America's weaknesses lay."

Natesh said, "Okay, let's calm down. Lena is one person. If no one else will, I will play devil's advocate. I highly doubt that it's within the realm of possibility that the Chinese government would place all of us here with one person from their intelligence service."

David said, "I agree. But that doesn't mean that this hasn't been staged by the Chinese. To me, that just suggests that we need to watch our backs. They wouldn't try to do something like this and leave her alone with all of us on an island. Right? Just like you're suggesting, that sounds too risky. So—who else is helping her?"

They each looked at each other.

"The major? That guy's weird as hell," said Norman.

Brooke nodded. "And he's been here from the start. I could see that. *And* he carries a gun. He's also got access to the Communications building."

"So do I," said Natesh.

The others went quiet.

David broke the awkward silence and said, "Sorry, Natesh. It's just—"

Natesh said, "It's alright. Go ahead and be suspicious. Ask me anything. I would, if I was in your shoes. Again, it's only prudent. However, I can guarantee that I'm most definitely *not* a Chinese spy. I'm not a traitor."

He was telling the truth. David could see it in his eyes. David said, "No one is accusing you of being a traitor. But—what do you think about the major?"

Natesh grimaced. He said, "I...I can't back anything up with facts..."

Brooke said, "Can't back what up with facts?"

He said, "I just get this feeling. Like he is enjoying this too much. He almost enjoys being on a team that's outsmarting the US."

Brooke said, "That's what they said about Robert Hanssen. The FBI agent who spied for the Russians. He didn't do it for the money. He did it because he loved the ego boost. You think Combs is like that?"

Norman said, "He's pretty old to be just a major. Maybe he was prior-enlisted or something. But if he wasn't, that means he was probably passed over for promotion a lot. A guy like that would probably get disgruntled and jaded after a while. But that doesn't mean he is a traitor."

Henry said, "No, but maybe Lena used that as a way in."

Natesh said, "Please, let's remember that this is all speculation."

Norman said, "Bill being dragged into a helicopter unconscious was speculation?"

Natesh sighed and held up his arms in surrender.

David said, "Alright, calm down. Look, I needed to tell someone. I thought I could trust this group. But if it's all the same, let's keep this information to ourselves for now. We need to figure out who we can trust. And personally, I just don't think Lena's acting alone."

Brooke said, "You think this place is bugged?"

They all looked around the room. David said, "I honestly didn't consider that."

Henry said, "It's not bugged."

Norman said, "How do you know?"

Henry said, "Because they'd be running in here right now, guns blazing. Right? Look, we know she's not acting totally alone. The computers transmit and receive to someone, right? The stewards, the daily resupply flights. Hell, she got a helicopter to arrive within a few hours. She must have an *immense* amount of support. But what I don't know is what support she has on the island. And if she is playing for the Chinese, the isolation factor may be our greatest advantage."

David said, "Actually, I think you're right. Natesh, you told me that you think you could hack past the firewalls in the Comms building. Do you still think you could do that?"

Natesh glanced around the room. "Yes. I do."

"Good. Because right now, I think you're the only way that we know of to get a warning out and send for help."

Henry nodded, "That's a good idea. But I would think that they'll know somehow. I mean, Lena would know. The major would know. Natesh might be able to get in there, but wouldn't he get caught and shut down?"

David said, "Not if we've got Lena and anyone on her side as our prisoners."

Norman said, "I'm in. I don't even know what you're planning yet, but I'm in. I know some of those law enforcement and military guys that are on the Defense team would have to be with us if we told them what's going on."

David looked at Natesh. "If we gave you the time, could you do it? I have to imagine there is some kill switch if whoever is pulling the strings finds out what you're trying to do."

Brooke said, "That would be easy to set up."

Natesh said, "Let's slow down. Please. Can we first make sure that we have in fact ruled out all possible legitimate reasons for what David saw happen to Bill?"

Henry said, "Of course, but—"

Natesh held out his hands. "If we find out that Lena indeed is anything other than what she says she is, then I'm confident that if you get me thirty free minutes in that Communications building, I will be able to send out a warning message, and contact friends on the outside that could lead rescuers to our location. I've seen enough of those computers and operating systems. I can do it. But, please, let's continue to do our jobs until we know for sure."

David nodded. "That's fair. First, we need to figure out what's really going on. If it is the worst-case scenario, then we need to come up with a plan to escape. And warn people. Right now,

Natesh is our only hope. And getting him alone in that Comms room will be the goal if we confirm that Lena is not CIA. She and any of her accomplices are people we'll have to deal with. But I'm not convinced they're the only ones on this island that could be a problem..."

Natesh said, "What do you mean?"

David said, "The fence."

"What about it?" Norman said.

"Why would you need a barbed-wire fence on an island? Who are you trying to keep out?"

Henry said, "Animals? I don't know, orangutans? They're pesky beasts, if you ask me. Never trusted 'em."

David said, "No, seriously. This island is relatively large. I don't know exactly how far around it goes, but I don't think that fence is for our protection. I think it's to keep us from finding out what else is here on the island. Maybe this is just part of a larger base. Maybe this is the part that was *meant to hold us*."

Norman said, "So what else is out there?"

David said, "I don't know. But I'm willing to bet it will help us figure out what's going on. So I'm going to find out."

Natesh said, "Find out what?"

David said, "Find out what's beyond the fence. For now, let's *all please* agree to keep this just among us. Let's keep meeting like this at night. We can call it a poker game if anyone asks, but keep it exclusive to this group until we know who else we can trust. Keep your eyes and ears open—tomorrow night I'll share what I've seen and we can decide where to go from here. But promise me that none of you will tell a soul about any of this until we come up with a plan."

The others nodded.

Brooke asked, "How are you going to find out what's on the other side of the fence?"

David said, "Leave that to me."

## 7

*Before I built a wall I'd ask to know.*
  *What I was walling in or walling out...*
  —Robert Frost

David's eyes snapped open as his watch alarm went off. It was 4:45 a.m. He kicked his legs over the side of the bed and put on his running gear and sneakers. He needed to hurry. Dawn approached.

A few minutes later he was once again running on the pavement of the island's lone runway. By his estimate, the sun should rise at 6 a.m. That gave him a good forty-five minutes of darkness.

David tried to scan the starlit runway for signs of other people as he ran. He didn't see Lena this morning. But that was one of the reasons he was up so early. It was a full hour earlier than he had seen her the last time she was out here. He wanted to avoid being seen by anyone, but especially her. To his knowledge, Lena and he were the only two real runners on the island. A few of the consultants worked out lightly in the afternoon. He had seen them with their trendy workout clothes on, doing push-ups and sit-ups on the beach for a few minutes and calling it a day. But if he even heard footsteps on the tarmac, he had to assume that it was Lena.

David finally arrived at the far end of the runway, about a mile from the barracks, cafeteria, classroom, and Communications building. He walked off the tarmac and towards the shore. The waves were picking up. This must be that weather they were talking about during the morning brief. Not perfect for swimming, but David would manage...as long as there were no sharks out for a morning feed.

He placed his shoes, socks, and shirt behind a small bush fifty yards from the end of the runway and halfway to the fence. It was hidden so that if Lena were running by, she wouldn't spot the pile.

David waded ankle-deep into the ocean. The salt water was warm against his skin. He walked farther out into the pitch-black water, wondering what was beneath the surface. He could feel the sand packed in soft rolls under his feet. He plowed through the moderate surf. Every once in a while, he would feel something hard touch his toes. Maybe a crab. Hopefully there were no sea urchins under there.

A million magnificent stars lit up the sky, and a sliver of bright moon reflected off the ocean. The water was up to his neck when he started swimming breaststroke, careful to keep an eye on the razor-sharp top of the fence. He had to swim against the waves so that he could get far enough out before he turned left to parallel the shore and start swimming around the island. That way, he wouldn't get lodged up against the jagged metal spirals of razor wire that followed the fence in a straight line fifty feet out to sea. David swam an extra fifteen feet past the point where the fence sank under the water. He was beyond the breakers, and the waves carried him up and down as he swam. He didn't want his legs kicking into the razor wire.

Once he was out far enough, he turned ninety degrees away

from the base and swam parallel to the shore. He picked up the pace and switched to freestyle.

In a way, it felt good to break the rules by swimming out here, past the fence. It was also terrifying. David was vulnerable out here. He didn't want Lena to catch him, and he wasn't sure what he would find. He had a hunch that something or someone would be there. Would they have a security guard? Would they be armed?

As he swam, he began to feel the swells of ocean pick up slightly. He realized that there must be stronger winds on one side of the island. Muscles that hadn't been tested in a few weeks were starting to burn, which felt good and made him push himself harder. His legs fluttered through the water, kicking but trying not to splash and make too much noise. Every few minutes he would take his head up a bit farther when he breathed, to gauge his distance to the shore. He tried to keep the same distance so as not to go too far out and get caught in a current.

He swam for twenty minutes that way, riding the waves up and down, breathing out his left side every few strokes. The waves were bigger than he had anticipated. It was hard work, but he pushed himself onward. Every few minutes he checked his watch, and then the shore.

David stopped and floated, taking a moment to get the salt water out of his eyes so he could clearly see the island. It always frustrated David that he had been medically disqualified for flight training for having bad eyesight. It frustrated him because, while he sometimes had to wear glasses to read, he could see faraway things just fine. The eastern sky was light blue now, and at any moment, the sun would begin to creep over the horizon. While the lightening sky made him nervous since it would be easier for someone to spot him, it also made it easier for him to scan the shore for any sign of suspicious activity.

He checked his watch. Damn. This swim was taking too long.

He didn't have much more time. As he pondered turning around and heading back, David realized that he was further out to sea than he had originally intended. He was a good seventy-five yards from the shore; far enough out that he almost missed the dimly lit concrete structures about a half mile further down the island.

His eyes widened when he saw them. He had suspected that he would find something else outside of the fence. Still—it was one thing to suspect it, and another to see it with his own eyes. He swam on to get a closer look.

The buildings looked like they were made with the same solid concrete design as the ones on his side of the island. But these buildings had some type of enormous netting draped over them. The main structure was about the size of a small college dormitory, and it slanted down from the hill toward the beach. Like the Comms building, there were dozens of antennas and satellite dishes on top. Just next to the main building was a large concrete square that looked like it must have been a helipad. David bobbed up and down in the rolling blue waves, studying the structures. There was a line of dim lights at the top of one facing of the building. It looked like a bunker. Lights shined through slits at the top of the bunker, just like the windows in the Comms building. David could just barely make out their glow.

He just floated there for a bit, bobbing in the warm sea. His nervousness told him he should head back, but his curiosity kept him stationary. It didn't look like there were any roads leading to these buildings from his side of the island. Hell, there weren't any cars to drive on roads. So who'd built these structures and how were they kept supplied? Who *inhabited* them? They looked like they could hold a hundred or more people, but he didn't see anyone. Why would this island have a fenced-in base on one side with these isolated structures on the other?

As the horizon began to turn greyish blue, signaling the coming dawn, he could just make out a small pier near the shoreline, adjacent to the buildings. Two motorboats were tied to the dock. Beyond the building and the pier was a sheer wall of rock rising up from the shoreline. It was at least one hundred feet high, and then gradually turned into the jungle-covered mountain above. The longer David stared at that cliff, the more it looked man-made. It was too perfect to be a natural rock facing. The smooth surface was rounded at the top and he could barely make out a vertical line splitting its center. It looked strangely like a gigantic door of some kind. An enormous closed stone door that opened into the sea. Very curious...

The noise froze him.

It was the high-pitched whine of a boat engine combined with the sound of its hull bouncing up and down on the water. And it was getting louder. Behind him. He swiveled to look...and immediately dove underwater, holding what breath he had.

The world went from light and loud to dark and silent as he plunged into the ocean. He swam deeper and deeper, trying to get under the boat that had looked like it was coming straight for him.

The boat had looked like a rigid-hull inflatable boat, with its bow protruding upwards. A high-horsepower engine probably weighed down the aft end. In the flash David had observed the boat, he thought he had viewed multiple people on board. He guessed three. Had they seen him?

The seconds inched by as David held his breath, waiting for the boat to pass overhead. He was desperately pushing himself downward, trying to fight the buoyant yet precious lungful of air that wanted to raise him up to the surface. He heard the dull noise of the boat passing above. It sounded like it was right on top of him. He looked up, eyes burning in the salt water.

There was a blur of dark motion on the light blue surface of the water as the vessel passed overhead, followed by circling bubbles of white foam. Time moved in agonizing slow motion. David's lungs screamed at him to breathe, but he kept pumping his arms to stay deep, away from the engine. And away from the eyes of the men on the boat.

When he couldn't hold his breath any longer, David let himself drift up as slowly as he could manage. He surfaced and breathed in deep gulps of satisfying air. His eyes were on fire with salt water. He wheezed and coughed, treading water. He did his best to stay right at the waterline, out of sight. He could only hope that the passengers on that vessel were far enough away and hadn't seen him before he dove under, and that they weren't looking in his direction now. The sky was grey now, and it was light enough for them to see him if they were looking. As the waves carried him up and down each crest and trough, he watched the boat continue its bumpy journey over the water, toward the pier that David had been looking at moments before.

He could see the men on the boat clearly, their bodies bouncing in rhythm with the speeding boat as it skipped across the waves. David had been wrong. There weren't three men on board—there were four.

Two of the men were Asian, and they wore black uniforms, with submachine guns slung over their shoulders. *Not good.* One uniformed man piloted the boat. He had one hand on a small silver wheel and the other on a black plastic power control lever. The other uniformed man was gripping a side rail, watching a prisoner.

A prisoner—that's what the third man looked like from the way he held himself. He held his head down, dejected. His arms and shoulders were slouched together like his hands were restrained.

David couldn't see the face of the prisoner, but he didn't need to. He knew who it was. The prisoner's fluorescent-white hair was a very distinct feature. Very easily recognized. That was one of the reasons he had spotted him the other night, in the dark, being hauled unconscious to a helicopter.

Bill.

David was numb. One part of him felt a strange satisfaction that his hunch had been right. A much bigger part of him wanted to panic.

The fourth man turned from facing forward and David almost lost it. The fourth man looked angry and unpleasant, just like he had the week before when he had convinced David to get on a jet to this godforsaken island. The fourth man's mouth was moving, and he looked like he was saying something to Bill, his prisoner. *His* prisoner. However impossible that seemed, David could see it in the body language. The fourth man shouldn't have been in the same hemisphere, let alone on that boat.

David tried to make sense of it. He tried to understand how that could be possible. As the military-style speedboat zoomed off to the dock, David wondered if he had a chance of surviving this ordeal.

He now knew with certainty that this gathering on the island wasn't to help the United States plan its defense. It was to provide China with its defense plans. No. It was to give China attack plans. They were outsourcing their war planning to the best consultants they could get. And at least some Americans were in on it. Seeing the fourth man confirmed that.

The fourth man was Tom Connolly.

## 8
---

In a time of universal deceit—telling the truth is a revolutionary act.

    —George Orwell

David swam back to his side of the island with determined intensity. There was a slight current working in his favor, not against him. He was lucky for that. In fifteen minutes, he crept out of the water and walked back on the beach near the runway. He hobbled over toward his pile of shoes and clothing. His wet feet were picking up grey bits of sand as he walked.

There was no one out on the runway. David kept looking up to make sure. And he kept his ears peeled for Lena's footsteps, too. He didn't want her sneaking up on him and catching him red-handed. He placed his sandy wet feet into his socks and got moving. He looked at his watch. He needed to hurry to make it in time for the first meeting this morning. Now more than ever, he didn't want to look suspicious. But he needed to tell the others what he'd seen. The question was—how?

Thunder crackled in the distance. He looked up and saw a line of storms approaching from the west. It was still another thirty minutes out, by the looks of it, but the wind was already picking up.

They needed to act soon. As he jogged the length of the runway back to his barracks, he thought about what he needed to do. David didn't think that the situation could get any worse. He was very wrong.

* * *

Henry slouched in his chair in the back of the auditorium, half-listening to the guys next to him. The classroom was alive with chatter. The intellectual exercise of plotting America's demise and learning interesting bits of classified security information fascinated most of the members of the Red Cell, and everyone seemed to be discussing their groups' plans. Apparently, the "compartmentalization" rules had been thrown out the window. Rumor was that everything was getting shared today anyway.

Henry scanned the class. David was still missing. It was very unusual for him. And worrisome to Henry. He had said that he was going to find out what was on the other side of the fence. Hopefully he was alright.

The conversation Henry was half-listening to was between two members of the Defense team, who were talking about how wired all our military technology is today. He couldn't remember their names. Henry was terrible with names.

The first guy worked as a Navy defense contractor out of Norfolk. He said, "So let me give you an example. A few years ago, one of our Navy warships bumped into a tanker as it was going through a strait. Just a little love tap—probably nothing compared to what a few missiles would do. But this little bump caused a ton of damage. Let me ask you something, do you have any idea how many *cables and wires* are in a Navy ship?"

The second guy shrugged.

"*Thousands*. That little bump from a tanker turned one of our most advanced warships into a floating barge *real* quick. The lights went out, its radar went black, and its guns couldn't be fired. Think it could shoot a missile? Forget about it. Contractors had a field day, though. Huge maintenance job to fix it up. But my point is—you think that in World War Two, one of Henry J. Kaiser's ships would have stopped being able to fight a battle because of one little bump against the hull? Hell no! You ever read about the Tin Cans? They took hits from the Japanese and kept on fighting. They had to. If one part of the ship gets destroyed, the rest can't be affected. That's what real sea combat is. It's messy. Comms go down. Wires get cut. Those old World War Two ship drivers knew that. If one part of the ship got hit, the others had to keep on fighting. But today—it's the *wires*, man. The *wires* are the problem."

"The wires?"

"Yeah—there's too many of 'em running all up and down the ships. Everything's all interconnected, so that if one part goes out, another is affected. It's just like what's his name—Natesh—it's just like he's been sayin'. Our technology is our Achilles heel. I'm not even talking about what our Defense team came up with, the EMP tactics. I'm just talking about a regular shooting war. If one missile gets a hit on one of our warships, my guess is that the Chicoms would just storm right through and finish the job. Because our ships would be dead in the water—lights out. All these years our politicians have been signing bigger and bigger contracts to add on weapon systems and radars and the latest computers...probably all made in their districts. Great! You got a floating high-tech boat that's gonna be useless once the first round hits it in combat. Meanwhile, the Chinese don't even have computers on a lot of their ships—that's what the books say. How crazy is that? But you know what? All this time, we've been thinking that we're the genius nation with the advanced technology and that they can't achieve our level of sophistication. But I'm looking at these plans that we're making and I'm starting to wonder—was this their strategy all along? Did they create ships and aircraft and tanks that would operate *better* in a low-tech environment as a *strategy*?"

The second guy grunted and shook his head.

"Because I start thinking that all this time, we've been thinking that they just don't have the ability to create technology like we do. That they're too poor or not advanced enough. Let me ask you something, who makes all the iPhones in the world? China. You think that they aren't advanced enough? You think they couldn't computerize the shit out of their ships and tanks if they wanted to? I'm telling you, man, all these years I think the Chinese have been playing us. It's been a strategy for them to create their military so that it isn't reliant on technology. It's lower cost that way. We spend all the money. They've got ten times the men. When the technology that we think is so advanced crashes from a computer virus or electromagnetic pulse, ten men beat one man. You know what I'm saying?"

Henry stayed still, casually looking at the two as they spoke. He glanced at the front of the classroom. It was past eight o'clock in the morning. In the four days that they had been here on the island, every meeting had started right on time. Henry watched as Lena, Natesh and the Major spoke in hushed voices at the front of the classroom. Something was going on. They were huddled close together and Natesh was frowning. Lena was speaking to him calmly. But her eyes looked at him with force. Henry knew a guy that always looked at people that way. He was a short Italian guy —a boxer. He was a quiet guy, always looking up at people. He never blinked. Henry had once been at a bar where a few big drunken guys had made the mistake of underestimating the Italian. They'd regretted their mistake very much. Lena had this look. It was a hungry, confident look. Like she owned the world, or soon would.

Henry looked a few rows down and saw Brooke. He caught her

eye and nodded down to Lena, Natesh, and the major, as if to ask her what was going on. Brooke just shrugged. She mouthed to him, "Where's David?" Henry had been wondering the same thing. It worried him. He shook his head. He didn't know either.

Henry looked back over at the two guys that he'd been listening to. He said, "Hey, what were you guys talking about with EMP?"

The first guy said, "Huh? Oh, that's one of the main parts of the Defense team's plan. Lena and Major Combs gave us the idea. I mean, people were already talking about it. But Combs seemed to know a little more about the Chinese EMP capability. Did you know that they have shelters for their military that they've built to shield them from electromagnetic pulse? Apparently the Chinese have these air bases that have hangars built into huge caves. They're essentially turning mountains into large man-made bunkers. And it's not just for aircraft—even their ships and submarines have these cave-like structures that they've been working on for the past few years. They build them into coastal mountain locations—I can't imagine the cost. But these things are enormous—giant caverns big enough for ships and submarines to float into and dock. They must be stacked right next to each other two or three deep in there. But they dredge the water right from the canals up into the caves. US intelligence thinks that it's to protect them from EMP in case they want to drop a few on their home court."

Guy number two grunted.

Henry said, "What do you mean, drop them on their home court?"

The first guy said, "I mean like the South China Sea. Let's say a US carrier strike group was over there. Or the Japanese Navy or Taiwanese or whoever. The Chinese could park all their assets in those caves, launch a couple of dozen EMPs, and while all our jets are crashing to the ground and our ships are blacked out with no electrical power, they can unleash their military on a bunch of sitting ducks."

Henry said, "No shit? Well, how many caves can they really have? Does that really even work? And isn't our military protected from electromagnetic pulse? I know the telecommunications companies I've worked with try to protect from it."

The second guy spoke up and said, "From what the major was saying, both the military and corporate assets are only protected up to a point. It's all about cost. But the Chinese have apparently been developing *very* powerful EMP weapons that are able to overcome our hardened electronics equipment. From what the group was discussing yesterday, they stole most of the tech from us when they hacked in to Los Alamos."

Henry said, "And this is what you guys are planning—or, you know, saying that you think China will do?"

The two nodded.

The first guy said, "That's part of the plan. We think they would use EMP to get past all the US military assets that are based in the Asia Pacific region. The plan is to detonate a lot of these EMP devices at lower altitudes...like thirty to forty miles above sea level—or was it kilometers?—well, anyway, they detonate them close enough to US forces in the Pacific that it hurts them and minimizes damage to the Chinese mainland. That's the plan we're writing up. It's what we would do."

Henry said, "So then what?"

As he spoke, he saw Natesh and the Major leave the stage and sit down in the front row of the classroom. The audience went silent.

The second guy whispered over his response, "Then, they head *east*—a *lot* of them." He looked at Henry knowingly.

Henry raised his eyebrows and looked back toward the front of the classroom.

Lena stood on the stage, upright and poised.

She said, "Good morning, everyone. First, I'd like to thank you for all the hard work you've put in over the past week. The plans you all have put together have been remarkable. I'm amazed at the innovative thinking and new ideas that you've presented. You all have shown us that there are definitely some holes in national security that will need to be addressed."

She looked at Major Combs. "Before I continue, Major, would you mind showing us the weather brief right now? I'll continue when you're done."

"Yes, ma'am. Of course." The major rose, his crisp blues wrapped tight around his oversized waist. He walked up to the podium and read from his notes. "At twenty-three fifty-two last night our weather forecaster updated us on the latest track of what is now tropical cyclone number sixteen. It appears there is now a greater than ninety-five percent chance that we'll be in the direct path of the storm, which is already starting to impact us. Winds are projected to be over sixty knots, with waves over twenty feet out at sea and eight to ten feet ashore. There will also be a slight storm surge of three to four feet."

Major Combs looked up from his notes. He continued, looking at the members of the classroom, "The buildings that we're working and staying in are all high enough up and secure enough that this shouldn't be a major safety concern. But we ask that you all stay inside unless you're conducting official business—so that means just going to eat or to the classroom. No horsing around here. Beginning at zero nine hundred today, the weather is really supposed to pick up. The bad stuff should all be over within about twelve hours. But it's going to get a bit hairy during the day today. Because of this, there won't be as much external support. No incoming plane today. We also may lose external satellite communication, so get any external information search requests in to Natesh and me by noon today. There is a small chance that we could lose communications for a bit longer. The computer link that we use has been known to go down in these storms. The wind might dislodge our satellite radar dishes. That is all."

Lena nodded thanks to the major and walked back in front of the stage. The major sat back down.

She said, "With that information, we want to take some precautions. Because you all have overdelivered on the speed and quality of your plans, we've decided to pause on the individual teamwork and send a summary of where the combined group plan is today. I've spoken with Natesh, and he's agreed to modify our schedule. Today you will all be in this classroom, working on bringing together your individual group plans into one congealed script. We will then transmit that out by lunch at the latest. What we don't want to happen is a scenario where we lose communications for a prolonged period of time and can't get any of the great work that you all have completed to those that need it. We're on a tight timeline as is."

Henry thought this didn't really make sense, considering the unknowns of the supposed timeline, but he didn't object. He also wasn't sold on some satellite communication disruption causing them to totally change Natesh's schedule. David's concerns seemed more valid by the minute.

Lena said, "Alright, I would like to thank you once again. I'll step aside so that you may all get to work. Natesh?"

Natesh stepped up on stage and Lena walked up to the back of the classroom. She stood in front of the large glass panoramic window, jotting notes down in her black leather book.

Natesh said, "Good morning, folks. Lena has asked us to make a change in our schedule. The weather is indeed moving in. Instead of breaking up into teams, today we'll stay in one big group and create the integrated first draft outline for the Chinese attack."

The door opened and David stumbled into the class. Ten minutes late. His hair was damp and he looked even more anxious than normal. Henry thought that he saw glistening on his forehead, like he had been running again. He looked upset. He wondered if he'd seen anything new that had spooked him this morning.

About half the eyes in the classroom shot over to him. He didn't say anything. He just walked to the nearest seat and sat down. Henry tried to act casual as he peered behind to where Lena was standing. She was looking right at David. Then her eyes darted over to Henry and he looked away.

Natesh called up the team leaders for a quick huddle in the front of the class. Everyone else continued talking. Lena walked down the stairs and out the door. Once she left, David looked over at Henry. David was mouthing something to him, but he couldn't make it out. Henry finally got what he was trying to say: *we need to talk*. Henry just nodded back and pointed at his watch, made a circle gesture, and then pointed to his notepad. Unofficial sign language was one of his specialties.

David looked back at him, confused. Class was starting. Henry would have to talk to him during the next break.

There were no official breaks given. People trickled out by themselves for the occasional trip to the bathroom, but Natesh was a slave driver this morning. He plowed the members of the Red Cell through plans, and wasn't taking any shit from the usual argumentative characters. Henry wondered why Natesh was so hellbent on speeding through this. Natesh had heard David's story last night. Lena might not really be CIA. Natesh even had his own concerns about the major. But he sure was doing a good job for Lena right now. Henry could see why he made the big bucks from all these companies. Natesh was a thinker. He made connections and processed information faster than anyone Henry had ever met.

By a little after 11 a.m., the class had a comprehensive invasion outline written up. They'd worked for three hours straight. Major Combs captured it all in a presentation which was projected in front of the class. Henry had listened with growing alarm as the time dragged on. These were scary good invasion plans. If a country with China's capability and resources really wanted to follow through, he didn't want to think of what might happen. Every once in a while he looked over at David, whose face looked pale.

Tess asked, "So is this supposed to be a final version? This is our actual recommendation?"

Natesh shook his head and said, "No, Tess. Think of this as a first draft. But it will be a first draft with all of our plans integrated together. I realize it got a little messy today as we prioritized, but I appreciate everyone's patience as we went. Today we've created the integrated holistic plans. Now we'll go over them briefly and make sure they match up with the original objectives that we were given. Sorry for the pace. We will break for lunch in a few minutes. I will submit this to Lena now and we can split back up into teams this afternoon."

It was a funny thing. While the twenty or so members of their group were probably horrified at the thought of any of these plans actually occurring, they were all so proud of the work they had done. Henry could see it in their eyes. Everyone was listening to Natesh speak so carefully, happy to hear that their contributions had created the optimized blueprint that could potentially destroy their country. *They think they're helping to improve their country's defenses*, Henry reminded himself.

Their inner circle of David, Brooke, and Norman were quiet. None of them said a word in contribution during the morning session. They each stole nervous glances at each other but none of them had done anything to stop it. Why was that? Groupthink? Fear? David had seen something today, Henry could tell. Maybe the others were following his lead. And if what he had seen was enough for him to keep his mouth shut, then it was probably a good idea for Henry to do the same.

Henry wondered how Natesh did it, knowing what David had said about Bill. Natesh didn't look nearly as comfortable as he had when speaking to everyone the day before. His voice carried well, but he spoke like he was under a lot of stress.

The major was clicking through slides as they lined up the different pieces of the war plan. Henry read through the outline on the screen. The slide they were on showed some of the high-level initial activities by geography.

Phase 1

1.Iran

    2.Assassination—incite anti-US fervor

    3.Arabian Gulf City attack—destabilize region via Iranian military attack on Western targets and provide immediate demand for large-scale US presence in Arabian Gulf

    4.US beltway & school attacks—enflame US and promote support for Iran-US war

    5.Panama

    6.Pre-stage Chinese subs

    7.Secure Panama Canal Zone with Chinese ground troops (First-wave troop/cargo transport via retrofitted merchant vessels)

    8.Establish large-scale troop transport and logistics supply chain to Panama Canal Zone (Post ARES, EMP Strikes)

Natesh said, "Team Psyops, your number one objective was to

create an environment where the US populace would—eventually
—be open to and accepting of a new government that the Chinese
would eventually install after the fighting subsides. So we said
that meant no nukes. We said it meant that we needed to have the
US civilian population cut off from any modern communication
and official media. We also said we would need to create a situation where the civilian population was in a sort of 'disaster mode'
to begin with, in order to..." Natesh was searching for the right
words.

Dr. Creighton said, "So that the American populace would be
highly receptive to foreign aid and supplies. We intend to create a
situation that makes Americans vulnerable and in need. They will
not have access to normal supply chains for food and utilities.
Thus they will be very happy when a solution shows up—in the
form of a large-scale foreign aid program. We talked about China
going in under the guise of a UN peacekeeping force. In addition
to this, we're recommending that external and internal covert military operations take place that encourages both the US military
and civilian population to focus their resources and anger on
someone else. Like we said before, our suggestion is a combination of Iran and a large terrorist group—maybe ISIS, although I
don't think that their goals align. It shouldn't matter, though.
Never let the truth get in the way..."

Henry couldn't believe this guy. It was almost like people
couldn't see how inherently evil these plans were. Everyone
needed to wake up.

Natesh reached down to the podium and took a sip from his
bottled water. "Okay, so once again—this would allow the US
populace to believe that the Chinese are actually there to help?"

Dr. Creighton said, "Right. Because when communication was
cut off, the American people wouldn't know any better. After the
ARES cyberattacks and the subsequent communications and
infrastructure attacks, all the American people would know is that

the electricity, gas, and food have run out. They wouldn't know who did it, and there would be no way of finding out. Riots and starvation would occur pretty quickly. If this happens in the summer or winter months, the effects would be magnified. Because of how hard and quick this stage would hit, we recommend a pre-staging of invasion personnel and assets as a first wave. They would be the ones with the UN uniforms. On the other side of this equation, we would also recommend giving consideration to having the Chinese soldiers actually *believe* that they're there to help unless that becomes impractical."

Natesh said, "Right. That's the part that Tess was talking about."

Tess said, "Yes, it would be quite a challenge in today's climate for the Chinese government to convince their people that they need to make war with the US. For the most part, the Chinese love Americans. So that's going to have to be a major variable in this equation that the Chinese string-pullers are going to have to solve. How are they going to get one point three billion Chinese to want to invade America?"

Norman said, "Wait, I thought we were just talking about the first wave of Chinese troops thinking that they were there to help America?"

Dr. Creighton said, "Those troops would, potentially, think that. But realistically, that won't work in every situation. The Chinese will have to control the information very carefully—"

Tess said, "Something they're very good at."

Creighton said, "We haven't talked about all the details today, but we're designing our plan so that different Chinese groups would get different bits of information. The submarine commanders that are tasked with sinking American naval vessels will be told one thing. And the Chinese troops going in with UN stickers on their helmets will be told another. But this is just for the first stage of the invasion. Eventually, the bigger piece of communication to the Chinese people will focus on something else entirely. And that message will gain consistency during the post-invasion phase."

Norman said, "And what will that be?"

Tess said, "We've talked about this at length. It's a big problem —how do you motivate a nation of Chinese that, relatively speaking, love Americans to suddenly pick up arms and invade them? The Defense team has coordinated with us and they call for even larger numbers of troops than are currently in the Chinese standing army."

Dr. Creighton said, "Simply put—we make religion the enemy. Lena actually helped us with this one. But it makes sense. Chinese Muslim terrorists have made a lot of headlines already. You probably have read about the Uyghur terrorist attacks in China over the past few years. Our idea is that we link these attacks to a Muslim-Christian war. We then create a series of very public attacks in China by both Christian and Muslim groups."

Henry said, "Wait. You're saying that China should attack its own citizens? Fake terrorist attacks?"

Dr. Creighton said, "Why not? That's what we're advocating that we plan for in Iran and the US. Every politician needs a scapegoat. And over the years, religious groups and ethnicities have served wonderfully in this capacity. The message will be that religion is the source of all war and terrorist violence. The Chinese government will call upon its citizens to enter into a crusade, if you will appreciate the irony, to root out religious extremism. This includes Christian extremists in the US that want to hurt China. The exact message track needs some work, but you get the point."

Norman said, "Do you really think the Chinese government would kill some of its own citizens just to motivate the rest?"

Henry heard someone in the back say, "That's a good idea—a little scary—but good."

Natesh continued, "Okay, I'm sorry but I must insist we move on. Objective two: our Chinese invaders want the economy to still be vibrant and capable within a few years of the initial occupation. For this, the team looked at East and West Germany and how different their long-term economic conditions were compared to how the Soviets and the Allies allowed the nations to develop. So we recommended that the invading force help the occupied nation to set up their own government that they put in place, but allow them to flourish within limits. This means that the rebuilding nation would have restrictions on their military as it's rebuilt. The invading force shouldn't hit any of the moneymaking economic centers, only military targets and utilities. This one is hard due to the Communications team's need to cut the Internet and the American economic reliance on telecommunications, so we've agreed that only power will be taken out, not the submarine cables. There will still be global economic collapse—but we aren't creating any mortal wounds here, just flesh wounds that will heal over time."

Natesh took another sip from his water bottle and continued. "Okay, almost done..."

Henry saw on the outline that he too had made strong contributions to the plans. During day two, Henry had designed how the Chinese would solve one of their biggest problems: how to get tens of millions of troops and all their equipment across the Pacific Ocean. The answer was pretty simple—shipping containers. Henry had drawn out loose plans for how to create a fleet of makeshift troop transports out of the countless container ships that were in and out of Chinese ports each day. Many had argued that the scale of such a project would surely attract the attention of US intelligence. But Henry had pointed out that they only needed the first few ships to reach Panama when the attack began. The rest could be loaded up after the blackout, when the US wouldn't know what was happening.

Henry looked at the outline and saw how valuable Natesh must have been to the companies he worked for. He had integrated all of the project pieces in such a way that they came together perfectly in a terrible and efficient plot. One ship would be loaded and sent. It would have to leave one month earlier than the others. But its preparation would have to be kept secret. The US blackout would be executed just before the first ship left port. It would capture the Panama Canal and hold it while the rest of the fleet was formed. The psychological operations would then ensue. The Chinese people would be made to believe some story that would call them into action. A massive military buildup would begin in China and troops would begin ferrying across the Pacific in container ship after container ship.

The US, meanwhile, would be going through weeks without electricity, transportation, or communication. The nation would be thrown into a very scary month of chaos and uncertainty. Grocery stores would go barren. Gas stations would run dry. Small elite teams of Chinese special ops would be inserted into key areas to make sure that things stayed chaotic. Orchestrated events just prior to the blackout would mean that the US was blaming Iranians or Middle Eastern terrorists. The blackout would make the US populace thankful for any help they could get. When the Chinese rolled in posing as UN aid workers, handing out food and water, the Americans would be grateful. But as the lights were turned back on, the Chinese would be controlling communication. During the blackout, the Chinese special ops units would have taken out US leadership. A new puppet government would be installed. The military would be turned mostly into an unarmed rebuilding organization, cleaning up the rubble. There would be a tense few months as Chinese law was implemented and the Americans had to adjust to new rules and censorships. But the Chinese troops would continue to pour in. And so would their families. They would be there to stay.

One of the main objectives was to capture and hold the United States. The only way to do that, the team had agreed, was to get as much of the Chinese population over there as possible. It had to be a new way of life for everyone. The influx of Chinese children would give the new government an excuse to reshuffle the courses they were taking. Subjects had to be standardized across the nation. All children would learn both English and Mandarin. There would be years of social transformation.

Henry had heard rumors about these plans over the past few days. Seeing them now, however, scared him half to death. If this was all really going to be used...

He needed to talk to David.

## 9

_It only stands to reason that where there's sacrifice, there's someone collecting sacrificial offerings. Where there's service, there is someone being served. The man who speaks to you of sacrifice is speaking of slaves and masters, and intends to be the master._

—Ayn Rand

_14 Years Earlier_

Sweat poured off Lena's forehead and onto the hard-packed dirt that surrounded Burke Lake in Northern Virginia. Her chest heaved as she caught her breath, recovering from the five-mile run. She wore a tank top and runner's shorts that were one step up from a bathing suit. She turned as she heard the footsteps pounding pavement behind her.

"You were really kicking out there," said Greg.

"Yeah. Had some extra energy that last mile. How long a head start did you give me?"

"Maybe thirty seconds. I may have lost count." He smiled a cute, boyish grin. She felt that tug at her heartstrings that she was trying so hard to ignore. She *must* ignore those feelings today. Sacrifice was a virtue.

"I'm sure." She smiled.

They sat down on the grass median next to their parked car and stretched. It was the only one left in the lot. The sun had set almost a half hour ago and dusk was quickly fading into night.

"Wow. Did you see the moon over there?" Greg pointed over toward the lake. Beyond the boathouse, just above the tree line, an enormous red moon began its ascent.

"Oh, I heard something about this on the radio. They call it a blood moon. There will be a lunar eclipse. The red is from all the sunrises and sunsets that reflect off of it."

Greg leaned over to her and kissed her cheek. "Sounds romantic."

She turned to face him and they kissed deeply. When they separated, they stared into each other's eyes. His held a hunger in them. Hers held back a flow of tears.

"What's wrong?" Greg asked.

"Nothing." She looked away, back towards the moon...then down to the boathouse. She could see the reflection of the moon in the lake. "I have a...fun idea. I think you are going to like it."

Greg raised his eyebrows, "Oh? This sounds exciting."

"Follow me." She raced up and began jogging down to where the rowboats were stacked up on the shore. She didn't need to look. She knew he would be running behind her, his strong legs propelling him with ease. She would miss their runs together.

Lena arrived at the boats and took another look around. No one in sight.

"Come on, let's go for a private row." She winked.

Greg grinned and began sliding one of the bottom boats off its holder. The low-pitched echoes of wood sliding on metal sounded throughout the inlet, but no one heard. They were alone.

Together they slid the boat across the gravel shore and into the water. Greg grabbed two large wooden oars that looked like they had seen better days. They slid the metal rings into the locks and pushed off, bobbing and rocking as they began to float.

They both giggled as Greg almost lost his balance. Then he slid into the rower's seat and took long, strong pulls.

Stroke.

He stopped one arm and pulled with only the other, turning them towards the center of the large lake. It was getting darker. The blood moon cast red light across the water and onto the faces of the two young lovers.

Stroke.

Lena sat in the front of the boat, gazing into that copper-red orb. The sounds of water bubbling by were relaxing.

But she wasn't relaxed.

She was fighting a strange mix of emotions inside her. Sadness. Nervousness. And a third, stirring feeling that *shouldn't* be there but strangely was...*excitement*.

Stroke.

They looked at each other as he rowed, a knowing gaze passing between them. She watched his body as he moved and felt his eyes on hers. He wanted her. Out here in the cool fall air where they were completely alone, surrounded by crimson moonlit water.

Stroke.

It took about ten minutes for the rowboat to reach a darker part of the lake, shadowed by tall pines. When he stopped rowing, they drifted, silent ripples following in their wake. Lena crept to his middle bench. He reached for her and they kissed. It started off slow. A few romantic pecks gradually became more intense. Then she straddled him and wrapped her legs around his waist. His hands were moving up and down her back. Her heart was beating faster. He started to reach a hand up the front of her shirt and she stopped him.

"Wait," Lena whispered.

"What?"

"I thought I heard something." They were near the other side of the lake, where the running path cut through the forest and followed the winding shoreline.

"What is it?" Greg asked. He leaned forward, looking in the same direction.

They both peered into the dark shadows of the woods.

Lena slipped her hand under her shirt and up to her damp sports bra. She reached until she felt the small hard plastic device that had been resting there for the past two hours.

"I thought I saw someone. Over there," Lena said.

She held it behind her back, where Greg couldn't see. She removed the plastic cap, careful not to touch the needle.

"I don't see anything," Greg said. He turned back to her, smiling.

She said, "Kiss me."

They each leaned forward, careful not to lose their balance as they kissed.

Her hands were behind his head. He only felt a pinprick on his neck. But he must have heard the sound. The *phssstt* as the $CO_2$-pressurized container shot a dose of paralyzing liquid into his body that would take down a four-hundred-pound man almost instantly.

Greg's face contorted. And Lena's heart raced with euphoria.

Her eyes were wide with anticipation. She had never killed anyone before. She hadn't been sure how she would feel. She'd assumed sadness, given who it was and the relationship they had. But the excitement that filled her now was better than any high she had ever had. Greg's neck muscles tensed. Then the rest of his body seized and his face turned beet red, the veins on his neck bulging. She still had her legs wrapped around him. She didn't know why, but she found herself caressing his back. But she didn't kiss him. She wanted to watch his face as the life drained from his eyes. She was torn between losing one of the only romantic relationships she had ever had and the excitement of finally using her training. Or was the excitement something deeper? Did she like *killing*?

"Shhhh...shhhhh..." Lena whispered.

He was looking at her, not comprehending. His convulsions were getting stronger now. And the boat began to rock. She put her feet on the deck for stability. Then she grabbed his arm and knee, and lifted up with all her strength. Cool water splashed her face as his stiff, unresponsive body plummeted into the lake. She could hear incomprehensible noises coming out of his gritted teeth. He floated for a moment, still facing up...until she reached in and turned him over. After that, there was a grotesque gurgling for a few moments, and then...silence.

She watched with wide eyes. When it was over, a single tear streaked down her face. She had a strange taste in her mouth. Adrenaline. For a moment, she wanted to sob. Then to scream... then she was calm. This was a heavy sacrifice, but she had done her duty. An enormous sense of pride washed over her. She had proven herself. And now she would become one of Jinshan's rising stars.

Lena picked up the oars and began to row back the way they'd come, away from the floating corpse. Halfway back to the boathouse, she threw the small plastic syringe into the lake.

\* \* \*

*Present Day*

Lena walked out of the Classroom building and into the humid wind. It was truly blowing now. The tropical storm was here. By the looks of the soaked ground, she had just missed a band of torrential rain. She hurried down the gravel path.

A minute later, she typed her code into the digital keyset and opened the Comms building door. Once in, she felt a rush of cool air as she walked down a dark and narrow concrete hallway. The two desktop computer fans whirred.

"Hello?"

No answer. Natesh Chaudry and Major Combs were the only two people she had given access to this room, and they were both in the classroom. She walked to the back of the room, where the other door was. She typed another, longer code into that digital keypad and entered the back room of the Communications building.

The walls of the back room were covered with charts and de-energized computer screens. There were also radios and radar screens. This would eventually serve as an air traffic control center once more people got here. But for now, while Jinshan had her on this island, it was her living quarters. There was a weapons locker, a shelf for her clothes, a bathroom with a shower, and a small kitchen that she seldom used. On the concrete floor she had a small mat slightly thicker than a yoga mat. That was her mattress. Each day she did forty-five minutes of calisthenics on the concrete floor, then another forty-five minutes of martial arts practice. She lived a Spartan life.

She approached a round metal hatch in one corner of her living quarters and spun the large metal wheel that sat atop it. It was stiff at first, but then it unwound quickly. When the hatch was completely unlocked, she opened it and crept down the ladder inside. She shut the hatch behind her and continued down the ten-foot cylinder that was big enough for a man carrying supplies to fit through.

The vertical shaft she climbed down emptied into a round concrete tunnel. She had only walked it twice, but both times she had been amazed at how long it went on. It took her about fifteen minutes to get from one side to the other. Fifteen minutes to walk across—or through, to be more accurate—the island. She began her third trip through the tunnel, ignoring the pain she felt as she realized that her black low heels weren't the most comfortable shoes she could be wearing. She had endured combat in some of the harshest spots on the planet. She could handle uncomfortable shoes.

The tunnel was dry and well lit. It curved back and forth through the dark rock of the island. There were no doors or alternate paths to take—just rounded concrete ceilings going on and on as far as the eye could see. Like the entrance to the Comms building, the door on the other side had a digital keypad. There was no vertical shaft to climb this time, however. Just a large metal door. She typed in the code and heard an electronic beep followed by a click as the door unlocked. The door opened to reveal a long, steep set of stairs that went up into oblivion. She began marching.

Lena's footsteps echoed as she walked up the stairs. As she ascended, she heard more and more voices speaking Mandarin. She also heard the digital orchestra of computers, keystrokes, and high-tech communications. The stairway curved around into a cavernous room with dim blue lighting and the bustle of a dozen Chinese military and intelligence operatives going about their daily routines. Several sat in front of TV screens that had live feeds of the consultant meetings on the other side of the island. They typed furiously as they listened, taking notes and adding commentary that would later be carefully scrutinized. Others monitored radar and radio transmissions to a nearby fleet of Chinese naval vessels.

A lone white man—the American—walked up to Lena and held out his hand. "Lena Chou, nice to finally meet you." He looked her up and down. "You having fun over there?" He was the only one in the room who was speaking in English.

Lena ignored the American and turned to the watch supervisor. "What's the latest?"

A short, serious man with grey eyes and a raspy voice answered in Mandarin, "Ma'am, the latest weather report remains similar to this morning's. Additionally, our amphibious support ship is now in helicopter range, but they've told us that it will be very difficult for them to fly in this weather. They asked me to convey to you that it would be wise to request air support in emergencies only until the storm fully passes."

Lena frowned. "I understand." She looked up at the TV screen that showed the classroom. "Keep your men's eyes on David Manning. I think that he suspects something. He was out that first night. I think he saw the helicopter. Watch him carefully."

The American cocked his chubby head and said, "David saw something?"

She studied the American's face. She didn't know how he had been allowed to spy for the CIA. She saw him as a disgrace. His disloyalty to his own country was despicable, regardless of the fact that he now claimed loyalty to her own. She would rather slit his throat and have fewer men than rely on him in a combat situation. He embodied all that was wrong with Americans. He was fat, lazy, pompous, and obnoxious. Worst of all, he had no sense of honor. To think what she'd had to sacrifice, all in the name of duty and honor. This man knew *nothing* of sacrifice.

Lena replied to his question. "Yes. David Manning likely saw something."

"What did he see?"

"The second night. When Bill Stanley was extracted. You know Bill now. I believe you accompanied him back here this morning, correct?"

Tom said, "Yes."

Lena said, "Well, David may have seen that extraction process.

And if he did, that has likely compromised our position on my side of the island."

"How do you not know whether he saw it or not? I saw those camera feeds in your control center just now. Can't you see everything that's going on over there?"

Lena sighed. This man was beneath her. "We have video feed for the classroom only. We are constrained by time, I am afraid. The opportunity to host the consultants here on the island did not come with much prior warning. We prioritized the classroom. It is, unfortunately the sole area under surveillance. I monitor the status of our consultants, and I check in every few hours with the control center. The control center supervisor has standing orders if I don't call in."

Tom looked amused. "Really? That gets a little dicey for you now, doesn't it? Think you can handle that all by yourself?"

"Yes, actually. But I'm not by myself. I have an assistant with me."

Tom raised his eyebrows and said, "Just one?"

"Just one."

"Who is it? Anyone from the list I saw?"

Lena didn't answer. She turned and walked out of the room. A young Chinese soldier with a clipboard followed her. She dictated orders to him as she walked and he wrote down everything she said. Tom hustled to keep up.

They walked down a hallway with metal grate floors, then went up several sets of stairs. Tom was huffing and puffing by the time they got to the fifth floor. Lena walked with the endurance of a marathoner. They left the stairway and entered another long, narrow hallway. One side of the passage was the same dark grey concrete that all the structures on the island were made from. The other wall had long plexiglass windows that looked into an enormous cavern. Lena stopped and stared out the window. A dozen men in hard hats were working inside. One had on a welding mask and sparks sprayed from the torch he held.

It was a spectacular work of construction. One of their newest submarine pens. The dark blue water on the ground level was empty of submarines at the moment. Two nuclear fast-attack submarines would fit, however, when they arrived. The opening of the cave was four hundred yards down and emptied into the ocean near the pier. Lena had been told that several dozen of these covert bases had been constructed in the past three years. It gave her a sense of pride to see the quality and precision with which the Chinese military worked.

Lena looked at the production site and said, "Tell me, Thomas, why did you betray your country?"

His face flushed. He said, "It's Tom. And screw you."

"Oh, please...take no offense. I simply wanted to understand how the transformation occurred."

Tom shifted his weight and looked at her suspiciously. He said, "Fine. You wanna know? It's because America isn't what it used to be. I was in the CIA for eighteen years. I worked my ass off. I spent more time in shithole countries around the world than I care to remember...swatting at mosquitoes and listening to bad guys talk on cell phones. The pay was shitty. The job was shittier. After Iraq, the private sector got hot. And they paid real nice. So I jumped ship."

Lena could see his eyes darting around as he replayed his life. What was sad was that he probably hadn't given much serious thought to it. He lacked depth. He wasn't a thinker. He was a pawn. That was fine. The world needed pawns. But she despised this one.

Lena said, "And?"

He looked at her. "And...the private sector played by a different set of rules. They weren't driven by patriotism but by dollars. Everything started to become clearer for me. The game you and I play, Lena...it's the same no matter what side you play it for. Once I went to the private sector, I got access to a lot of information. Sometimes our company sold it to the Americans...sometimes to other countries. And the thing about the private sector is...you can move around a lot. Competitors will pay you more money to come work for them and spill your guts. So this loyalty thing really started to get overrated for me. I bounced around a few times... worked for all of the major players. I started doing work in Beijing for a small shop there. When you guys approached me...I saw it as just another opportunity to join a competitor. An opportunity. That's all life is. A collection of choices and tradeoffs. There is no loyalty. No country or company is going to look out for you. They only care about themselves. Patriots are idiots. They can keep their flags and medals. I'll be rich and on the winning team."

Lena listened without betraying her emotion. This man was truly a pig. Mr. Jinshan had coaxed him into this role. Tom had helped them, that much was true. Much of his information had assisted their project greatly. They wouldn't have been able to get many of the consultants if not for him. But she despised what he stood for. Meeting Americans like Tom made her believe in this cause. Lena knew that religion and those who loved it would serve as a scapegoat and motivator for many of the common folk. But to her this war had nothing to do with religion. It had everything to do with strength and weakness. This man was weak. Weak in the mind and weak in his convictions. He gave in to his desires. Probably went whoring any chance he got. He sacrificed nothing and believed in nothing of true value. That was how he'd gotten so fat. America had gotten fat. Europe had gotten fat. While much of the world starved. Lena would help to trim the fat and reset the balance.

She motioned for him to approach her. He leaned forward.

She bent in close to his ear and whispered, "I want you to know how thankful we are here for your service. But please...in case you have any doubt, know that my personal belief is that you're nothing more than a highly paid prostitute."

She backed away and stared straight into his eyes.

His mouth dropped open. His face grew red. "I...I have helped you. And your country. How dare you..." He fumed, but didn't add anything else.

She stood facing him, not backing down. After a moment, she turned and walked away, leaving him standing there, questioning everything.

She called back to him as she walked, "Come on, Thomas, let's go chat with our friend Bill..."

* * *

Bill's cell was eight feet by eight feet, and the ceiling was fifteen feet high. It was almost pitch black. A small crack under the door where the hallway light peeked in was the only illumination he had. They played some type of white noise at all times. It was beginning to drive him mad. He didn't know how, but they must know when he was trying to sleep. That was when they turned up the volume. It was like a cross between the old sound of static from a wrong analog TV channel and a bee buzzing in his ear.

A jingle of keys. Then the door opened and the light from outside temporarily blinded him.

Lena and the American that had escorted Bill from the Chinese ship both stood at the door's entrance.

Bill cowered when he saw them.

Lena gave him a bright smile. "Hello, Bill."

He didn't answer. Bill ran his hand over the stubble of his unshaven face. He was a mess. He looked back at Lena through tired, watery eyes. His stomach ached with hunger, and he was *so* exhausted. He wanted nothing more than sleep and a hot meal.

They treated him the same way here as they had on the

Chinese ship. They piped the noise into his cell at all hours on the ship, too. He didn't know how often they fed him because they had removed his watch on the first day on board. The first few nights on the boat he'd felt sorry for himself. He'd cried and been scared and missed his wife. But then he'd gone through a few days with little food and even less sleep, and he'd stopped feeling sorry for himself. He'd willed himself on, and started praying a lot. For food, mostly.

When they did feed him, it was just a little rice and some water. Usually they emptied his piss pot, too. He didn't even smell the stench anymore.

This morning's boat ride had been bumpy and confusing. He couldn't understand why the American guy, Tom, would be helping *them*. But Bill had been so fatigued that he'd barely spoken to him. This was the first day the Chinese had let him out of the ship's brig since the helicopter had dropped him off a week ago. One quick ferry to the island this morning and he'd been thrown right back in a cell. At least this one didn't rock. The relentless seas had made him dry heave.

Lena repeated herself with an edge in her voice. She said, "*Hello*, Bill."

Bill spoke through parched lips. "What do you want from me? Are you going to let me go?"

Lena said, "No, Bill. I'm afraid not. No one can leave. That's why you're here. Because you wanted to go home. And because you had knowledge of the timing of our ARES execution that others did not. I may have been able to convince you to do your patriotic duty and stay on the island for a few more weeks. But I couldn't have you alerting the others that the attack is planned for much sooner than they believe. If they found out, they might not see the need to keep quiet and make all these excellent plans. And we can't have that."

Bill curled up into a ball, holding his knees on the floor.

"Bill, you're going to be alright. I just wanted to come by and say hello. Pretty soon you'll be reunited with many of the other consultants. Your work will continue. If you do well, you'll be treated well. If you do poorly, you'll be treated poorly. Is that clear?"

Bill sniffed, looking up at her. He then looked at Tom. "You took me here on the boat today. You're American, right?"

Tom was still frowning from his recent interaction with Lena. He said, "Yeah."

Bill said, "How can you do this to people from your own country?"

Lena looked at Tom. She cocked her head, interested in hearing his answer.

Tom grew defensive. He said, "I'm not the only American helping out. I'm not even the only American on this island that's helping out. It's a new world order, bud. Better get used to it."

Bill said, "Who else? Combs?"

Tom looked at Lena. Neither said a word.

Bill didn't need to hear the answer. That was one of the few things that Bill had given thought to as a prisoner. He knew Combs was dirty. Ever since he had seen that disgruntled, balding excuse for an officer glaring at everyone over his clipboard and thrilled at the prospect of having authority over them—he'd known he was a strange guy. In his cell, Bill realized that he was exactly the kind of eccentric, loner oddball that got off on spying as a way to prove that he was better than everyone else. It was obvious in the way he held himself that he felt superior to everyone in the room.

Lena and Tom didn't need to tell Bill that the major was in on it. He *knew*. And the smart-ass grin on this guy Tom's face was all the confirmation he needed.

Tom just smirked and looked at Lena. She didn't smile back.

Lena said, "You'll see all of your friends soon enough. Tom will be back to go over some questions with you here soon. Some details that we need. I just wanted to let you know that I expect to hear good results from these conversations. Bill—do you understand?"

Bill nodded. He would try to resist. But if they offered him food, he would probably end up telling them whatever they wanted to know. He was so hungry.

"Good."

Lena and Tom backed up and closed the cell door with a loud clang.

They walked back toward the room filled with Chinese personnel and computer screens.

**10**
———

*All the forces in the world are not so powerful as an idea whose time has come.*
  —Victor Hugo

It was lunchtime when David was finally able to speak to Natesh and Henry alone in his room. He had tried to talk to them in passing throughout the day, but with the major and Natesh whipping the class into production mode, there was no time. He felt sick listening to all the plans and seeing them written up in the summary document so precisely.

David siphoned Henry and Natesh over towards the barracks before they went into the cafeteria to eat. They started to ask him questions, but he shushed them until they closed the door in his room.

David said, "We need to act today—while the storm is moving in. I saw the other side. I swam there this morning."

"You *swam* there?" said Natesh.

"Yeah. Listen. I *saw* Bill. They have him as their prisoner. I didn't get a good look, but I'm pretty sure he was tied up. There were two Asian guys and they both had machine guns slung over their shoulders. I'm gonna go out on a limb here and say they were probably Chinese. And I saw the guy that *sent* me here. One of the directors at my firm. Name's Tom Connolly. He must be in on it. I mean, there can be no doubt now, right?"

Henry said, "Oh my God…"

"Are you sure it was them?" said Natesh.

"Positive. I've been thinking about this. I could see how, if this were a legitimate CIA operation, Tom could be here to help out. By itself that doesn't mean anything. But with Bill on that boat—and the way they looked. It was *all wrong*. Lena said that she sent Bill home to his sick wife. We now know that she lied about that. And they all looked Chinese. I'm sorry, but that's too strange to be legitimate."

Natesh said, "I'm not as familiar with how the CIA does business, but is it possible that these Asian men are just CIA employees or contractors that they have working for Lena?"

Henry frowned.

David looked skeptical. He said, "Natesh, I think that the holes in the Swiss cheese are starting to line up. Sure. Maybe the CIA hires a bunch of contractors that are from the local regions they operate in. But that boat sure looked like the kind that's used on board Navy ships. If I was a betting man, I'd guess it came from a Chinese warship."

Henry said, "And why do you think Lena and the Major are pushing us to get this done today so quick? Do you really think they're worried about communications getting knocked out? Or does Lena suspect that we're on to her? I think she's trying to suck as much out of us as possible before the hammer drops."

A howling wind blew in from the open window. The palm trees were starting to bend the way you saw on the Weather Channel when they did their storm coverage from down on the Gulf Coast of Florida. It wasn't raining heavily yet, but the clouds looked vicious. There were large, violent black clouds and fast-moving, low-hanging grey ones. It reminded David of the way it looked before a bad summer thunderstorm.

Outside the shut door, David heard muffled voices in the hallway. Several of the consultants were on their way to lunch.

Natesh said, "Are you sure about all this? I mean, I know this is highly questionable, but perhaps we should just *ask* Lena?"

Henry said, "Are you *crazy*? Didn't you *hear* him? There were *Asians* on that boat. First of all, I make it a rule never to trust an Asian with a machine gun. And sometimes I just don't trust Asians."

Natesh cleared his throat and said, "Um, I'm from India. India is in Asia."

Henry said, "Yeah, but I mean like *real* Asia. Sorry. That's probably insulting. I don't mean anything negative...I love naan bread."

Natesh rolled his eyes.

David shook his head and glared at Henry. He said, "Natesh, seriously, it's extremely suspicious that both of those men were Asian, and Lena is Asian. And they're holding Bill prisoner. And the guy that flew me here is on that side of the island with no explanation from Lena."

Natesh said, "Lena's English is perfect. And last time I checked, there were plenty of Asian-Americans in the US military and government."

David said, "I know, but come *on*. Do you want to bet your life that Lena and the Major are legitimate? More than that, what happens if this is really China, like I now think it is? What happens when they execute these plans without any warning? We sat here and we told them what the most effective way to attack America was. Now we have a responsibility to neutralize those plans by getting word out. And, Natesh—we can't do it without you."

Henry said, "Natesh, we need your help on this. You're the only one we trust who can access those computers in the Comms room.

No one else has the codes and the capability. And the major would probably take that gun out and shoot us if we ask him. You need to be with us one hundred percent on this. You're the one part of our plan that we have no substitute for."

David said, "Natesh, he's right. Trust me, this isn't a Red Cell being driven by the CIA. Let's be real. This is some sort of foreign intelligence op. They're trying to tease out important and classified information, and create or improve plans to attack the United States. We need to stop this. We can't stay quiet and watch anymore. It's gone too far. With the storm moving in, we might have a window to act. They said it themselves. We're going to be at minimal shore support. That's what they said. I think that means that Lena and Major Combs and whoever is on the other side of this island are out on a limb for the next twenty-four hours."

Henry paced the room and looked up at the ceiling, deep in thought. "What do you say, Natesh?"

Natesh sighed. He looked like he was struggling with the right decision. His eyes looked out the window, toward the clouds and the crashing sea. He said, "Alright. You've sold me."

David looked tense. He looked at his watch and said, "Alright, time to let people know what's really going on. Let's go round up the troops."

* * *

David watched from Brooke's window. He could see Henry and Norman shielding themselves from the heavy rains as they ran to the Comms building and knocked on the door.

"Lena, open up! We need help. Brooke's sick!" Henry said.

The door beeped and then swung open. The major was there, hand on his sidearm. He looked wary. Lena stood behind him, hands on her hips.

She said, "What is the problem?"

Norman said, "It's Brooke, come quick! She's having some sort of seizure or something. We need to get her help. Come on!"

The major looked back at Lena as if unsure of what to do.

Lena said, "Of course. I'll be right there, let me get a medical kit. I think Dr. Creighton has some medical training. Major, please go help them out. I'll be right along."

The major nodded and followed the two men. They jogged back towards the barracks and up the staircase to the second floor. Combs was out of breath by the time they got into Brooke's room. He was huffing and puffing and completely unprepared when he saw five of the larger male members of the Red Cell waiting for him as he entered.

He still hadn't processed what was going on when they jumped him. Norman removed the M9 while the others wrapped a series of tied-together socks over his mouth. They used a belt to bind his arms and legs. He was on the bed and out of commission in a matter of seconds.

David served as the lookout. He was at the window, trying to get a look yet stay out of sight in case anyone glanced up from the outside. He was waiting for Lena to show up.

One down, one to go. From Brooke's window David had a clear line of sight to the path that Lena would take from the Comms building to the barracks. Large drops of rain pelted the dark ground.

Norman said, "Is she coming?" Tense eyes.

"Not yet." David looked at his watch. "What did she say when you guys talked to her?"

"She said she'd be right here. She was going to get a medical kit."

"Seems like it's taking too long. You think she's on to us?"

Two agonizing minutes went by before there was any sign of Lena.

David said, "Hold on. Here she comes. She's got Dr. Creighton in tow. Alright, get ready."

Everyone was quiet. A drip of sweat rolled down David's forehead. His palms were wet. He could feel his heartbeat. It seemed like it took forever for Lena to get to the door. There were seven men waiting for her. Seven on one. *Let's see how good you are, Lena.*

Footsteps in the hallway. Norman was at the half-open door. He stuck his head out in the hallway so Lena would see him. In his hand on the inside of the door he held the M9 that he'd commandeered from Major Combs. The hallway was empty. It was never empty. She knew something was up. David was sure of it.

Norman said, "Brooke's in here. She's not breathing."

Brooke was across the hall, with several other team members who had been briefed on the situation. They'd only told ten people. The ten they thought they could trust the most. There was the chance that someone they hadn't explained everything to would come by and screw it up. But Henry and Natesh had decided that telling everyone posed too many problems. Right now there were still a half dozen of the consultants eating their lunch, unaware that Lena was about to get jumped.

David heard Dr. Creighton's voice say, "What happened?"

Norman said, "Come in, we just found her like this..."

Major Combs had been silent until then. But as Lena entered he let out a muffled noise from behind the makeshift gag. Right when Lena crossed the threshold to the door. The timing couldn't have been worse.

The voices all yelled at the same time and David could barely tell what was happening. He heard Norman yell, "Get her!" and then bodies literally began flying. David had seen martial arts movies. He had even taken a few judo classes when he was a junior at the Naval Academy. But movies and amateurs were nothing compared to witnessing the real thing.

Lena was an artist.

Her movements were quick yet deliberate, powerful yet graceful. There were seven men in the room. Eight if you counted Dr. Creighton, who stood dumbfounded in the flurry of fists and limbs moving around him. Of the seven men who tried to apprehend Lena, three were on the floor almost instantly. One was grabbing his neck, another his groin. The third man, Norman, was knocked unconscious when he cracked skulls with someone else —David couldn't see who. As he fell to the ground, his gun tumbled across the room, letting loose a round from its chamber. The deafening sound froze everyone in place. That gunshot was followed by a shriek that turned to pain-filled moaning.

Lena's eyes locked onto the gun that lay on the floor. She darted for it two seconds too late.

That was her one moment of error. Her one mistake in what could have been a devastating defeat to the seven men in the room. The four men who remained standing saw her objective and dove on towards her. By an act of divine grace, the gun had fallen two feet from David, who reached down and scooped it up just before Lena could do the same.

He grabbed it in his hands and, shaking, raised it up and pointed it at Lena's beautiful face. She was on all fours. Before the three other men collapsed on top of her and tied her up, David swore that he saw a faint smile form on her lips.

\* \* \*

Tom stood in the back of the Control Center. That's what he called the room where all the Chinese military intelligence men—or whatever organization they were from—observed the Americans on the other side of the island.

He looked at his watch. Three p.m. He looked around the room. Everyone was busy typing away or watching their monitors. Some of them were translating the reams of script that had been transferred over to them by Natesh and Major Combs earlier that day. Some were communicating with the two Chinese Navy ships one hundred miles to the north.

There were fewer men than earlier. Most of them normally were tasked with watching the daily meetings. Since it was lunch break, there was little attention being paid to the screens. But the afternoon sessions were due to begin any moment now, and Tom decided he wanted to watch. He wanted to see how twenty Americans were really planning China's invasion of the United States.

One of the screens showed the main classroom. It was an auditorium of sorts, with four rows of tiered seating and a large Plexiglas window that wrapped around the upper level in the back of the class. People were starting to file into the room, Tom noticed.

He looked around the observation deck and didn't see anyone watching the screen—or watching him. He removed the flask from his breast pocket, took his third swig in as many minutes, and put it back. Lena could say whatever she wanted. It was nothing Mr. Johnnie Walker couldn't drown out.

The short watch supervisor entered the room, talking in Mandarin to his subordinates. He looked up at the same monitor that Tom had been watching and let out something in Mandarin that Tom didn't need translated. Every language had that word. As soon as he said it, several of the other men in the room began yelling and typing furiously. Two were pointing at the screen and yelling at each other.

Tom couldn't understand what all the fuss was about. He squinted and looked up at the screen. It was low resolution. The men that were monitoring it all had headsets on, so Tom couldn't hear what was being said in the classroom.

Then he saw *exactly* what all the fuss was about. Lena and some guy in a military uniform were both being carried into the classroom. They were tied up. Bound with something around their arms and legs. Holy shit. *Somebody better do something about this.*

The next thing Tom knew, the one man in the room was on a satellite phone, screaming bloody murder in Mandarin. Tom had no idea what he was saying, but it sounded like he was repeating the same thing over and over. Then the supervisor picked up a handset bolted to the wall and started talking, and his voice was transmitted over the loudspeaker. A minute later, several dozen men, including the supervisor, were running by Tom, heading down the stairs. They were all armed, and they looked scared.

The room was almost empty after they left. There was one young soldier at his monitor. He typed away. It looked like he was typing in some sort of chat room. Must be updating the Chinese high command on what was going on. Something like that. Maybe he was telling Jinshan himself? Nah. Guys like that had minions do the work for them. Tom had met Jinshan. That guy was probably in a hot tub with a cigar in his mouth. That's where Tom would be soon. Screw Lena.

He looked around, didn't see anyone watching, and took another swig from the flask. He squinted up at the screen and saw that Lena and the military officer—it looked like an Air Force uniform—were tied up in the middle of the center stage of the auditorium. Everyone was in the classroom now. There were several animated conversations going on, by the looks of it. Tom sure as hell couldn't hear anything. He could ask sonny boy on the computer to put the sound on. Kind of like turning the volume up for the football game.

Shit. Football. Probably not gonna have much football for a while. That was a definite downside to all of this. He let out a deep sigh. Tom was already sick of all these Chinese assholes here. It was going to be a long few months until he could live like a king in the new version of America. He decided to go talk to the prisoner. Bill. Maybe that would cheer him up.

\* \* \*

A few minutes later, David stood looking at Lena and the Major
tied up in chairs on the stage in the middle of the classroom. This
was the best place to gather everyone, Henry and he had agreed.

The major wouldn't stop screaming bloody murder behind his
gag, so they left it on. Lena didn't say a word. She just watched
everyone behind those cold eyes. Everyone in the room was
soaked from walking through the rain outside. The storm was in
full swing.

David and Henry were surprised how easy selling the others
had been. It had only taken a few minutes. They had taken a few
at a time into Henry's room and let them know what David had
seen. Some were skeptical, at first. But after this many days on the
island, people knew and trusted each other. They believed David's
story. Henry outlined their plan and explained why they needed
to act fast. The initial group of consultants that they told were all
military and law enforcement. They went for the bigger guys who
they thought would know how to handle themselves in a fight. If
David had known how close the contest would be to take Lena, he
might have tried to wait until they could recruit everyone.

The second group of people they told were the civilians of the
Red Cell. Some of them were just now getting the full explanation
as to what was going on. Dr. Creighton and Tess McDonald had
first argued vehemently that David should immediately untie
Lena. But after David had explained what he had seen, and they'd
witnessed Lena's cold, silent stare, they'd quieted down.

Henry looked at David and said, "People are all the same.
We're scared of our shadows. Every one of us here is frightened.
We just need to know what to do. David, this is your show now.
You gotta take charge. Let everyone know the plan."

David nodded and walked to the center of the crowd.
Everyone was talking at the same time. Some of the consultants

were hysterical. Dr. Creighton and one of the military guys were helping to mend the gunshot wound of the guy who had been hit when the M9 hit the floor and fired off.

David said, "Everyone quiet down!" He motioned for people to come closer. Natesh and Henry were by his side.

Even the stewards were here now. Communication with them had been against the rules. But the rules had been thrown out the window. Tess, who apparently was fluent in Mandarin, discovered that they were all hotel employees at some Macau resort. They had been sent here two weeks ago. None of them spoke English. As David spoke, Tess translated for the stewards.

David felt the crowd's eyes on him, looking for answers. He had become their situational leader. Even Natesh seemed to be looking to David to figure out what his plan was.

David said, "As all of you now know, this place isn't what we thought it was. Bill wasn't sent home. I saw him dragged unconscious by Lena onto the helicopter a few days ago—"

Someone said, "Why the hell didn't you say anything then?"

Norman yelled, "Don't freaking worry about that now! Let him speak."

David said, "...and this morning I saw Bill again, a prisoner on the other side of this island. There is some sort of base camp there as well. And the occupants look like members of a foreign military. My guess is Chinese. I think that we've all been taken here by the Chinese as some part of...I don't know...an intelligence-gathering operation. As a way to extract information from us."

The voices in the room went silent. Angry faces looked back at him. A loud wall of wind and rain hit the classroom's window. It startled several in the audience. The cyclone was picking up strength outside.

David said, "So let's assume it is the Chinese. We don't know how long we have until they come get us. But we want to start ransacking this place and figuring out what tools we have to work with. Priority number one is communication. Norm—you and Natesh go to the Communications building. Our best bet is to let Natesh try and hack through the computers they have over there and get word off the island so that we can get rescued."

"Got it," Norm said. Both he and Natesh stayed put, waiting until David was finished speaking.

David said, "Brooke, you start questioning Lena and Major Combs." He nodded over to them. They both were watching David speak as they were tied up in their chairs on the middle of the stage. Lena betrayed no emotion. Major Combs, with his mouth still covered, was wide-eyed and crimson. He looked like he had a lot to say, although David suspected that it wouldn't be pleasant.

Tess said, "David. I've just been talking to some of the cooks and caretakers here. They say that there is a basement behind the kitchen that's filled with supplies. We might be able to use some of them. They say it's very large, but the door is locked and they don't have a key."

Norm said, "I got a key." He stood over Major Combs and ripped off his keychain from his belt. There were several keys on it. "I bet you one of these suckers will work."

David said, "Okay, Henry, can you go with Tess and a few others to go check it out? See if there are any pieces of communications equipment or weapons that we could use to defend ourselves."

Lena laughed.

A few of the consultants looked at her with disdain.

Henry said, "Will do." They grabbed the keys and scooted after the head steward.

Natesh said, "David, I think that Norman and I should take Lena with us. I'm confident that I can hack into their computer systems. But she will likely know some of the names and passwords that I will need."

Brooke said, "Who are you going to talk to if you can get word out?"

Natesh said, "My company has an encrypted email system. If I can send several of my employees a message, they will immediately act on it. I know them. They'll figure out what to do and move quickly. I don't know who I would go to if I was to try and go through some sort of government channel. This way, they'll make sure the problem gets solved and word gets out."

David nodded. "That sounds like a good plan. Do you trust them?"

Natesh nodded. "Yes. Very much."

David said, "Okay. Lena's tied up. Old Norm over there looks like he could bench press a Mack truck if we asked him to. You think you two can handle Lena by yourselves if we send you all over to the Comms room?"

"I think so, yes."

David looked at Norm, who was still rubbing his head from the beating Lena had given him earlier.

Norman said, "I'll be fine this time. I've got Harold's nine mil. And Lena's tied up. Hopefully she'll get forgetful on these passwords and I will have the pleasure of making her remember."

David said, "Alright. Everyone else, let's stay in the classroom and keep an eye outside. We know they've got a few small boats and a helicopter. Be watchful and yell if you see anyone coming." About half the class walked up to the top level of the classroom and began looking out the glass window.

A few of the military guys took the role of prison guards.

Natesh walked out the door of the classroom with Norman in tow. Norman carried Lena on his shoulder the entire way to the Comms building. Her legs and arms remained tied together.

David walked over to Brooke and the group of military guys. They were standing just off the stage, quietly deciding what to ask the major.

David said, "Okay. Listen, I need you to help question Major Combs. Try and find out what was really going on here and what they're planning to do with us. Figure out how many people are on the other side of the island and how well armed they are. And see if you can figure out how far away we are from a populated area. I saw a few motorboats tied up to the dock on the other side of the island. If we're five hundred miles from land, those things are useless. They might have been just using them to go back and forth to ships in the area. But if we're less than twenty miles from another island with people on it...or from a mainland...even if it's China, that gives us a chance."

Brooke said, "Okay, I'll do my best. What are you gonna do?"

Henry ran up to them, huffing and puffing and holding a large black box that looked like a cell phone from 1989.

David said, "What's that?"

Henry said, "It's beautiful is what it is. It was the first thing I saw in the supply room downstairs. They have rows and rows of stuff down there. Dozens of these babies."

David looked at the writing on the black metal box. Chinese. He had no idea what it said.

Henry said, "It's an *HF radio*. We might be able to reach a boat or a plane. But what I really want to do is call MARS."

David looked at him like he was crazy. He said, "You're going to call who?"

"MARS. The Military Auxiliary Radio System."

"Never heard of it."

"How were you in the Navy and you've never heard of it?"

"I wasn't in the Navy for long. Henry, we need to hurry up here. Are you going to get to the point?"

Henry said, "It's only the coolest club on the planet. They're regular guys—like you and me—who listen to a HAM radio and relay information for the military. If I can reach one of them, I can probably make a phone call. The frequency is thirty-three megahertz if I remember correctly. A lot of Vietnam troops used to use them to make phone calls back home when they were deployed. The MARS radio operator would hook up the radio to a phone and make the call for them. Some guys still even do it today. This HF radio can broadcast at a pretty far range if the conditions are right. I'm going to need to set up the antenna. It looks like it rolls out ten or twenty feet. I think I'm going to go up to the barracks and put it out a window."

David questioned Henry's characterization of a regular guy, but was excited at the prospect of a new means of communicating off the island. "That's great, Henry. Nice work."

Brooke said, "HF radio ranges are pretty far. If we get lucky, we can reach someone as far as six hundred miles away. And if we hit a relay..."

Henry was smiling ear to ear. "Exactly. The MARS guys have relays set up all over the place. If I can get someone on the line, I might be able to make a phone call or just tell the MARS operator what is going on and what to do."

David nodded. "That's great news. Okay, you go to the barracks and try and set it up."

Henry said, "I'll need some help. Can you come give me a hand?"

David looked at Brooke. "Are you going to be alright questioning the major?"

Brooke looked over at the military Red Cell team members standing next to her. She said, "I've got a lot of support. I'm sure I'll be okay."

David looked at Henry, "I'm gonna see if Henry can get that radio working. If Natesh can't get word out on the Internet, maybe there is a boat or plane nearby that we can call for help on. Oh, that reminds me. See if the major knows our GPS coordinates... our latitude and longitude. If Henry can get the radio working and we can send out a distress call, that will be crucial." David turned to leave and then said, "And watch your back. I don't know how long we have until Lena's friends arrive."

Brooke looked nervous. She said, "Okay."

David and Henry walked out of the classroom and went down the hall. On the way, they saw Tess and the stewards, running around with the set of jingling keys. The stewards were opening up all of the previously locked compartments—most of them supply rooms, David realized. Tess had told them that there were apparently rooms all over the building that were filled with batteries, parts, tools, and emergency materials that looked like they were meant for a lot more people than just the consultants.

They opened up one door to a supply closet, and Henry's eyes lit up when he saw the trove. He said, "Jackpot." His hands moved quickly over the rows of plastic bins. He snagged a roll of duct tape and a few other items. When he was done, he turned to David and said, "Come on."

The two raced back to the barracks and up to Henry's room. They talked as they ran.

Henry said, "So this should take me about ten minutes before I'm ready to transmit. I'll need to run a wire on the outside of the building for about twenty feet. I'll probably just drop it out the window to you and you can secure it on the ground floor."

David yelled over the wind, "Okay, I'll need to grab a few things from the barracks first."

"What are you getting?"

"Shower curtains...and rails."

"What for?"

"Nothing. Just a backup plan."

"We have a backup plan? I didn't even think our original plan was that good, and this guy's got a backup plan."

David said, "Lena was too calm. Something still doesn't feel right."

"You wanna tell me about your backup plan?"

"Don't worry about it right now."

Henry beamed with pride. "Shower curtains. And here I thought I was the only MacGyver in the group."

* * *

Brooke's experience with interrogations was limited to watching Jack Bauer in episodes of 24 and trying to use what she had learned when interviewing her sister's constant flow of unworthy boyfriends. She didn't know exactly what to do here, but she figured that she would learn quickly. Brooke had one of the military guys tear the gag off Major Combs. As soon as he did, Combs let out a river of profanity that normally would have made her blush. Today, however, she wasn't having any of it.

She simply said, "Are you done?"

David had asked her to do this. She didn't have time to worry about her inexperience or dwell in self-doubt. The team needed her. She would just be straightforward with him and ask him exactly what she needed to know. If Major Combs wasn't cooperative, she might ask one of these large military helpers by her side to physically encourage him to be more forthcoming. That tactic may have been picked up from the TV shows. But she was confident that it was probably effective.

The major's chest was heaving. His eyes were bloodshot, and he had several minor cuts and scrapes on his face...remnants from the wrestling match that he had quickly lost in the barracks.

Brooke took a seat on the chair that Lena had been sitting in a few minutes prior and turned it to face Combs. She looked Combs directly in the eye, not saying a word. He stopped yelling.

She said, "I need to ask you some questions. I assume that you really are an officer in the Air Force. Or maybe you were at one time. If you have any honor left, please tell me the truth and do so quickly."

He looked at her aghast. "Of *course* I'm an officer in the Air Force. What the hell is this? You people are completely out of line. There are *protocols* to be followed. Lena is the site *supervisor* for Christ sakes. I don't know who's responsible for this, but you need to get her back here right now. This is ludicrous!"

Brooke shook her head quickly like a dog shaking off rainwater, trying to absorb what she was hearing. She hadn't expected him to continue the charade at this point. They were past this, weren't they? Why was he still pretending?

She said, "What do you *mean*, why did we tie you up? You *know* why we tied you up. Look, David saw what was on the other side of the island. We know this isn't really an American operation. We *know*. The game is over."

He had a look on his face like she was from another planet.

She said, "Look, Harold, if that's your name. We just want to get out of here safely. Listen, I don't know what made you betray your country—"

"*What the* hell *are you talking about?*"

He said it so loud that the two military guys standing behind him jumped. They went over and stood right next to Brooke as if to emphasize that he should behave better. Brooke liked the muscle, but she couldn't understand the outburst.

Brooke sat there staring at Major Combs. She was new to this interrogation thing, sure. But he sort of seemed like he was being honest. This might take longer than she was hoping for...

\* \* \*

Lena and Natesh sat in the only two chairs in the communications room. Each chair was in front of one of the two computer terminals, which were only a few feet apart. Lena was restrained with duct tape around her forearms and her calves. Norman stood behind them, watching. The wind howled outside. Every few seconds Norman could see flashes of lightning through the windows at the top of the stone walls.

Natesh typed away. The letters were in English, but it must have been code or something, because it looked like gibberish to Norman.

They were in there no more than two minutes when Lena started talking. She hadn't said a word in the last hour. Now she looked right at Norman and she spoke with all the confidence of someone who knew they were going to win.

"They'll be here soon." Melody in her voice. Taunting. Playful.

Norman shifted his weight. "Who will? How do you know? That weather's pretty bad. Do they have cameras? Do they know we've taken you?"

She said, "Of course."

"How many?"

Lena said, "More than enough." Again with the tone. It was like she was an elementary school teacher.

Natesh looked away from his screen and at the two of them for a moment. His forehead was sweating. He looked back at the screen and typed faster, if that was possible.

Norman said, "Natesh, how's it coming? Any progress?"

Natesh kept typing as he said, "Just give me a few more minutes."

Norman looked at Lena and said, "How will they come?"

She smirked. "Well armed."

Norman eyed the 9mm in his hand. The one he had taken from Major Combs. He said, "Well, I'm armed too, lady."

Lena let out a quick laugh, and then went quiet.

Natesh was hitting keystroke after keystroke at a rapid clip. Then he lifted up his hands and hit one final key with a flourish. He turned around from the monitor to face Lena and Norman and said, "I think I just sent a message out. Give me a few more minutes. I'm going to see if I can get access to their servers."

"Whose servers?"

"The people that we were sending emails to. I might be able to find out who they are or where our emails were going. Just give me a little more time. I might need her for a password."

Norman turned Lena's chair around so that she was facing him. He stood, towering over her. He was closer than he needed to be. He holstered the 9mm and checked that her hands were taped up nice and tight. They were. She gazed up at him from her swivel chair. Silent. Thinking, perhaps. He could feel his heart pounding. He kept wondering how long they had.

David dropped a large roll of shower curtains and rails on the floor of Henry's room. He had taken a roll of duct tape from the supply room and used it to hold the shower curtains all together like a big Persian rug. He hoped that he wouldn't have to use it. But the voice in his head kept whispering. He needed to be ready.

Something still didn't feel right. David had missed something; he just didn't know what it was.

Henry saw him enter and said, "Okay, buddy, I'm about ready for you to secure this line down outside. I'll unravel it down the window. I might need you to walk around a bit until I can be sure it's positioned right. I'll be watching the needle from in here. Once I say it's good, use your roll of tape to secure it to something on the ground." Henry didn't even look up as he spoke. He had taken his alarm clock apart and was connecting wires and circuits to other metal pieces.

David said, "Got it. I'll be down there. Just yell when you're ready."

* * *

Brooke was exasperated. She'd been questioning the major for the past twenty minutes and he was still playing dumb. Worst of all, she was starting to doubt how much he really knew. She thought she could read people pretty well. He was reacting just how the others had reacted when they'd found out that Bill was being held prisoner on the other side of the island. He was enraged. And he was insistent that he knew nothing about it. At first, he had also insisted that Lena wasn't a part of it. But the more he heard about what David had seen, the less sure he seemed to be.

Brooke said, "So you had access to the computer room every day. Who would you talk to on the other end? Did Lena ever tell you who that was?"

"Like I said, she's always told me it was members of her CIA team. People that were piped in to this closed network. I guess I figured they were in Langley or some covert CIA Internet lab somewhere."

"But she let you carry a handgun. Why would she do that if you weren't in on it?"

"In on it? Look, let's say you're right. Let's say Lena isn't who she claimed to be. I mean, first of all I can't explain why she would let me carry a gun—"

Dr. Creighton was standing nearby. He said, "Because she wanted to create the illusion of reality in all of our eyes. The same reason that she made us sign nondisclosure agreements and get security badges when we checked in. Giving Major Combs a gun is a large risk to take. But it creates a compelling reason to believe that she is a trusting and trustworthy American CIA official, does it not?"

Combs said, "That's insane. I could have shot her if—"

Dr. Creighton said, "But you were the last to suspect anything. And the most loyal due to the trust she gave you. She had you as one of her henchmen up until an hour ago. Other canaries would have fallen before she needed to remove the gun from your possession. My hypothesis is that it was a calculated risk on her part. One that worked well, until David's swim this morning."

Major Combs looked very different than he had a few minutes ago. Where he had started off cursing and angry, he now looked defeated and sad.

Brooke said, "So what can you tell me about how Lena got that helicopter here? Or the airplanes every day. How did she coordinate all the logistics? We were told that you helped with all that."

Combs frowned. "No. The only thing I did was send and receive emails on those computers. I didn't actually do any of the planning. I relayed information to and from Lena. Half the time I didn't even understand what was being said."

"Natesh said otherwise. He said that you and Lena were by yourselves in some secret back room of that Communications building. He said that was where you got the gun. And that's where he thought you kept anything that you guys didn't want us to see."

Major Combs looked like he would explode. "Bullshit. That's total bullshit. Natesh is a liar. He was the one that was always back there with her. It actually pissed me off."

Brooke's eyes narrowed. "What?"

"She made me the administrative officer, not him. He was just supposed to help facilitate some of these meetings with people. But then when we got here it wasn't the way she said it would be..."

Brooke shook her head in disgust. Even now, after being told that Lena was very likely a Chinese spy, he was still upset that she had given Natesh more attention. Still...what he was saying about Natesh was very odd.

"...She was always having private conversations with Natesh in there in the early morning and when I got into the room they would stop talking. She would go into the back room for hours and Natesh and I would go on the computer. I didn't know if it would be like this for the whole three weeks. She told me and Natesh when we met last year that—"

Brooke said, "*Stop.*"

He looked at her, startled. He said, "What?"

"What do you mean she told you and Natesh *last year*?"

\* \* \*

Norman leaned forward, pressing his hands into her shoulders and holding his face just inches from her own. He said, "I want you to tell me what's on the other side of this island, and when and how many people are going to come for us. Do you understand?"

Lena winked a sexy, defiant wink. It infuriated Norman.

He raised his hand as if to strike her. She smiled back at him, a daring glint in her eye. He thought about hitting her but couldn't bring himself to hit a girl. Even if she was an enemy. She was a woman, and he had been raised never to lay a finger on a woman.

He shoved her chair away in frustration and let out a snort.

"Are you frustrated?" Lena asked, a weird excitement in her voice.

Norman said nothing. Natesh continued to type.

"You should let go of your frustration. This situation will be resolved soon enough."

Norman clenched his jaw. "How so?" he said.

"Soon my support will arrive. They will take all of you into custody. I will be released. That is what will happen."

"That so?"

"Undoubtedly."

Norman stepped over to speak into her ear. He kneeled down. His face was red and he was angry enough that he started doing things he wouldn't have otherwise. Like pressing his weapon into

her temple. He unholstered the gun and jammed it against her
skull.

Lena closed her eyes and inhaled. A deep, pleasure-filled breath.
"Don't you just love moments like these?"

Natesh looked at them and said, "Norman, cool it."

Norman said, "Tell me how many people there are on the
other side of the island."

Lena turned her head so that the barrel of the gun was pointed
straight at her forehead. She caressed the tip of the gun with her
lips. Norman's face was red with fury.

Lena said, "More than enough, I assure you."

"Will they send helicopters in this weather? Can the people on
the other side of the island take boats here? How will they get
here? Do they know that we have you? How much time do we
have?"

Lena said, "Relax, Mr. Shepherd. Trust me, there is absolutely no way out for you or the other members of the Red
Cell—"

"Stop calling it that. This never was a Red Cell. It was all a
sham. A waste."

"A sham maybe, but definitely not a waste. Trust me, the information will be put to good use."

Norman was losing control of his emotions. He said, "You
*bitch*. Is this *noble* to you? Do you think this is right? To kidnap
people and attack a peaceful nation? I assume you're Chinese,
right? Why the hell would China want to attack us, anyway? Don't
you guys already own half our country and sell everything to us?
What more do you want?"

Lena stared at him, the slightest of smiles on her mouth.

Natesh leaned over and said, "Calm down, Norman. I'm almost
done."

Norman took his eyes off Lena and looked up at Natesh. He yelled over to him, "How much longer?"

He heard a loud, rapid ripping sound.

Norman looked down at Lena. She had somehow torn apart the duct tape that had tied her forearms together.

Her hands grabbed at his gun and he tried to pull it away, but she was incredibly quick. They wrestled over the gun, Norman forcing its aim toward the ground. He tried to pull the trigger, hoping that would win him control, but she had jammed her finger behind it, blocking his pull.

With her free hand, she grabbed his shirt, twisted it around, and shifted all her weight so that she and her chair fell to the ground, acting like a fulcrum and slamming Norman to the floor.

Natesh was on his feet now, mouth gaping, looking unsure of himself. He saw Norman on the ground, his eyes growing wider with the first hint of panic.

Lena's legs were still taped together at her calves, but now she was on top of Norman, free from her chair, her knees balancing on his chest. One of her hands was still blocking the gun trigger. The other hand—the free hand—moved faster than anything Natesh had ever seen. It was the last thing Norman would ever see. Her fingers became weapons, gouging his eyes with lightning strikes of her long fingernails. Norman twisted away in crazed pain and let go of the gun, holding his now bloody eyes and screaming.

The gun clattered on the concrete floor, but Lena didn't go for it.

She took both her hands and twisted Norman back so that he was facing straight up toward the ceiling. With one strike, she forced her fist into his Adam's apple. She let out a guttural yelling noise as she hit him. Her fist was tight, and her knuckles struck

like a hammer. The stone floor behind Norman meant that there
was nowhere for the pressure to go but straight into his larynx and
trachea. His bloody and scratched eyes shot open and his hands
instinctively went to his throat as he tried to breathe.

As soon as his eyes opened, Lena attacked them once again.
She simultaneously dug the pointer and middle fingers of each
hand into the corresponding soft tissue of his eyes. The eye
sockets caved in about an inch, and Lena squeezed and tore. Dark
blood streamed down his face as Norman wailed.

Lena rolled off him and sat on the floor, next to the gun.
Natesh stood, facing her.

Behind Lena, the far door in the room—the one that led to her
private quarters—opened. Natesh saw dozens of armed Chinese
men in military gear looking into the room. Lena looked back at
them. They could see the bloody mess on the floor but remained
stationary. They appeared to be waiting for her command.

Lena looked back at Natesh. "I see you sent your distress
message."

* * *

Combs said, "A year ago. We met out in California. Near Edwards
Air Force Base, where I worked. I was retiring. I didn't want to get
out of the Air Force, but they wouldn't let me serve any longer. I
didn't get promoted. I was being forced out. Mandatory retire-
ment, they said. Then my boss told me that they had an opening
for a special assignment. It would give me another year in the Air
Force. I was thrilled. A week later I met up with Lena and Natesh
and they told me all about this job. Supposed to take about a year
to eighteen months. They needed a lot of data. My boss helped me
with that. We did IT security audits at all the Air Force bases on
the West Coast. So it was easy for us to get access. This operation
was all highly classified. At the time, I thought Lena and Natesh

were both private contractors, but they were pretty easy to work with. They didn't tell me about Lena being CIA until just before we came to the island."

Brooke's eyes were wide. "*Wait*, you're saying that you, Lena, and Natesh were accessing government computers on the West Coast for the past twelve months?"

"Yeah, why?"

"How long have you been planning to come to the island like this?"

"The whole time. We didn't find out the exact location of course until just a few weeks ago. Everything moved quicker once the Chinese got hold of ARES. But we knew we were going somewhere. They said that they needed me to check our base cybersecurity and to be the administrative officer here."

"Haven't you been listening or talking to anyone while you've been here? No one else has been working with her for more than a few weeks. The ARES codes were just found in the satellites a few weeks ago. And the operation that killed our CIA operative in Shanghai took place over the past few weeks. The whole premise for us being on this island is that Lena and members of our government found out about a Chinese invasion plan over the past few weeks. So if you and Natesh have been working with her for the past twelve months on plans to come here, that directly contradicts what we've been told about just recently finding out about the Chinese invasion."

Combs looked confused. Brooke realized that he was not guilty of treason. He was just guilty of being an idiot. Perhaps that was why he was chosen.

Tess yelled down from the top level of the classroom, near the window, "Brooke, Natesh is on his way back. He's by himself, and he's running."

## 11

---

*Force always attracts men of low morality.*
   —Albert Einstein

*Two Years Earlier, San Francisco*

Natesh drove his Tesla Model S up to the entrance of one of San Francisco's most exclusive restaurants. He flipped the keys to the valet and strolled through the large rotating glass door. A petite Chinese woman in a business suit was waiting for him next to the hostess.

The Chinese woman said, "Right this way, Mr. Chaudry."

He followed her up the stairs to the second level of the open-floor restaurant. The smells of fresh bread and spiced meat filled his nostrils. The woman led him to a table next to the railing that overlooked the diners below. The downstairs dining area was packed. The bar was standing room only. Up top, though, every table had been cleared. Natesh saw a manager shooing away a busboy who tried to clean a nearby table. They escorted him to the only table that had place settings and he sat alone. The Chinese woman stood ten feet away, waiting.

Natesh looked at her and said, "I'm sorry, miss, but do you know when he'll be here?"

She held up a finger and touched her ear with her other hand. She was listening to an earpiece. A clear one like Secret Service agents wore when they protected the president.

Natesh looked at the entrance of the restaurant and saw a half dozen men in black suits enter and spread out. Several of them were holding a hand to their ears as well. Security.

The second floor was a good twenty feet above the ground floor of the restaurant. It was wide open, with colorful glass decorations hanging down from the immensely high ceiling. A jazz band played, though it wasn't too loud up there on the second floor. The bar was buzzing, and waiters and waitresses flew through the crowd while balancing food and drinks. It was busy. And yet, when the man who had to be Mr. Cheng Jinshan entered the room, he immediately looked up at the exact spot where Natesh was sitting.

It took Jinshan a moment to get up to the second-floor table. He was an older gentleman, but looked very fit. Jinshan had hard eyes, sharp cheekbones, and thick wrinkles on his forehead. His suit looked very expensive, as did his shoes. An entourage followed him up the stairs, but they dispersed as soon as Jinshan reached the table. Natesh rose as he arrived, and they shook hands. Jinshan spoke in thickly accented English. "I am happy that we were able to meet. Your reputation precedes you. You have done excellent work with your company, Natesh. You should be very proud."

Natesh was used to wining and dining the clients he worked with. It was part of the job. But usually he arranged everything and was able to do his homework on who he was meeting ahead of time. He knew a little about Jinshan, but other than his wealth and business success, it was hard to find details in such a short amount of time. There was surprisingly little about his personal affairs on the Internet. This meeting had been popped on him only a few hours ago by one of Jinshan's subordinates. *Mr. Jinshan is in town on business. He wants to meet you. We will call in a few hours with a time and place. Be ready.* There was no choice in the matter. When your client was one of the three most powerful men in Asia, you dropped everything.

"Thank you, Mr. Jinshan," he said.

"Please excuse my direct line of inquiry. But my advisors keep me on a tight schedule. So I will get right to it, if you don't mind."

"I'm all yours, Mr. Jinshan. How can I be of service?"

Jinshan offered a polite smile. "Where do you see yourself in the next five years? What is your vision for your company and yourself?"

*No chitchat. He gets right to the point.* Natesh gave him his normal elevator speech. He told him about wanting to transform the consulting and product innovation world. Big companies had the means. Natesh and his crew had the ability. Natesh had hired some of the best innovators in the world and wanted to help create and disrupt industries.

"Create and disrupt, you say—two very different words. But often people in your line of work use them together, don't they?"

Natesh said, "Yes, I suppose they do."

Jinshan said, "Natesh, I have a question for you, and I want you to answer me truthfully. I've read your file. I saw some things in there that intrigued me. My question is...do you have a strong loyalty to the United States?"

Natesh opened his mouth to answer, but nothing came out. He'd expected a business proposal. An opportunity for his consulting firm to work with one of Jinshan's companies, perhaps. This question was completely unexpected.

He said, "You were born in India and lived there until you were ten. You are an American citizen. Your father still lives in India. But not your mother..."

Natesh felt a flash of concern. Why would this man be looking up things about Natesh's parents? "I'm not sure how that is relevant," he said.

"It is."

"Well, I'm not fully comfortable—"

Jinshan looked over his shoulder at the small Chinese woman who had greeted Natesh earlier. She stood out of earshot but hurried over when he caught her eye.

"Please bring us a bottle of wine. And let the chef know we're ready to begin our dinner." She nodded and scurried away.

He turned back to Natesh and said, "Relax, Natesh. I don't care what your parents did a long time ago in Kashmir. All I care about is that you have the frame of mind that I am looking for. And that you are not your parents."

Natesh said, "My parents were...very political..."

"And are you?"

"No."

"Then what does motivate you? What do you believe in?"

Natesh laughed nervously. This man was digging quick and deep. He said, "I believe in myself. And I believe in the power of reason."

Jinshan said, "And what motivates you? Why do you work so hard in life? What do you long to do? To create? To become?"

His mind raced. "I'm only twenty-seven. I think I have a lot of time—"

"Don't tell me that. I don't believe that you haven't thought about this. Men like us don't go through life aimlessly. We conquer. Now—what is your goal?"

He was off-balance. He said, "I...I guess I've always wanted to be one of these titans of technology. Every day we create new ideas for companies and they use our ideas to create more value for themselves. I'd like to sift through these ideas as we create them, and find the one or two that are really big. Then I would like to form my own large technology company and build it up. I would like to form it into one of these titanic firms that shapes the world."

"So you want power?"

"Yes."

"You want to create and control how the world works?"

"Yes. If we're being honest. Which it seems we are."

"You are. I haven't said a word."

Natesh flushed. "Well, your reputation stands true. I've heard that your interviews were more like interrogations."

Jinshan laughed. "I don't interview."

"Isn't that what we're doing now?"

He shook his head. "No. Interviews are a waste. I decided to give you the job before we met. I've already done my research. Now I need to convince you that my job and my objectives are worthy of your dedication."

"And what does that have to do with my loyalty to America?"

Jinshan said, "Are you loyal to America?"

The two paused their conversation as the wine came. A second waitress placed a plate of artisan breads and cheeses in between their plates.

Natesh arrived at the conclusion that this man didn't care whether he was loyal to the US and might even look at it as a negative. If he was honest with himself, Natesh really didn't harbor many patriotic feelings about the US. It was just a matter of whether his answer would hurt or help his future relationship with this client.

"No. I am not especially loyal to America. It's just a set of lines over land and laws over men. Both of which will change over time," Natesh said.

Jinshan said, "Natesh, what if I told you that those lines and laws were about to change very soon? What if I were to tell you that the *world* was going to change drastically in the next few years? And what if I offered you a major part in shaping and controlling how that happens?"

Natesh wasn't sure what to make of this man. He saw the look of fierce intelligence behind his eyes. He said, "I think what I do would depend on the details, Mr. Jinshan. The first thing I always ask when encountering a new problem is: what are my options?"

Jinshan's face filled with wrinkles as he truly smiled for the first time that evening. "I'm glad you asked. That's what I wanted to talk to you about."

Natesh looked down onto the sprawling restaurant scene below. Bright incandescent bulbs lit up the bar. Waitresses in elegant yet revealing black dresses maneuvered through the tables to bring high-priced fare to some of San Francisco's elite.

He took a sip of wine and said, "I'm happy to hear what you have to say."

Jinshan studied him. "Tell me the answer to this question: Let's say that you built corporations and began to take on the world... much like you are already doing. When would it be enough?"

Natesh considered that. He'd asked himself versions of that question a hundred times before.

He said, "It would never be enough."

Jinshan pointed his finger at him and grinned. He said, "This is why interviews are a waste for me. I always research my investments heavily before I make a decision—especially my investments in human capital. I knew that I was right in my decision to choose you before we even spoke."

"Thank you."

"Natesh, a hunger for life is never something that you should be ashamed of. People will call it greed. But greed doesn't fully capture the reason for the statement you made..."

Natesh's gut reaction was to say that he wasn't greedy. It was the natural response to such an accusation. But he could tell by

Jinshan's tone of voice that this was not meant to be a negative charge.

Jinshan said, "Ambition gets us closer. That word gets closer to what really drives many of the men and women who prop up this world. But *why* do they have ambition? You have to keep peeling back the layers to see that it's all about two things: control and *fear*. People want to be in control. They want to be in control because they fear what happens when they aren't."

Natesh smeared some Brie on a slice of a baguette and listened while he chewed.

Jinshan said, "Do you believe in God, Natesh?"

Natesh moved uncomfortably in his seat. He debated how to answer. He went with truth.

"No. I don't," he said.

"Good. I don't care why you don't. It's irrelevant. But the reason people fear God is because they think that he is in control of their lives."

Natesh chewed, not sure how to respond. The conversation was taking yet another unexpected turn. Yet he was intrigued by Jinshan's ideas.

Jinshan said, "However, if you don't believe in God, it is quite liberating. If there is no divine spirit controlling your destiny, then why shouldn't *you* be in control? And what would *real* control look like?"

Natesh wasn't sure if he was supposed to answer.

Jinshan sipped his wine. He looked up at the ceiling and kept talking. "If you don't believe in God, and you achieve greatness in this life, then eventually you realize that you can *be* one."

Natesh didn't know what to say. What was this man leading up to?

"Natesh, I'm going to tell you something, and I need you to suppress any worry or disbelief that you may have until I'm done. I made my decision on you long ago. When I'm done talking, you need to make your decision on whether to join me. It's a onetime offer."

Natesh said, "Okay."

Jinshan said, "Over the years I've developed many contacts in the Chinese government. For that matter, I've developed many contacts in governments all around the world. Some are politicians and businessmen. Some of them are in the military or intelligence community. The point is, I have my fingers in everything, so to speak." He smiled. Natesh could see that he was proud of his network.

"That's very impressive."

"I've needed to keep my businesses competing at the highest level each year. These contacts help me to get information I need, and to overcome hurdles that would otherwise impede my success. And my businesses have done well...very well, as you know. But it's time to cash out."

Natesh raised his eyebrows.

Jinshan continued, "Some of my contacts—ones who are very good at predicting things like this—tell me that China's economic growth is unsustainable. I know—people have been saying that for years. But this time, I believe it to be true. So, what does that mean for me? It means that it is time to take the next step in achieving my goals. It is time for me to make a bold move. Over the next year, China will get a new president. I will put him there. Our economy will begin to falter before that, and this new president will promise the people a way out. But...*there is no way out*, Natesh. Not with the way the world is set up. You are a student of business. What do you know when you see a stock price rocket up at an impossible rate? That rate of acceleration, most likely, will correct in the opposite direction. The stock will come crashing down. The same occurs on a larger scale with national economies. They either expand or contract in endless cycles—some more violent than others. This next one will be quite violent, I am afraid."

Natesh said, "So you are selling your businesses?"

Jinshan shook his head. "Not at all."

"What, then?"

"I will lead China into a global expansion, and I want you to be a part of it. I want to give you the control that you truly desire. You won't just lead businesses. You'll shape nation-states. You'll lead decisions on all aspects of people's lives. And you know what? It will actually help them. You will get the control and the power that you've wanted all your life. For once, there won't be the bureaucracy and political infighting drowning progress. The masses that have formed failed democracies and corrupt governments will get the growth and leadership that they never could have put into place on their own. Look at history—look at what the Roman Empire did under proper leadership—look at what Kangxi of the Qing dynasty did.

"Natesh, I've been watching you for a long time. I want you to help me rule a new empire that unites our globe and brings an era of peace and prosperity that the world has never seen. Great men have been asking themselves this question for ages. What is more desirable? Money, or power? Let me save you from a life wasted— the answer is power. Control gives us power. And I'm offering it to you, if you'll work alongside me."

Natesh did all he could to keep his mouth from opening. Was this real? He didn't know what to say. His mind wrestled with whether he was hearing the lunatic rant of an eccentric old billionaire or whether Jinshan was actually capable of such things.

"How?" Natesh said.

Jinshan said, "Tell me, Natesh. What do you know of my country's policy on having children?"

"The One Child Policy? Not much. I think it's pretty self-explanatory. Of course, I've heard rumors of..."

"Go on. You won't offend me."

Natesh looked away, embarrassed. He said, "Well, I've heard rumors of things like late-term abortions or killing newborn babies in order to maintain the law."

Jinshan scoffed. He said, "The Western media, I assure you. The One Child Policy, as you call it, was a magnificent achievement. It serves as an example of the sensational results that can be achieved when real leaders make decisive moves. Do you know how many poor, jobless souls would be crowding the streets if we hadn't put that law into place? China would be weighed down by starving criminals. Instead, we carved out the excess waste like the cancer it was. But something like that can only be accomplished if those leaders have the *authority* they need. And today, we can. Just imagine the improvements to our global society that we can produce. And in the new global empire that I will create, we will have the capability to make these choices."

Natesh said, "What do you mean, the capability?"

"The Internet. Your specialty. Mine too, really. In China, I work many jobs. Some of them in business, others in a more public capacity. One of my jobs is to consult with our Cyberspace Administration. Natesh, I can control the information that over one billion people see. If I want them to hear that the sky has turned pink, then that is what they will hear. If I want them to stop reading CNN, then it will not be available to them."

"Censorship?"

"More than just *censorship*. Total control of information. And with that, the power of shaping of opinions. Today, true national authority must have this power to succeed. In a connected world, the government administration that cannot control the information that shapes public opinion is doomed to be a slave of rivals who can. If I want the Chinese people to read that America suffered a great cyberattack, and will be without power for months, they will. If I want them to read that our Chinese countrymen must perform our brotherly duty and bring military aid to America to make sure they don't suffer, they will read that. If I want them to hear that a growing element of radical American Christian terrorists have murdered innocent Chinese, they will. And if I want them to believe that the solution is that we must rise up and defend ourselves by invading the United States...then *that* is what they will believe."

Natesh's pulse raced. He said, "That doesn't sound ethical."

"You may question my ethics, but you can't question my logic. Or my influence. Or my *power*. And that is what I offer you now... power. Like no other man on earth can offer you. Today you cash checks that you have earned playing a game. It's an entertaining game, business. But it's not the real game. Statesmen would say that the real game is politics, and they are right. For that is where the real power is. Businesses can be crushed by politicians overnight."

Natesh was getting light-headed from the wine. He said, "And dictators can be overthrown overnight."

Jinshan looked down at the crowd below. He said, "True. But to win in *that* game—the game of nations—you must be willing to exercise every option. And that is where I have an advantage in placing logic over ethics. You said you didn't believe in God. Well, neither do I. If there is no God, who will stop wars from destroying the world? Who will stop economies from crashing due to Wall Street gamblers' mistakes? Who will save the people of this world from themselves? It has always been the same answer to these questions. The great emperors throughout history have been the men with the vision, the capability, and the authority to shape the world. *You* have great ambition. *You* have great strength. *You* have great intellect. *I* have chosen *you* to be a part of this great shaping of the world."

Natesh said, "I'm flattered to hear you say that. But, sir, you only just met me. How can you possibly know whether I'm suitable for—"

"I know."

Natesh paused. He took another drink of his wine. "How do you know I won't disappoint?"

"You won't."

Natesh shook his head. "I have reservations."

Jinshan said, "I have no doubt that you are apprehensive about some of the things I have mentioned. The road ahead will require hard work and sacrifice. Things that I believe are part of your nature. But before I continue providing you with details, please give me an answer to this question: do you choose power or wealth?"

* * *

*Present Day*

Brooke looked up at Tess from the stage at the bottom of the classroom.

Brooke said, "Natesh is running here?"

Tess said, "Yeah."

"Alone?"

Tess said, "Yeah, he should be in the building now. I can't see him anymore."

Brooke walked quickly over to the classroom door that led to the outer hallway and building entrance. She didn't know what she would say to him, but she knew she had to confront him. What Major Combs had just revealed didn't paint him in a good light. And it raised serious questions about things Natesh had said. She liked him, sure. He seemed honest. But if he had lied about how he'd met Lena, and how long he had known her, what else could he be lying about? Why would he lie about those things? And why was he alone now? Why would he leave Norman and Lena in the Comms building by themselves?

Brooke pulled on the classroom doorknob to open it, but it didn't budge. She frowned. Her fingers tightened around the knob. She twisted and pulled again. It was locked. The only exit to the room was locked from the outside. She gave it another tug. She looked down and didn't see a lock handle. Just a keyhole. *That's odd.* Shouldn't the lock keyhole be on the opposite side? She looked back through the small glass square at the top of the door.

Natesh stared back at her.

She stared at him, confused, yelling for him to open the door. Other people heard her yelling in the room and came over. Then Brooke heard a scream from up on the top level of the tiered classroom. Her eyes shot up to see a cluster of people leaning towards the window.

Brooke yelled, "What is it?"

She could barely hear Tess over the panic. Tess was frantic. "They're *coming.* There's so many."

Brooke looked back through the small glass window. Natesh stood looking at her. A serious look in his eyes that she hadn't seen before.

The last thing she saw before he walked away was his lips as he mouthed, "I'm sorry."

## 12

---

*The object of war is not to die for your country but to make the other bastard die for his.*

　—General George S. Patton

Tom Connolly opened the cell door and looked inside.

Bill lay in shambles on the floor. He looked up at Tom and said, "Just you this time?"

"Yeah. Just me."

Bill said, "What do you want?"

Tom almost gagged as he got a whiff of the air. It stank in this cell. It smelled like human waste and rotting food. He said, "I decided that I would check on you. See if you needed anything."

Bill squinted. His voice was ragged. "You helped put me here and now you're worried about my well-being? Lena said you were gonna come back and question me. Maybe that's why you're here. More likely."

Tom looked away. He swayed in the doorway, thinking about leaving. Maybe this was a bad idea. What was he doing here, anyway? Was he lonely, the only American on this side of the island? There would be others here soon, but they would be locked up like Bill here.

Bill said, "So why'd you do it? What do you think they're going to do? Make you a prince? Where are you going to go?"

Tom said, "What did you say?" He flexed his fists.

Bill spat on the floor of the cell. He said, "I assume they made you promises."

Tom said, "Yeah, they did. Pretty big ones."

"And you're okay with that? With selling your soul like that?"

"I'll live."

"Will you? Where are you going to go? It looks to me like you came in here because you didn't know where else to go. You're already having regrets."

"I'm not having—"

Bill's voice was raspy. "So what are you gonna do? They gonna send you back to America? You gonna be a king there?"

Tom didn't know why he kept listening, but he had a bit of a buzz going and didn't yet care to move. "That's the plan."

"Well...your servants will despise you. They'll know. Somehow they'll know what you did. And if they don't kill you, what will you do when the guilt hits you like a ton of bricks?"

Tom stared at him, stone-faced. Bill was lying on the floor, filthy and tired. And yet he looked stronger than Tom felt.

"Go to hell," Tom said.

"Oh, I'm going to heaven, my friend. I've got a seat waiting for me there. I've lived a good, honorable life. I've got a wife and family that love me and memories of..." Bill's voice cracked. He said, "I'm satisfied with what I've done with my life. Will you be able to say the same, when your judgment comes?"

Tom glared at him. He took another swig from his flask. "It stinks like shit in here."

He turned and walked out of the cell, slamming the door behind him. He walked down the empty hallway. Almost all the

Chinese soldiers were busy hustling over to the other side of the island. There was no one around.

He approached one of the steel doors that led out to the docks and the beach. He opened the door and stepped outside. He needed a smoke. Rain and wind struck him, but he continued on.

Tom shielded his eyes from the pelts of rain and walked around the side of the large concrete building he had just come out of. He removed a cigarette from his pack and tried to light it. The wind and rain made that nearly impossible. After a few minutes of cursing, he got one good drag before the cigarette was too wet to smoke. Tom flicked it into the air and the gusts sent it cartwheeling down away on the sand. He took out his flask and took a swig, walking down to the beach. Tom's clothes were already drenched. He looked at the waves and decided he would go pick out a seat next to the motorboats. A drink in the rain on a beach in a hurricane. A sure cure for whatever ails you.

Bill didn't know what the hell he was talking about, anyway...

* * *

Henry tossed the antenna cable out the window. It unraveled down the side of the building, where David caught it two stories below. A hellacious wind and rain beat against David's face as he grabbed the end of the cable. The rain was coming in bands now. One moment it would be a downpour, and the next moment it would be just wind. David kept thinking the storm was letting up when the next band of rain would pelt down on him.

Henry explained to him that the longer they made the antenna, the lower the frequency they could transmit and receive on. And the lower the frequency, the greater the range. That was the idea, anyway. David hoped it would work.

Henry yelled out the window of his second-floor barracks

room, "Back! Step back about five feet! Okay. Stay there. I'm going to try and transmit."

"Okay, let me know if—"

The wind was blowing so bad that David didn't hear the noise at first.

It started off as a dull hum. Like millions of bees flying towards them. David looked up the mountain, its peak just barely visible in the storm. When the first of the large helicopters came into view, ducking under the low, thick clouds and hugging the green treetops of the island, David kept thinking how enormous it looked. It was a dark grey steel dragon, much bigger than the one that had landed on the runway the other night.

The closer the aircraft flew, the louder its rotors became, until the rapid chugging sound was so loud that it drowned out the storm's wind. The giant machine flowed down the ridge with a grace and precision that both captivated and terrified him. Then two more helicopters appeared behind it, trailing the first as they dove down the curvature of the mountain like they were part of a giant roller coaster.

David looked up at the window. Henry appeared, staring at the helicopters, his mouth open. They looked at each other. They both knew what this meant. No time for an HF transmission. If any last shred of hope remained in David's mind, it disappeared as a large red star came into view on the tail of the first helicopter.

David yelled, "Henry, bring down the pile of shower curtains. I'll meet you at the entrance to the barracks."

Glickstein nodded frantically, and his head disappeared from the window.

David ran around the building and huddled inside the entrance. He peered through the large vertical glass panel just to the right of the door that rose from the floor to the ceiling.

David could see everything from his vantage point. The barracks was uphill from the Classroom, which was uphill from the Communications building and dining hall. Below all those buildings was the runway. He watched the three helicopters as they plowed through the rain and wind and banked left, getting ready to land on the runway. The nose of the three steel beasts pitched up dramatically, and they slowed until they came to a hover over the taxiway. As they did, they formed ferocious vortices of rainwater, spreading out in white sheets below.

David thought that it would take any troops in those helicopters at least ten minutes to get to their position. More, if they stopped at the Classroom first. Good. That would give Henry and him time. Maybe they could run down to the Classroom and gather some of the others while—

Down the gravel path, beyond the buffeting palm trees, he saw Natesh walk into view, standing alone in the open area between the Classroom building and the Communications building. What was he doing there? Why had he come from the Classroom? Then Lena walked up and stood beside him, unrestrained. She held Natesh's shoulder and spoke into his ear. Lena looked toward the Communications building and made a large waving motion.

They came in droves. Dozens of armed men in black tactical gear ran past Lena and Natesh, towards the Classroom. These men weren't coming from the helicopters. They were coming from the Communications building. David saw Natesh walk, unescorted, back toward the Communications building. Lena followed the soldiers into the Classroom.

David's head was spinning. Natesh. He must have helped her. That was the only way to explain the way they were just talking with Chinese troops running beside them. David felt so stupid for trusting him. He had access to the computer room. Of course he was in on it. He just hadn't seemed the *type*. David wanted to scream, but he didn't have time for regrets.

Much farther down, toward the runway, David saw several dozen more troops running out of the helicopters. Two of the men were hunched over, vomiting near the runway. It must have been a bumpy ride. The rest ran full speed up the path and towards the buildings.

Henry hopped down the stairs, dragging the clunky plastic roll of shower curtains, duct tape, and metal rods.

"How bad is it?" Henry asked. He joined David, looking out the window.

David said, "Bad. We need to hurry. Henry, how good of a swimmer are you?"

Henry said, "I can do doggy paddle. Well...okay, not very well."

David said, "Okay, here's what I need you to do. Take no more than two minutes to try and gather any food or water that you can stuff into a pillowcase. Bring as much as you can. And any razors or something we might be able to fish with. Shit, I don't know... think of something. We're going to get out of here. I'm going to get us a boat. I don't know how far we've got to go, but plan for the worst. I count at least forty armed men down there, and I'm not sure how long we've got until they come up this way. Don't waste time. I'm going to the other side of the island. There were boats there. We've got a few more hours of daylight. I think we might be able to make a run for it with one of their motorboats at night. If we can get far enough away from this island, we can try to make a sail out of this tarp once we run out of gas."

Henry laughed nervously. "MacGyver." Then he looked back out at the buildings. He said, "What about the others?"

David said, "The best thing we can do for them now is make it out of here and get word out."

Henry nodded and started running up the stairs, then looked back and said, "Hey—where should I meet you?"

"Follow the barbed-wire fence east away from the buildings until it reaches the runway. Hide in the trees there until you see me come back. Just keep an eye out for me. I'm going to make one run up to land with the motorboat. When you see me, you need to run to the boat and get in. I'll be vulnerable then, so I'll only come to the beach once. If I don't see you, I'm leaving."

"How are you going to get the boat?"

David said, "I don't know."

"Oh. Good plan."

"To be honest, with the waves from the storm, even if I can get us a boat there's a good chance we'll drown."

Henry nodded, eyes wide, and said, "Oh. I see. Good, then. See you in a few." He dashed away up the stairs.

David looked out the window and saw the Chinese troops with submachine guns pointed forward, getting ready to enter the Classroom over a hundred yards away. Lena and Natesh were both out of sight. No one was looking in David's direction. He took a deep breath, opened the door, and bolted past the barracks toward the fence. He turned right and sprinted uphill on the long, narrow path in between the fence and the jungle.

He could feel his adrenaline pumping as his feet strode over the uneven terrain. A canopy of wet leaves reached out from above. He looked up as he ran, drops of water landing on his face. They felt cool in the warm air. There was less wind here. He was protected by tall rainforest on either side. The vegetation grew denser the farther up the fence he got. Fine with him. Better for staying hidden. He ran as fast as he could, fighting the urge to stop and look back. It was only this morning that he'd swum halfway around the island. His muscles reminded him. His quads and hamstrings already ached and he hadn't even gotten to the beach. David forced the pain out of his mind. He eventually made his way to the apex. It was the far corner of the barbed-wire fence, where it turned a sharp right and went downhill towards the sea.

David cycled through the recent events in his mind as he ran, trying to focus on something other than the growing pain in his legs. The apprehension of Lena and the Major. The helicopters diving down over the mountain. Natesh, standing in the middle of a herd of Chinese soldiers. Was Natesh really one of them? A part of him couldn't believe that Natesh had betrayed them. But the exchange between him and Lena? The troops running right by? He had to assume that Natesh had betrayed them all.

It was no longer safe to stay on this island. There was no guarantee of survival. At least not without being taken captive. There were boats on the dock on the other side of the island. He hoped that they were still there. David didn't know how far Henry and he could get on one of those small rigid-hull inflatable boats, but it was likely their only shot. How far from land were they? The prospect of dying of dehydration while at sea didn't appeal to him. If they reached mainland, where would it be? Was it China? What would happen if they rolled up on a boat in Hong Kong?

Each stride down the hilly path took David closer to the beach. With the winds pounding the seas, the waves were pretty big now. Much bigger than just a few hours ago. He could hear the surf from hundreds of yards away. The rain had stopped for the moment, and hints of blue afternoon sky peeked through the low black clouds. The sea, however, remained angry.

Whether it was drowning or dehydration, David didn't want to die at sea. But if he didn't leave this island, he could die a prisoner. He thought of his family, his friends, and his country. As he approached the end of the jungle where the path gave way to gravel, sand, and runway, David kept thinking about his family. He teared up thinking about Lindsay and his two girls. He had to force those thoughts away for now. He had to focus on the problem at hand.

If David didn't get word out, America would never know what was being planned. There would be no warning. This thought drove him on. He had to warn people. David believed that a Chinese attack on America was truly coming. And the Red Cell had helped the Chinese gather important information that would make this attack more potent.

His heart pounded. He came to a stop at the part of the path where the jungle ended. He would have to sprint across an open area. He prayed that no one would see him. If he could get to the water, he thought he could make it to the docks on the other side of the island without being seen. The only problem there was surviving the waves. *One thing at a time.*

He sprinted, stretching out his legs into long strides on the dark ground. As he ran, he looked to his right, down the long, wet runway. The three helicopters sat motionless on the ground. There was no sign of the Chinese soldiers.

He closed in on the shore and tore off his sneakers, placing them near the corner of the runway. They would only slow him down in the water, and he needed all the speed he could get. His eyes widened as he saw the colossal surf close up. Yesterday there had been a picturesque line of turquoise breakers. This morning the waves had been bigger, but nothing like this. Ahead of him now lay a whitewash of violence. A reminder of nature's strength. It was loud and intimidating. There didn't seem to be any pattern or lull in the waves, just one spew of forceful white salt water after another.

The barbed-wire fence that just this morning had sloped into the water was now a disjointed mess of metal, bent and broken. The raging surf hid the points where the barbed wire remained. This frightened David. He needed to get out past any remnants of that fence, but the force of the waves made that almost impossible.

He was like a fireman walking into a fiery building. Every instinct told him to stop, that the danger was too great. He thought once more of his family, and of the dozens of members of the Red Cell that had probably been taken prisoner by now. He thought of what would happen if China used the plans they had developed to launch a surprise attack on the United States.

He took a few fast breaths, gritted his teeth, and marched into the surf.

When he was in deep enough that the waves began pounding his chest, he dove and swam freestyle as hard as he could, directly out and away from the beach. He tried to time it with the waves, going under as the big ones broke overhead. It wasn't perfect, and a wall of salt water clobbered him more than once. But eventually he made it far enough out that he felt he could turn left, toward the other side of the island.

He turned, angling his aim to swim around the area where the metal fence was. That's when a big wave hit him. A fast-moving wall of water. It enveloped him and sent him tumbling over. He was disoriented, blind, and swallowing a lot of salt water. He fought to get upright. Just as he broke the surface, another wave hit him and pulled him under, back toward the beach. It had taken him five minutes of excruciating physical output to get that far into the water, and two waves were sending him rapidly back toward the shoreline...and toward the razor wire.

His head broke the surface for the second time. He was sucking in oxygen, kicking his legs and pumping his arms, doing everything he could to breathe and stay above water. He coughed up seawater from his lungs, and his eyes shot wide open as he saw sharp glistening metal circles protruding from the sea. The undertow was pulling him towards the broken array of barbed wire much faster than he could swim. He tried to swim parallel to the shore. If the waves were pushing him back to land, he could—

It felt like a combination of fire and ice was streaking down the length of his left arm. It was like someone had dumped ice cubes in a straight line from his shoulder to his elbow, and then lit a match that caught on fire in the exact same location. The sharp spikes of metal had just torn a gash in his arm as the waves twisted and pushed his body further toward shore. He was helpless. He started to panic. He was afraid he would get caught like a fish on a hook.

Then another wave tore him loose and carried him the rest of the way to the shore. The wave dumped him onto the black, sandy beach on the other side of the fence. The side that he was trying to reach.

The beach itself was almost nonexistent. The waves were coming right up over the sand and past the palm trees, temporarily covering the jungle floor in a few inches of surf. He got up and looked at the gash in his arm. It was bleeding badly, and he had nothing but his tee shirt to cover the wound with. He trudged along the edge of the jungle, stopping every few seconds as another large wave came ashore and covered his feet. He tore his tee shirt at his stomach and ripped off a rag, which he used to dress his wound. He put pressure on it and kept walking, toward the buildings and docks, where he hoped to find a boat to steal.

He wondered what was happening to the other consultants of the Red Cell. David hadn't even tried to save them. He pushed away the guilt. *There was no other way.* He hoped that Henry would be at the rendezvous if David could get a boat. *If.* It was a big if. What would he find near the docks? The seas had been much calmer when those boats had been tied up there before. David had been a sailor in college. Anyone who had ever taken care of a boat knew that you couldn't leave it tied up in the water during a storm. So where would they take them? Would they drag the boats up to higher ground? Would they be guarded? No. There was no need for security. They were on a remote island. No one would be outside in this storm, would they?

Ten minutes of painful walking later, David got his answer.

He arrived at the beach adjacent to the base on this side of the island. It was there, two hundred yards from where the buildings and docks were, that he saw the boats. Someone had pulled them up away from the beach, out of reach of the waves, just like David had suspected. There were two boats, each with a single outboard engine. He was wrong about there not being anyone outside, though. He saw one person.

Tom Connolly. *Unbelievable.* What was he doing out here?

Tom sat in the sand no more than twenty yards from the boats, staring out at the waves. His knees were up near his chest, and he was taking occasional sips from a steel flask. David stayed twenty feet inside of the tree line. That way he was pretty well concealed from view, but still able to keep his eye on Tom as he walked toward his position. David wanted to approach from behind if he was going to have any chance of pulling this off. *Pull what off, exactly?* What was his plan, now that there was someone he would have to deal with? David had no weapons. Could he take someone's life with his bare hands? Hell, could he even take someone's life? He pushed the thought away. Now was not the time for pondering. Now was the time for execution.

The closer David got, the more nervous he was that Tom would see him.

David stepped through the wet jungle. He was now 180 degrees from where Tom was looking. Directly behind his line of sight. As David approached, another band of rain began pouring from the sky. David worried that Tom would get up, wanting to get out of the downpour. But he just tilted his head back, letting the rain fall against his closed eyes. What the hell was he doing?

The bleeding on David's arm had slowed, although the wound still hurt badly. He looked on the ground for a weapon. A stick, a coconut—anything would do. He was desperate. And a desperate man needed very little in a fight. *And a desperate man could kill, if he had to, right?* Finally, he came upon a large rock, about the size of an orange.

David crept out of the jungle and toward where Tom sat. He looked to the left, toward the concrete structures. They were about fifty yards away, and slightly obscured by the heavy rainfall. He looked over toward the buildings to make sure no one was watching. The structures looked very similar to the Communications building. They had small slits in the top of their tall concrete walls. A dim blue light illuminated them from inside. But there was no sign of anyone outside. Was it possible that all those people he had seen on the other side of the island had somehow come from here? Were there people still remaining in these buildings that would be able to see what was happening? David didn't see any windows that looked like they had a view of the beach. It didn't matter. This was his only chance.

David took another step towards Tom. He gripped the rock in his sweaty palm. He decided the best way to do it would be to deliver a deathblow with the first strike. No talking. No second-guessing of Tom's level of guilt. Just one decisive blow to the head. Any doubt over this intended course of action was silenced by David's anger. Anger that Tom had taken him from his home and from his wife and family. Anger that Tom had betrayed his country. He thought about asking him why he did it. But even that seemed pointless. No—not pointless—wasteful. David had a mission to complete. Any deviation from the most efficient path of getting himself and Henry safely off the island was a possible detriment to the mission.

David stepped closer. He was about twenty paces away from Tom now. Tom was still facing the sea. Loud waves masked David's footsteps. Tom took another swig from his flask. David got a whiff of something. Rum. He was probably drunk, David realized.

He needed to strike Tom's skull with this large, hard rock. He needed to swing his good right arm as hard as he could, in one violent motion. That rock needed to crush through Tom's bone and into his brain and kill or incapacitate him. Only then could he begin to move the heavy motorboat through the sand, hoping that no Chinese military men came out from the buildings with machine guns.

David had to force all the excess noise out of his head. His sister, the Navy pilot, called it compartmentalizing. Could he really kill this man? Would he be able to pull this heavy boat?

Would he ever see his wife again? Was Henry even going to be there if he could get the boat to him, or would the Chinese be waiting? All the questions. All the emotion. David pushed it into a box and locked the thoughts away.

Ten paces away.

Each step was painfully slow. David's heart pounded as he lifted the rock up above his head. He could feel the shells and sand crunching beneath his feet. Tom faced forward now. David came from directly behind where Tom was looking. What was he doing just sitting here drinking in the midst of all of this?

Five paces away.

Tom sat there, hugging his knees, looking straight ahead. Every few seconds, he took another quick swig from his flask.

Two more steps.

Tom shook the flask like he was trying to see how much was left.

In one quick, sloppy motion, Tom let his head fall backwards, into the sand. His eyes were open this time, and he stared upward.

Their eyes met.

David was frozen six feet away, holding the rock above his head. Tom stumbled up and twisted around to face him. The rain was falling hard enough that they both were squinting. They stared at each other, both in a defensive posture, the magnificent white surf pounding the dark sand behind them.

Tom looked at the rock and then up at David. He slurred his words as he spoke. "You gonna hit me with that?" He laughed. His eyes were red and unfocused. Tom swayed slightly as he stood. He let the flask drop to the ground and held up his fists like he was ready to box.

David didn't let go of the rock, but he stood in a similar fighter's stance. He said, "Why'd you do it?"

Tom scoffed. "Goddammit, I'm getting tired of that question. What's it matter?"

David's eyes darted over to the buildings and then back to Tom.

David said, "How could you betray your country?"

Tom snorted and said, "Don't get all high and mighty on me. You haven't walked in my shoes. If you had, you'd have done the same." He looked around, toward the jungle. "How the hell did you get over here, on this side?"

David took a step toward him. He didn't seem to notice.

Tom said, "You think your country is loyal to you? There's no loyalty. Not with companies. Not with countries. Not with wives. Not with people. There's money and there's power and there's you and that's *it*. You want to know—"

David's first blow went into Tom's stomach. He drove the rock into him with an uppercut. Tom doubled over, but David drew the rock back up and then down again into Tom's temple. He felt it connect. It was a good, solid impact of stone and skull. There was some give, like the hard bone shield had been dented and caved in slightly. Tom went down and there was a lot of blood oozing from his forehead.

David dropped the rock and picked Tom up with both hands. The walk to the water's edge took about twenty seconds. The gashes on David's arm opened and bled more, but he didn't care. Expedience was more important than anything right now. David dragged Tom's body towards the ocean. He was heavy and left a deep track behind them. But he didn't make any noise or move. David thought he might be dead already until they got to the water.

When the first layer of seawater covered Tom's face, he started fighting. He kicked and thrashed.

Tom tried to get up, but he was weak and David had leverage. David pushed him under. Tom's arms flailed wildly now, his face just below the surface. David could see his wide eyes looking up from below the waterline.

The ocean's pull was incredibly strong. Even in just three feet of water, it took all of David's strength and balance to hold Tom under without falling down. David's legs and back muscles rippled. Blood flowed from the gash on his left arm. He could feel himself sinking as the rush of water eroded the sand around his feet.

David looked into Tom's eyes as the struggle ended. There was a distinct moment when Tom couldn't hold his breath anymore, and the ocean started pouring into his lungs. And then it was over. Tom's eyes fluttered up into the back of his head and he stopped fighting. David kept pushing him down for a few more seconds, just to be sure. He didn't want to take any chances. He counted to ten and couldn't feel any resistance in Tom's body. Just a limp, wet sack of traitor's blood and skin and bones.

It was strange. David didn't feel any remorse. He let go of the corpse and let the sea take it away. Then he turned and ran back up to the boats.

There were wheels underneath the boats. They were on a rig that allowed it to be towed. Probably meant to be hooked up to a machine. David hoped he would be strong enough to do it on his own. Thank God there were wheels. He moved as fast as he could go. There were chocks on all sides of the wheels, meant to keep them from slipping. David ran around each one, pulling out the chocks, and then pushed the boat into the ocean. Every few moments, he peered over his shoulder towards the buildings, but no one ever came out.

Tom's body was being tossed by the waves. It was already fifty feet down the beach.

When the boat reached the water, bow first, it floated off the rollers. David pushed hard as soon as that happened, careful to keep the bow pointed straight into the oncoming waves.

David knew boats. He had grown up on them and sailed up and down the East Coast of the United States for four years as part of the Naval Academy sailing team. Thankfully, the surf on this part of the beach wasn't as bad as the waves David had thrown himself into on the other side of the island. Here the waves were breaking much farther out—about a hundred yards out. There must be a reef. He was able to hold the boat steady as he pushed it deeper and deeper into the surf.

He got the vessel a good fifty feet out before he was chest-deep and decided to jump in. David pulled himself up and threw one leg over. He shimmied and squirmed his way over the large inflatable tube that served as a rim to the hard-shell hull. It was a small boat. Maybe fifteen or twenty feet long. If the waves were really twenty feet high out at sea—like Major Combs had told them during the weather report—then he and Henry would get tossed around like rag dolls.

*Henry*. He needed to hurry. The sky was starting to dim.

As soon as David climbed in, he hustled over to the outboard motor and manually put it into the ocean, then locked it into place and primed the pump. He prayed that it would start without any trouble. He pulled the T-handle and cord, and after a few lawn-mower-like sounds, the engine chortled to life. He took hold of the steering wheel and slowly moved the power control lever forward, careful not to go too fast into the oncoming waves.

Henry hid in the last grouping of tropical shrubbery before the jungle ended and the runway cutout began. He looked at his watch. Almost 6 p.m. It had been a full hour since David had left for the other side of the island. The rain had stopped. If the soldiers were looking for them, how long would it take before they came this way?

After David had left, Henry had run through the barracks building. He'd grabbed two pillowcases and filled them up with anything he could find that might be valuable: water bottles, fruit, and snacks that he found in people's rooms. Someone had brought a whole box of granola bars back from the cafeteria. Henry grabbed it, feeling like he had won the lottery. He tried to think of what else they would need. He took someone's alarm clock and smashed it into the bathroom mirror, then took a piece of the mirror. Maybe they could use it as a reflector to signal for help. He couldn't find any sunblock but he did find black shoe polish. He figured they would use that to coat their exposed skin. It was an impulse grab. He had no idea if it would work.

As he waited in the jungle, he decided that covering his face with the black shoe polish might make him harder to see. He would be camouflaged, like a commando. Like Rambo—except that Rambo never looked scared shitless.

He still carried the HF radio and had tried transmitting several times on all the frequencies he thought might be used. Nothing. He had the volume down almost all the way, but the antenna was sprawled out flat on the ground. Not ideal. He decided to grab a piece of the duct tape and attach it as high as he could reach on one of the many palm trees.

Henry looked up the hilly path he had followed to get here. No sign of anyone. Then he looked to his right, down the runway. It was empty for a good mile, except for the three helicopters that were shut down on the taxiway. Their rotors wobbled in the heavy winds.

It was 6:10 p.m., according to his watch. He really hoped David would get here soon. If he didn't make it, Henry didn't want to know what would happen if he turned himself back in to the Chinese.

Henry was on one of the MARS frequencies. He tried one more time. David would be here soon...he hoped.

"Any MARS station, any MARS station, this is Hotel Golf, how do you copy, over?"

Henry put his ear to the receiver, listening to the static. Nothing. He sighed.

"...over...Hotel Golf, this is MARS radio transmitter seven-three, I say again, I read you...and garbled...over..."

Henry's heart leapt. He held down the transmit button and said, "MARS seven-three, this is Hotel Golf, request immediate connection to the following US phone number...break...area code..."

These days, Henry just didn't need to memorize phone numbers. And it wasn't every day that you needed to connect with someone via an HF radio enthusiast in order to save your life and stop an invasion. He thought about just telling the radio operator what was going on, but he would probably think it was some type of prank. No, he had to call someone he knew. Henry sighed as he realized who it would be. He gave David the only phone number he knew. His first ex-wife's. Henry spoke the number and listened as the radio operator repeated it back, then told him to wait.

Henry told himself that she would come through for him. They had shared a special bond, after all. Henry still thought of Jan fondly. He imagined that she remembered him the same way. They had been young, after all. And she probably wasn't sore about the details of the divorce at this point. Or that he'd dated two of her girlfriends in the year after they'd split. Hell, they'd had great times together. Henry thought so. Jan was a smart, reasonable woman. She would hear how important this was and act accordingly.

Henry heard the static change to a ringing sound and then to a brief conversation between a woman he hadn't spoken with in fifteen years and the pubescent-sounding HAM radio operator from who knows where.

"Ma'am, my name is Ron Jacobson, and I'm a MARS radio operator. I have been asked to connect you with—"

Henry didn't have time for radio etiquette. He couldn't wait for this young guy to explain the rules about saying "over" after every sentence. Henry said, "Jan, it's Henry." He hesitated. "Henry Glickstein. Look, I need a favor. I know I haven't talked to you in a while, but I need you to call—"

Henry heard her voice on the radio, "...*no*, I will not accept a collect call from that womanizing ass—"

"Jan, now hold on. *Listen.* I'm in trouble." Henry tried to control his voice. He wanted to yell, but he wasn't sure how well the noise would carry through the trees. It was less windy here.

"You tell that bastard that he can call me on his cell phone. Where is he? Is he in prison? Is that why he's calling collect? Well, you tell him he can rot for all I care."

"This is MARS radio operator—"

"Goddammit, Jan, listen for a second!" Henry spoke as loud as he dared, his eyes darting up the path to see if there was any sign of the Chinese. "I'm in serious trouble here!"

Static noise.

"Hotel Golf, this is MARS radio operator seven-three, over."

Henry rolled his eyes. "*What is it?*"

"Hotel Golf, this is MARS radio operator seven-three—break —I regret to inform you that the number you have been connected to has terminated the call, over."

Henry wanted to scream. That woman was literally going to be the end of him.

He was thinking about what to say to the MARS radio operator when he saw it. A raft-like black boat bounced along the waves and headed straight for the spot that David had told him to be at. Henry swiveled his head one last time, checking to see if—

Up on the path. A football field away, but walking towards him. There were at least six of them. Black uniforms. Machine guns drawn. They crept along, scanning their weapons back and forth as they walked.

Henry froze. He suddenly felt incredibly visible, wearing a

white tee shirt and greyish pants in a dark green jungle. He needed to run. He looked back at David's boat. He had to go now. He looked at the HF radio. The antenna was spread out fifteen feet, the end taped to a tree. Those men were getting closer. He dropped the radio.

Henry grabbed the pillowcases of supplies and heaved the large, heavy cylindrical roll of shower curtains over his shoulders. Then he bolted towards the beach, running as fast as he could while carrying the load of supplies. He looked up every few seconds to see David heading towards him, bouncing through the surf.

The boat practically flew onto the beach and lodged itself in the sand. David was looking all around. He said, "Hey! Get that stuff in here, quick. We've got to get this boat turned around and back out there right now."

Henry said, "Up on the path. I saw some of them approaching." They got to work turning the boat around. The engine was off and swung up so that the propeller wouldn't get damaged.

Henry hopped into the craft and started the engine as David instructed him. David was walking the ship by its side into the water, until the engine was in the water and able to push it along. As soon as that happened, David hopped into the boat and Henry pushed the power lever forward. Once David was in, he took the controls and drove them out to sea.

A gunshot rang out behind them.

The two men looked back towards the island and saw half a dozen men in black uniforms sprinting towards them. One man was on his knee, taking aim. David saw a flash from the muzzle. He heard a weird snapping sound as the bullet whizzed by, followed by the crack of gunfire a split second later.

"Holy shit, get us the hell out of here!" said Henry.

David gunned it. The boat heaved forward into the heavy waves, thick white foam and salt spray splashing up over the bow.

Henry lay pressed flat against the deck of the boat, holding on to metal cleats for balance. The bow hit a larger wave and they pitched up so high that David thought they might tip over. But then they came back down, hard, and kept driving forward, farther away from the soldiers on the shore. David turned left, maneuvering them back around the island and out of sight.

Several shots rang out behind them, but they were getting far enough away and bobbing so much that none of the rounds came close. After a moment, the gunfire stopped. David looked back at the men. They were running the opposite direction, no doubt going for reinforcements.

Henry said, "Are they gone?"

David looked down at Henry, huddled on the floor. He said, "What happened to your face?"

Henry waved him off. He said, "Shoe polish. In retrospect, it was an ineffective solution to a larger problem."

"Can you hand me the duct tape?"

Henry dug in one of the sacks and handed it to him. David ripped a long patch of duct tape and put it over the gash in his arm.

As they rose and fell with the waves, David began giving Henry his idea on how they could set up the makeshift sail out of shower curtains, shower rods, and duct tape.

"I think I can fix something up," said Henry.

The two men did an inventory in the boat and were thrilled when they found an emergency kit with some fishing gear and a water purification device. With any luck, they could make it to a mainland or get rescued by a passing ship.

They were still heading parallel to the shore, towards the other side of the island. David said, "We will need to turn out to sea now. If we keep going this way, we'll risk getting seen by anyone occupying the other base."

Henry looked out towards the ocean. White caps went on as

far as he could see. He nodded. "The weather looks like it's clearing up. Maybe the waves will slow down a little. We've got to go for it, right? It's our only shot to get word out."

"Yeah...our only shot."

David turned the wheel to starboard and they began their journey out to sea.

**13**

---

*Either you decide to stay in the shallow end of the pool or you go out in the ocean.*

—Christopher Reeve

David held the plastic bottle up, letting the final drops of water fall into his dry and open mouth. It was one of their last water bottles. He sat listening to the now-calm ocean lap the hull and wondering how far they would make it.

Only two days and they were almost out of water. At first Henry and he had planned to use rain to replenish their stores. Since the storm had blown through, however, they had seen nothing but clear skies.

David brought up the idea of using his tee shirt as a filter for salt water, but Henry assured him that it wouldn't work. Henry was now setting up one of the shower curtains like a tent so that any condensation would drain into the empty bottles—a sort of fresh water collector. But that was a long-term solution for a short-term problem—they needed fresh water soon. It was very hot. They could stretch out the collection of snack foods that Henry had gathered for another few days, but not the water.

David looked over at Henry. He seemed better than yesterday. His face was still a little green. At least he had stopped throwing up. He was not meant to be at sea, he kept saying. The experience they'd had in the storm that first night had been both frightening and physically draining.

The storm had tossed the tiny boat around like it was a bath toy. They could barely control the direction of the boat. The motor and rudder kept coming up above the waterline as they surfed up and down the gigantic white caps. After turning out to sea, David had put their supplies into a small storage chamber on the port side. Henry and he had spent the next ten hours throwing up while holding on for dear life. The waves were the biggest David had ever seen in person. Twenty-footers, easy.

He prayed a lot that night. There were moments when he didn't think they would live. There were moments when he wasn't sure if he wanted to, his misery was so great. But the thoughts of his wife and children would flash in his mind and he would pray some more. He felt guilty that he only called on God in times of need.

The morning after the storm, as the seas calmed down and the sun crept over the horizon, they finally were able to rest. That was when they'd heard the helicopters.

David had heard the noise and looked over the inflatable rim of the boat. He'd been slightly horrified to find that they were still within sight of the island. It was far in the distance, but he had still been able to make out its silhouette on the horizon. It had to be the same island because he could see the three helicopters taking off from it and flying in formation to the south.

They were miles away and weren't a danger to the two men. Still, David waited until the aircraft were completely out of sight before starting up the motor and moving them away from the island. He didn't want to create a wake that was visible from the sky and risk a chance of capture. The spare gas they'd found in one of the boat's storage bays only gave them an extra two hours of propulsion.

Now they floated, out of gas, hoping the wind would catch their makeshift sail. Neither Henry nor David knew which way they should head in order to reach the closest point of land. They had settled on west. Given the climate and the fact that the flight to the island had taken around nine hours from California, they both figured that they were probably in the South Pacific. Closer to Southeast Asia than not. West was as good a heading as any, he supposed. South America might take longer.

David looked at Henry and said, "How's your water purification contraption coming?"

Henry was taking little tiny strings of duct tape and binding the rings of the tarp to the metal handlebar that wrapped around the top of the inflatable rim of the boat. It created a small tent for shade. He used one of the shower rods to prop it up in the middle and placed bottles at the corners, hoping gravity would bring any drops of condensation down in to them.

"It's coming," Henry said. His face was sunburnt and tired. "You know, it's not so much the heat out here...it's the humidity..."

David tried to smile, but his mouth muscles wouldn't make the shape. "Yep."

"There," said Henry. "That should do it."

"Looks good. The shade will be helpful, too." David leaned as far under the tent as possible while still holding on to the wheel.

Henry's lips were chapped. His neck and shoulders were bright red and blistering from being in the sun. David imagined that he didn't look much better.

They had made the sail as soon as the boat's gas had run out. Henry's design. He was pretty crafty, David would give him that. He had used the rope from the small anchor, several of the shower curtain rods, and a half roll of the duct tape, and turned them into what David thought resembled a jib. Then they'd used similar parts to increase the area of the rudder. It was crude, but it did the job. There was a steady wind coming from a non-ideal direction, but David did what he could to make it work and maneuver them west.

Henry, putting away the "tools," said, "Okay, let's make a bet. We make it to land, get rescued by a boat, or die of dehydration. What do you think it's going to be?"

"Don't forget sharks."

"Sure. Good point. So you're taking sharks? I think we die of dehydration first, personally. But..." He stopped and froze his gaze to the west. His words became more rapid. "Actually, I'm gonna change my bet. David, look. I see something," Henry said.

David leaned over and peered in the direction Henry was looking. There was a dark shape on the horizon.

Henry said, "Do you see that? Just to the right of where the front of the sail starts. I think it's a boat."

David thought so too, although he couldn't make out what kind of ship it was. It would be a minor miracle to find someone else out here. Even more miraculous would be if they were spotted and rescued.

Henry said, "I'm going to signal it with the mirror."

"Wait."

"Look, we've been over this. We agreed that if we saw *anything*..."

David squinted as he tried to make out the features of the vessel. A mast, a radar, fishing nets...anything that might give them a hint as to whether it was a friend or foe. He said, "You sure you don't want to wait until it gets closer to make sure isn't a warship at least?"

"I'm sure. We might not want to pass up opportunities," Henry said. He held up an empty water bottle. "Beggars can't be choosers." He scratched at the peeling sunburnt skin on his neck.

David bit his lip and jiggled his empty water bottle, then

looked at the dark spot on the horizon. Even if they did signal it, that thing was so far away that whoever was on board probably wouldn't spot them.

"Okay. But assuming they're civilians and this doesn't get us killed or captured, let's remember the plan."

\* \* \*

Nathan heard one of his deck men yelling from the bridge. It sounded like Byron, his good-for-nothing nephew. Christ, now what was the matter? Their icemaker had been on the fritz for the past week. No fishing and a ten-day steam to Darwin. Could have been ten years, it would have been the same effect. You can't store fish without a working icemaker. They were over one hundred miles west of the Philippines by the time they'd finally fixed it, only to discover a major hydraulic leak that prevented them from reeling in their catch effectively. Once again, no fishing. The ship was going to need major maintenance. Nathan's chief engineer informed him that they needed to head back to port as soon as possible. Back to bloody Darwin.

Nathan climbed up the ladder to the bridge to see what that idiot nephew of his was blubbering about now. When he got there, Byron was looking through his binoculars—not wearing them the way he was taught, as usual—and getting more excited by the minute.

"Nathan, someone's signaling us! They look like they're in distress. Look."

Nathan frowned. What the hell was he talking about? They were in the middle of the Pacific. Quite a ways from land. Nathan didn't expect anyone else around these waters. He grabbed the binoculars from Byron's hand. The chief engineer was coming up the ladder behind them now. *Wonderful. Let's just get the whole crew in here.* A monthlong sightseeing cruise with no fish to show for it.

Nathan centered in on the raft. Or was it a motor vessel? The thing looked like a security boat you would see around a naval base. But there were tarps covering it, and he could make out two men huddled together in the shade. One of them was flashing something at them that reflected in the sunlight. That's what must have caught Byron's eye. A good thing, too. There wasn't anyone else out here for dozens of miles. This was one of Nathan's favorite spots to haul in a catch because no one was ever around. And these assholes were floating on some navy raft in the middle of his secret fishing territory. He sighed. Better go help them out.

Nathan said, "Come right five degrees. And wake up McCormick. Tell him we'll need him to put his nurse hat on today."

* * *

Seven hours later, Nathan tapped his fingers on the metal table in his personal cabin. His two recent rescues sat across from him. The door was shut.

They were a sad sight. Peeling skin and chapped lips. McCormick had checked them out and given them plenty to drink. They had taken showers and put on oversized clothes borrowed from the crew. They were still guzzling down water nonstop. Like they were afraid it would run out.

Nathan took in a deep breath and let it out through his nostrils. If it wasn't one thing it was another.

"So let me get this straight. You gents have been working for the US government on some type of secret project that you can't tell me about. There are well-equipped *Chinese criminals* after you, and you think that if I was to call or radio or email anyone and let them know that I've picked you up, I would be putting us all in grave danger. Is that about the gist of it?"

Henry nodded vigorously.

David said, "I know this sounds very unusual, but..."

Nathan held up his hand. "Unusual is picking up two Americans in the middle of the Pacific. What you're telling me is a plot out of one of them crazy books that my nephew's always reading."

David and Henry exchanged nervous glances.

The ship captain closed his eyes as he spoke. "Still, this has been a strange time at sea for me. I usually have good luck. Catch lots of fish. This time, though, my luck's been rotten. Maybe I help you two out, it will turn around, eh?"

Henry was back to nodding and smiling.

"But tell me, how do I know you two aren't wrapped up in something criminal yourselves? How do I know you aren't running drugs or girls or some such rubbish?"

Henry said, "I wish to God that we were."

Nathan frowned.

Henry squirmed. "I guess what I mean is that I wish that was our only problem. I don't mean additionally. I mean like as a substitute problem. For our actual problem. That problem being... the *sophisticated* Chinese criminals that are after us."

David said, "Uh...what he means to say is that we're in a lot of trouble, but not for something that we did wrong. Please, Captain, we need your help. We just have to get to a safe place without alerting anyone. Please believe me when I say that Henry and I could be taken prisoner or worse. And you and your men could get caught up in it."

"And what is *it* exactly? What might we get caught up in?"

David said, "We can't say."

Nathan scoffed.

He looked at each of them and shook his head. He didn't like not knowing exactly what they were running for. But he could tell that these men were harmless. Nathan knew the sea and he knew people. He could trust these men at their word, he was sure of it.

"I'm going to have to make sure my men don't call home and

blabber about any of this. That's all these kids want to do nowadays is text on their phones and apps about what they're doing. Nobody does anything. They just text or *app* people about it."

The two men sat waiting.

Nathan said, "The best way to do this is to secure all phone and email usage until we get back to Darwin. They'll be angry. The only way to send email is on my own computer, and I've got the only two satellite phones locked up in my room. I'll talk to my engineer. And to my nephew, Byron. They're the only other ones with access to my quarters who might come in here when I'm not around. The engineer's a good man. He'll oblige. And my dumbshit nephew will do what I bloody well tell him. What do you want me to tell my men? About your situation?"

David said, "Anything you want. We'll stay out of the way and help out however we can. We just need to reach land safely." David hesitated. "And it would be best if no one knew about our entry into whatever port you drop us off in."

Nathan said, "Well...now this isn't a ferry boat. We're heading to our homeport in Darwin. I need to go straight there and get this boat fixed. We've got room and food, but I'm not stopping and wasting time with drop-offs. My company'd have my ass."

David said, "How long until—"

"Twelve days, as long as nothing else breaks on this gal. She hasn't been very friendly of late, however."

Henry said, "I'm sorry, but are we still talking about the boat?"

David looked disappointed.

"You gents in a hurry?"

David said, "We'll be fine. Thanks."

Nathan tapped his fingers on the table some more. "As for dropping you off without anyone knowing, I think I can figure out a way. I've got a friend who works the tugs. He'll be good for a lift, no questions asked."

David said, "Captain, thank you so much. You have no idea how much we owe you."

"Well, like I said, maybe this'll all come back my way in the form of good luck. If not, you come pick me up next time I'm stuck out on the water, eh?"

* * *

David and Henry walked out of the captain's cabin and down the stairs to the galley. Through the lone oval window they could see that it was dark out now. They sat down across from each other in one of the three booth-style tables where the crew ate their meals.

Henry said, "Things are looking up."

"For *us*..."

"You worried about everyone back on the island?"

"Aren't you?"

"Of course. But like you said before, this is the best way to help them. It wouldn't make much sense to get all this way and get caught."

David said, "Yeah. I know in my head that we're doing the right thing. If we hear a helicopter out here, there's nowhere to run. No stormy night to give us cover. But it's still hard to leave people behind. And it's harder still not to ask the captain to borrow his phone and call my wife."

Henry said, "You might get to talk to her for a moment, but that could also be the last call you make. And you could put her in danger."

"Because they might be able to triangulate our position?"

"Yup."

"I really want to call her."

"Let it go, brother. It's the best thing for everyone. I know it sucks."

David said, "Yeah..."

"Now remind me, what was it you were telling me about transponders on boats?"

David said, "Lena's men saw us go out to sea. Maybe she assumes we drowned. Maybe not. But if she wanted to recapture us, a good place to do it would be while we're stuck on a commercial fishing trawler for twelve days. Now this fishing trawler has got a transponder. And just like every other navy in the world, the Chinese Navy tracks all those transponders so that they know where all the commercial shipping traffic is. If the Chinese version of the NSA intercepted our satellite call, they would be able to triangulate our position and get one of those helicopters or warships on top of us in a flash. And if we turned off the transponder, that might look just as suspicious. Either way, they would be able to find us."

Henry said, "So what's the plan from here?"

"Well, now we know we're going to Darwin, Australia. You ever been there?"

"No. Although one time I took a cruise to the Galapagos."

"Close, but I'm not sure that will help. Anyway, we agree that we'll make calls once we get there."

Henry, getting into serious mode again, said, "Alright, let's say they are monitoring all calls that they think we might make. Family, work, hell, maybe even some government or news station numbers. The NSA has programs that can scan for word patterns and hone in on the right voice or combination of words and flag that one for someone to monitor it. Same thing for email, but that's easier since it's just words."

David said, "And we think China can do that."

"Based on what we've learned on the island, I think it's a given."

"How do we know they won't be waiting for us once we get there?"

"We don't. But if they know we're on this boat, why wouldn't they just apprehend us out here, where there are no witnesses? I think if we make it to Darwin, it's a moderately safe assumption that Lena and company won't know we're there until we try to communicate."

"Darwin's reasonably far from China. I think we'll have a window before anyone tries to come and get us. So what will Lena do when she learns that we're there?"

Henry said, "I think she'll send some henchmen to come grab us—or worse. Let's call it a six-hour flight from there to China. I'd have to check for sure, but that sounds about right for now. Plus two hours for the Chinese SWAT team they send after us to get on a plane and find us in Australia. That gives us eight hours from our first phone call to when we're in danger."

David said, "So we need that first phone call to count. What should the plan be there?"

"I would think that we would want to get multiple government authority figures in the room. We know there are breaches— Chinese spies in our government. We need to spread out our information to a wide enough group of people that we don't get unlucky and have one of the spies end up being the person we're talking to. They'd hide whatever we tell them, call Lena, and it's game over for us."

David nodded. "You're right. I think I know someone at my work that I can trust. A guy named Lundy. I've known him for years at In-Q-Tel. Good guy, family man, trustworthy as far as I know. We can get him on the line. But that won't spread out the information like you're saying. If we've got eight hours, let's use the first call to tell my friend the quick information dump. Then we'll get him to round up people from the CIA, Pentagon, whoever we think needs to be on the call—and we'll give them an hour to get in a room together. He'll have the connections to make that work. He's tight with the CIA and has contacts in several other government agencies from the work we do. Then we'll call the whole group back and give all of them the details."

"We're still putting a lot of faith in your friend."

"I know. I don't see how we can avoid that. We have to start somewhere."

Henry frowned. "Can we just go to a newspaper? Or the Darwin police?"

David said, "How'd your phone call with your ex-wife go?"

"Less than ideal. It could have been better."

"Why do you think that was?"

"Because she's a spiteful old bitch?"

"No. It was because we hadn't established credibility and trust. Even if she did trust and believe what we were saying, she wasn't equipped to take the right action. The first time we tell someone about this, we need them to trust what we're saying, and have the ability to take the proper action. We can't go to the police without passports and talk about a Chinese invasion, just like we can't go to the newspaper. There's way too high a chance that they will think we're crazy and we'll be apprehended by Lena's goons before we can really do anything meaningful. We can't take that chance. We need to hit a home run with our first at-bat."

Henry cracked his knuckles. He nodded. "The two-phone-call plan could work. I'm a little worried about the Chinese version of the NSA jamming our second phone call. But I might have a way to get around that."

"What about the Chinese SWAT team they send after us eight hours later? We might be able to make phone calls and warn people, but how do we protect ourselves?"

Henry said, "We'll have to use our first two phone calls to ask for security. If they have the right US government pull, we should be able to get Australian protection. Or they can send us to the US embassy. Not sure where that is. Probably Sydney. I need to look at a map."

"What if the Chinese SWAT team gets there sooner?"

Henry said, "I might have a way to buy us some extra time with that too. Let me think it over."

David said, "Okay. We'll have several days to go over our plan before we get there. Now we just need to pray that the Chinese don't find out where we are—or where we're headed."

"With any luck, they'll think we drowned in the storm. We almost did."

David said, "Luck's fickle."

* * *

Two hours later, Byron lay in his bunk. He had just finished the second book in a new science fiction series. It was about thousands of people who were living their whole lives below ground in a dystopian future. Their days were filled with endless physical work and sheer boredom. It reminded him of working for his uncle on the trawler.

Uncle Nathan had made him stand the midwatch every night since they'd been at sea this time around. There was only so much holding a wheel and pointing it at the same compass heading that Byron could do before he drifted back to his books to pass the time. He loved to read. Sometimes they drifted a little off course. It was a big ocean, however, and there were very few reefs to worry about this far out.

Byron checked his watch. It was 10 p.m. A few more hours and he'd have to go on duty again up on the bridge. The midwatch ran from midnight to 6 a.m. It got so boring up there without anything to pass the time. Uhhh. They expected him to man the helm, navigate, and keep a lookout for ships for six hours through the middle of the night.

Byron decided that he needed to download the next book in the series for tonight. The problem was, Nathan had said that they weren't supposed to use the computers until they got home. That didn't make any sense to Byron. Nathan was always giving him more and more rules. Don't go on the computer, no reading on duty. Stupid rules. It was just like the underground society in the book he was reading.

It wouldn't hurt just to check and see if Nathan's room was empty. He could sneak in for a few minutes, log in to his computer, and download the next book. Sneaky like a fox. He walked down the passageway in his flip-flops and cracked Nathan's door, peering in. No sign of him. He must be on the bridge or out on the deck making his rounds.

Byron crept into the room and logged in to the desktop computer. Good satellite signal. The Internet was extremely slow, but the book file size would be tiny. He hooked up the USB cord between the ereader device and the computer and clicked through the options until the file was downloading. A time remaining box appeared: six minutes.

Hmm. A little longer than he was hoping. Hopefully Nathan wouldn't arrive and catch him red-handed.

While he waited, Byron opened up another Internet browser window and logged in to his Facebook account. He wondered if Wendy had written him back.

He had sent her several messages telling of his experiences at sea. He would write long passages recounting details of his day and his feelings about how their relationship was growing stronger while they were apart. Usually her replies were very short. Well, there was that long one that had said they were just friends and that he needed to realize that. Usually she didn't reply at all. But that was probably just because she was a no-nonsense person.

Hmm. Wendy hadn't written him in seven days. Byron looked at how many messages he had sent to her during that time. Seventeen. Huh. Kind of a lot. He didn't want to send a desperation signal. Better just "like" her posts to let her know he was thinking about her...and maybe send her one final message since he wouldn't be able to write anymore until they got home. Byron decided to keep this message strictly about how his day went. What would he tell her? His *rescue*. Of course he had to tell Wendy how he had single-handedly rescued the two Americans who were lost at sea. He typed her the story and hit send.

Byron checked the ebook file. Download complete. Excellent. Now he could read the next book while on duty tonight. He logged out of his uncle's computer and walked out of the room. He couldn't help but smile when he thought of how impressed Wendy would be when she read his latest note.

* * *

*Six Days Later, The Island*

Lena stomped out of the control room, the soldiers and communications specialists vaulting out of her way. The site supervisor and Natesh hurried to keep pace with her as she travelled down a ladder way.

Natesh said, "What did Jinshan say?"

She flashed him a stern look. "He wasn't happy. We may need to move up our timing."

"By how much?"

"Significantly."

Natesh said, "What does that mean for us?"

She stopped in the hallway, the two men in tow nearly falling on top of each other as they halted. Lena said, "It means that you two will be here alone running things. I am needed elsewhere." She looked at the site supervisor. "*Do you think you can manage?*"

The site supervisor nodded. He had been caught off guard

when Lena had been taken prisoner. Lena had taken many risks in this operation, so she could forgive how long it had taken him to respond. But allowing two of the prisoners to escape with one of the motorized boats...that was *not* forgivable. She continued walking down the hallway, talking as she went.

She made eye contact only with Natesh. "He's worried about the escaped prisoners. He thinks that they could alert the Americans."

"Manning and Glickstein?"

"Are there any *others* that have escaped that I should know about?" She glanced at the site supervisor.

Natesh frowned. "Isn't it highly unlikely that they survived the storm?"

Lena said, "Apparently not."

"What do you mean?"

"Jinshan's cyberwarriors believe that David Manning and Henry Glickstein were picked up by an Australian fishing trawler several days ago."

Both men had shocked expressions on their faces. Seeing that only angered Lena more. Lena said, "Natesh, let me ask you, what is the main goal of the Iran operation?"

"To force a military conflict between Iran and the US."

"And in order to do that, we will attack a target in Iran and link it to the US. Correct?"

"Correct."

"So what's the link? I can go to Iran tomorrow and kill someone important. That's not my issue. My concern is *the link*. It takes a bit more time and effort to make it appear as though the attack was an American action."

Natesh said, "I understand."

Lena stopped at an entrance marked *Medical*. She held the door open and motioned for the other two men to enter. "After you."

Inside, rows of empty gurneys and unused medical supplies filled the room. A single medical technician wearing green scrubs stood over a black body bag lying on a table.

The tech was a recent arrival. One of the several dozen new military men now inhabiting the island. The flights had increased threefold since the Americans had been taken as prisoners. The island was being stocked with soldiers, weapons, fuel, and supplies. The submarines were supposed to arrive in the finished pen next week.

Lena smirked at Natesh's reaction when the medical technician unzipped the body bag. His face was pale. He had probably never seen a dead body before. Well, it wouldn't be the last.

She asked the site supervisor, "Where did you find him?"

"Ma'am, he washed up on the beach, about a kilometer south of here."

"How did this happen?"

"He drowned. The waves..."

"*I realize that*. I mean, how is it possible that he drowned?"

The site supervisor said, "Ma'am, it must have been when we were...the majority of my men and I...we were almost all on the other side of the island, rounding up the prisoners. He must have gone outside during the storm and got too close to the waves. A big surf like that can have a strong undertow. Perhaps he was sucked in."

Lena leaned over the bloated grey corpse. "I doubt that. Tell me, would that have been around the same time that David Manning and Henry Glickstein stole one of your motorized rafts?"

The site supervisor looked at the floor. "I believe so."

Lena looked toward Natesh. "What do you think, Natesh?"

Beads of sweat on his forehead. "I think it's very likely that this was an intentional act of violence, and that it was related to the theft of the boat and subsequent escape of the two prisoners."

Lena nodded. "I concur." She was about to scold the site supervisor but Natesh spoke before she could.

He said, "Lena, I...I think that this could actually present us with an opportunity."

"How so?"

Natesh said, "You need a link to the US in Iran. Tom was at one time an employee of the CIA. Even after he went into the private sector, he often did contract work for US intelligence agencies. While Jinshan's network placed him in his In-Q-Tel job, no one knows that but us..."

Her smile widened. "I see. An interesting proposition."

"Thank you."

Lena said, "I will need to depart the island soon. Natesh, I ask that you ratchet up the pressure on our consultants. Expedite extracting any further required information. I will be in touch on our new timeline. Use the site supervisor here if you need help *motivating* the prisoners."

Natesh looked hesitant at the thought of further violence against people he had come to know personally.

Lena said, "Now if you'll excuse me, I need to go make another phone call before I leave."

* * *

*Interpol Asia Headquarters and Innovation Center, Singapore*

Philippe Shek looked at the picture on his desk. It was an image taken from his former home in the South of France. He was born and raised near Nice. He missed that part of the world. Interpol had had him stationed in Singapore for the past few years. Their innovation center. Philippe wasn't sure what about police work needed innovating. You found the criminal element and locked them up—normally, anyway. Sometimes there were shades of grey and bargains to be made. But usually he locked them up.

His cell phone buzzed on his desk. "Shek. Yes, this is he. I'll hold."

"Hello, Philippe," came the female voice. A voice he hadn't heard in years. A chill ran down his spine.

"Lena. Good to hear from you again."

"I have a request."

"Of course, name it."

"I'm going to send you two names. In a few days, these men will be wanted terrorists. I have information that they'll be heading to Darwin, Australia. It is a delicate situation. I would appreciate it if you would handle this personally."

Philippe said, "They *will be* wanted terrorists? Aren't they right now?"

She didn't answer the question. In all of Philippe's dealings with Lena, she usually only told people what she wanted them to know. The same thing today. Lena said, "I would like you to apprehend them. Take them away for a while. And this is important—ensure that they don't speak with anyone for a few weeks."

Philippe frowned. He got up, closed the door to his office and sat back down. He spoke in a lower tone of voice. "When will they commit this act of terrorism?"

"I'm going to put you in touch with someone who will walk you through some of the details. Expect an email shortly. Things will be happening pretty quickly. It will be global news in a few days. I need these men to be apprehended as soon as they arrive in Darwin. Is that understood?"

"Yes. Of course."

"It is imperative that they don't speak to anyone for a few weeks once you have them. Bury them in legalities or jurisdiction. Do whatever it takes. I just need them locked up for a few weeks. No communication. Can you help me with that?"

He was taking notes. "I'll be able to do that. Interpol is very good at creating complexity. I'm sure I can keep them locked up and alone. Are you going to make me famous, Lena?"

"For a little while. Yes."

"And…"

"And you'll get your usual fee."

Philippe smiled. "I guess I better get on a plane."

"Thank you, Philippe. We'll be in touch."

The line went dead.

He walked out of his office and said to his secretary, "I need you to book a flight to Darwin for me. As soon as possible."

She nodded and picked up her phone.

He walked back into his office and looked at his inbox. Sure enough, an email from Lena's contact was already there. He read it over, raising his eyebrows as he did.

\* \* \*

*Darwin, Australia*

A bearded David and Henry walked down the aluminum gangway and stepped onto dry land for the first time in over two weeks. It felt funny, not pitching and rolling anymore. David looked over his shoulder at the tugboat. The tug captain, Nathan's friend, tipped his hat at them from the bridge.

David nodded. It was an extra precaution, not coming in with the trawler, but one that Henry and David thought was prudent.

Henry said, "Well, it was very kind of Captain Nate to give us cash for lunch and a cab." He looked down at his Rolex and sighed. "I'm going to miss this watch. After I sell it I'm going to need a stiff drink."

"We should probably do the phone calls first before drinking."

"Of course. It goes: pawn shop, get phones, get hotels, make phone calls, and then happy hour. I wonder if they'll have a pool bar. Do you know if Australian girls tan topless?"

David gave him a weak smile. The stress was getting to him. A lot would be decided today. And there was more than one phone call *he* needed to make. David was so close to hearing his wife's voice. So close to letting her know he was safe. They would be reunited soon. He would take Lindsay in his arms and embrace his three-year-old, Maddie. He would hold his youngest, Taylor, and laugh at her gummy smile. He wanted this all so much and it was almost within reach. Just a bit longer...

A mile away from where the tug had pulled in, Philippe stood smoking a cigarette on a similar dock. He watched a blue-and-white trawler as it inched closer and closer to its berth. He looked up at the large "19" posted on the wooden beam adjacent to the boat. This was the right pier. No other fishing boats pulling in. This trawler was the one. This was where the email had originated.

He threw the cigarette onto the ground and squashed it with his foot. Then he walked toward the trawler. Two of the men were setting up the gangplank. They were almost ready to get off. From what the manager at the fishing company had told Philippe, they had been at sea for several weeks. A long time. But the size and quality of the tuna were worth the trip, the manager had assured him.

"Is your captain available?" Philippe held open his wallet. "International Criminal Police Organization."

A young man in his early twenties yelled, "Uncle Nathan, the International Police are here!"

A tanned man of about fifty, wearing dungarees and steel-toed boots, came down a ladder and held out his hand. "Name's Nathan. I'm the captain. How can I help you?" He looked nervous.

"Good day, Captain. I am Philippe Shek with Interpol. I would like to speak with you and your crew for a few moments."

Shek held up his phone so that the captain could see the screen. "Do you recognize the men in these photographs?"

Nathan's face turned red. Behind him, Byron said, "Hey, Nathan, it's the guys we rescued! David and Henry."

Philippe grinned. He said, "And where might they be now? Still on board? May I speak with them?" He looked down the pier toward the two black sedans. His men would wait for his order. Philippe preferred to do this part by himself. It created less suspicion.

Nathan said, "I'm sorry, but may I ask what this is all about?" He was looking at the sidearm holstered at Philippe's waist.

"I'm afraid that the details are confidential. Are the men in these pictures on board? I just want to speak with them and ask them a few questions."

Nathan looked at Byron and then back at Philippe. He looked like he had done something wrong.

* * *

Henry took half the cash that Nathan had given them and stuffed it in his pocket. He left David a few blocks from the pier, then took a cab to an open-air marketplace.

The market was charming. Fresh fruits and vegetables in baskets. Tourist trinkets and hometown artists hawking their work. The sun was shining and the air was warm on his face. He had never felt so free. It was almost lunchtime, and Henry was pretty hungry. There was one man selling sizzling chicken skewers. Henry took out the small wad of cash that Nathan had provided, careful to guard it from view. He handed the man a few bills for the meal. Delicious.

The pawn shop was one street over from the market. His first stop. Second, if you counted the chicken skewers, which Henry didn't. It was a big place, with everything from crossbows to lanterns to jewelry lining the walls and under the glass. The owner looked Chinese, which under the circumstances almost made Henry turn right around and walk back out the door. But the cab driver had told him that this was the only *real* pawn shop in Darwin proper, whatever that meant. Henry figured he would let the ethnic prejudice slide. Captain Nate had given them fifty dollars Australian, which was very kind—but it wasn't going to get them very far.

"I would like to sell you this," Henry said, removing the very expensive platinum watch from his left wrist.

The Chinese man behind the counter peered at the watch. He said, "Do you mind?" He had an Australian accent, which Henry found funny.

Henry handed it to the man and he looked it over. The man said, "How much you want?"

"Well, I got it for seventeen thousand dollars US. So I guess I would like to get that much back."

"No good, no good." He looked like he was mulling over what to say. "This is not real."

"Like *hell* it's not real. That's the genuine article, buddy." Henry hated pawn shops. "Look, just make me an offer and let's get this started."

The pawn shop owner scowled and said, "I'll give you three thousand Australian."

Henry wanted to strangle the man. He said, "Fifteen."

The man rolled his eyes and took out a calculator from behind the register. He started typing away as if this was going to tell him something new and interesting. He looked up and said, "Five thousand."

Henry cocked his head and looked around the store. He saw a section for pistols. *Hmm.* "You need a license for handguns around here?"

The Chinese man looked around the empty store. He leaned forward. "Depends on the price."

"I tell you what, how about you throw in one of them pistols over there?"

A few minutes later, Henry left the store with five grand in Australian cash and a small canvas bag with a handgun and a box filled with enough ammunition to "get him through the rougher parts of the Northern Territory."

Walking to the electronics store two blocks down the road, Henry was quite pleased with the purchase. Now he needed to get phones. Henry entered Darwin Cellular off of Edmunds Street. He purchased three unlocked smartphones, then walked three blocks to the hotel district.

Henry walked through the revolving door in front of the Hotel Norvoel. Captain Nathan had given them the names of the best hotels. From conversations with the crew, they were able to deduce which ones were right next to each other. Most of the hotels on Esplanade overlooked the deep blue water of Fannie Bay. Henry read that name on a brochure in the hotel lobby. Fannie. Silly Australians. They were kind of quirky—like the Canadians of the Southern Hemisphere, but tougher. Probably from fighting all the crocodiles. He hoped he and David could wrap up this China thing soon so that they could meet some of the local female talent. Probably a lot of pretty girls in the Northern Territory. Like this woman here at reception.

"Can I help you, sir?" she asked. Fair complexion. Nice smile. Lovely accent. She'd probably love to escort a mature American gentleman at the bar tonight.

"How ya doing? I was hoping to get a ground-floor room. One that looks out at Peel Street."

"Of course. But I'm sure we can do better than that for you, sir. You see, we're underbooked right now and—"

Henry waved for her to stop. "Nope. I just want one on the ground floor. Looking at Peel Street, if possible. Do you have a vacancy that meets those criteria? Ground floor facing Peel Street?"

She looked confused and said, "I'm sure we do. We have a special on our Economy Queen on that floor for one hundred and thirty-nine dollars. I'll just need your ID and credit card."

Henry fidgeted. *Here comes the hard part.* He looked around to make sure no one else was watching. "Actually, I was hoping to keep my stay here rather confidential, if it's all the same to you. I'm...a *private detective*, you see. You can put my name down as Merriweather. Dr. Alphonso Merriweather. Just one night's stay, please. And if we can avoid any use of IDs or whatnot, I'd like to provide you a nice tip *for your exceptional service*." Henry looked at her as he slid over three hundred dollars.

She hesitated, and then looked around the room. "Of course, Mr. Merriweather. I think we can make that work." She blushed and began typing.

When they were finished, Henry took his room key and walked outside and around the corner until he found the right door. He ran the card through the slot and entered. He took out two cell phones, powered them up, and placed them on the coffee table. He sat down on a chair and ran through the phones' respective setup screens for a few minutes until they were ready to be used. He then downloaded the app that he needed on both phones and made sure that it worked.

When he was finished in the hotel room, Henry walked out the door and across the street to the Mantra on the Esplanade, another touristy hotel. David met him in the lobby.

Henry said, "Any problems with the lack of ID?"

"Surprisingly, no. These Australians are pretty good about discretion as long as they have the right financial incentive."

Henry said, "The pawn shops are kind of stingy. I did get us some extra protection, though." He held open the bag so that David could see the pistol.

"Nice. I got us on the fifth floor. Let's get up there and stay out of sight."

## 14

*Half the lies they tell me about aren't true.*

—Yogi Berra

They waited until it was 9 p.m. in Darwin before calling. That worked out to 8 a.m. Eastern Time. David expected that Lundy would be in the office by then. The wait was excruciating. Henry set up their cell phone and placed it on the room's lone desk.

David looked at Henry and said, "You ready?"

Henry said, "I'm ready, but I'm not doing the talking. Are you ready?"

He took a breath and said, "Yeah, I think so. Here goes nothing."

David dialed the number he had found online. It took a moment before a female voice answered, "In-Q-Tel, how may I direct your call?"

"Yes, I was hoping to speak with Mr. Chuck Lundy. Could you connect me, please?"

"Who may I say is calling?"

"Tell him it's..." He hesitated. "Tell him it's David Manning. I'm an In-Q-Tel employee."

David listened for any reaction from the receptionist. If she recognized the name, she gave no hint of it in her voice. "Sure thing, Mr. Manning. One moment while I connect you."

There was nearly a full minute of silence before anyone came on the line.

"This is Chuck—*David, is this really you?*"

David's voice was a mix of gladness and stress. "Chuck, it's good to hear your voice. But please listen very carefully. I may be in danger. I need to tell you some things and I don't have much time. I'm going to talk for about two minutes and then I'll be calling back in about an hour. When I call back, I'll need to speak with representatives high up in the following agencies: the CIA, the Pentagon, the FBI, and the State Department. Can you make that happen?"

"*David, where are you?* Your family is worried sick. Does Lindsay know where you are?"

David looked down and sighed. Henry had urged him to move the conversation along as quickly as possible. If the Chinese were listening, the longer they talked, the more likely the call would get traced or shut down. "Chuck. This is life or death here. I need to brief people, but I need members from all of those organizations on the line. Please, help me out—can you do that?"

"Sure, David, whatever you need..." He sounded dumbstruck.

David said, "I'm going to tell you something and I need you to write it down. You got a pen?"

"Hold on...yeah, I'm ready. Go."

"Okay, don't stop me for questions, just write what I'm saying so you can refer to it later in case we get cut off. Chuck, about three weeks ago, I was taken somewhere by Tom Connolly. He told me it was part of a joint DoD-CIA Red Cell. That's legit. I'm on retainer for one of those projects. But this Red Cell wasn't real. Tom was working for the Chinese. Somehow, they were able to activate a US government Red Cell. I believe that Tom also helped them obtain ARES, the cyberweapon that you and I were evaluating for In-Q-Tel..."

David spoke for two minutes straight. He poured out as much information as he thought Lundy would need. He named as many people still captive on the island as Henry and he could remember. He told Chuck about the planning of a Chinese attack on the US, the decoy attack in Iran, ARES, and about possible spies already inserted in the US government. He told Lundy about Bill, the Chinese troops, the helicopters, and about Lena Chou.

When David was finished, Chuck said, "David, my God...did this really happen?"

"Yes, I'm afraid it did. Chuck, you're the first person we've called. Now we need your help."

Henry held up two fingers and whispered so only David heard, "Technically he's the second person we've called, but my ex-wife is probably a communist."

David ignored Henry and said, "Chuck, we need you to move as fast as possible. Contact the CIA so that we can brief them. I know that you have contacts there from work. Make sure they're people you trust. We need to rescue the other Americans on that island if they're still there, and we need to put a stop to any plans that are already in motion."

There was a delay due to the distance, and Chuck spoke over David. "David, I hear you loud and clear. I'll get to work on this right away. Hey, where are you guys? We'll send a team out to pick you up ASAP."

David and Henry looked at each other. Henry nodded. David said, "We're in Darwin, Australia."

"Australia? How did you get there? Okay, sit tight. What's your number? I'll call you back—"

David said, "Chuck, I'll call you back at this number in one hour. Sorry, but I need to get off the phone now. Please have someone from all of those government organizations on the line when I call back. Get whoever else you need on the line too. Talk to you then."

"Will do, David. I'll talk to you then."

David said, "Wait!"

"What?"

"One more thing...have you spoken to Lindsay? Is she okay?"

"She's fine, David. I spoke to her yesterday. She's upset that she hasn't heard from you yet, but she's alright."

David closed his eyes and said, "Thanks, Chuck."

David hung up the phone and handed it to Henry.

Henry said, "Okay. So far so good."

* * *

Philippe rode in the backseat of the black sedan. The sailors on the trawler had been of little help other than to confirm that the two men in question had been dropped off in the city of Darwin around noon.

He didn't want to think what Lena would do if they were able to communicate out before Philippe was able to arrest them. He didn't know what Lena was trying to keep secret, but he had witnessed what could happen when other men had disappointed her. He didn't want to suffer the same fate.

He felt his phone vibrate in his pocket.

"This is Shek."

A man's voice. "Manning has made a phone call. We are refining the call origin geoposition now. Initial assessment is near the intersection of Daly Street and Esplanade."

Philippe called up to his driver, "Daly and Esplanade. Go."

The man on the phone said, "We need you to find him soon. Ms. Chou wanted me to convey the importance of timing. She also said that using lethal force would not be looked down upon."

Philippe grimaced. "Understood. However, what you are mentioning...that is outside my normal scope."

A moment's pause. "You'll be compensated proportionate to the risk."

The line went dead and Philippe tucked the phone back in his pocket. The car made a sharp right turn and accelerated down the road.

\* \* \*

"You gonna call her now?"

David said, "You think it's safe?"

Henry said, "I don't know. But we already made one call. I doubt they're going to have a call quota. Either they know about us and they shut the connection down or not."

"I need to call her. I'm going to."

"Call her. Just...don't spend more than a few minutes on the line if you can help it." Henry was uncharacteristically serious when he spoke.

"Got it."

David picked up the remaining cell phone from the table and took a deep breath. His palms were sweaty. She was fine, he kept telling himself. He dialed the number.

There was a clicking noise and then the phone rang. David's heart was in his throat. He was breathing heavier just at the anticipation of speaking to his wife after such an ordeal.

It went to voicemail. *Son of a bitch.*

He dialed again and Lindsay's phone went straight to voicemail just like the last time. He dialed two more times before finally deciding to just leave a message. Henry watched David's frustration from the chair near the window. He turned away and looked out the window, across the street.

David was nearly crying when he recorded his voicemail.

"Lins. It's me, David. I love you, honey." He sniffed and wiped away the first of the tears that began streaming down his cheeks. "Listen, I want you to know that I'm okay. I love you. Please tell the girls that I love them and miss them. I've been...in some trouble for the past couple weeks. I think I'm almost in the clear now, but I'm going to leave it at that over the phone." David thought about leaving the room number where they were staying or the cell number for her to call back but he decided against it. And the application that Henry had them using for these phones meant that she couldn't dial his cell number. "I'll call back soon."

He hung up, wiped his nose and looked away from Henry.

Henry's eyes were low. "Sorry," he said.

David nodded. "You said text messaging and email wouldn't work, right?"

"Not with the way I've got it rigged up. Sorry. Just outgoing phone calls for now."

David said, "You wanna make a call?"

Henry took the phone from him and began to dial. He held the phone to his ear and then looked at the screen. He pressed the red button to end the call. He snorted. "Voicemail."

"You don't wanna leave a message?"

"Nah. It was my daughter. And we haven't talked in a while. She's the only one that I really need to call." Henry handed the phone back. "You got anyone else you want to try?"

David thought about that as he took the phone.

Henry said, "I'm gonna run down to the lobby and see if they have any beverages we can bring up." He walked out of the room.

David only knew a few phone numbers by heart anymore. He tried his sister's. The clicking sound came on the line and then it went to her voicemail. She was deployed right now, wasn't she? She probably wouldn't get this message for weeks, if not months. He hung up.

He called his brother, Chase. Now there was a guy that never answered his phone. David left a message. "Chase, it's David. I..." He had planned out every word of what he would say when he called Chuck Lundy at work, but now he couldn't think of what was appropriate to tell his brother. Should he unload everything on a voicemail? Did he even know that David had been gone? He must. When David hadn't called to check in, Lindsay would have emailed Victoria, regardless of any instructions to keep the "business trip" quiet. And David's sister Victoria, the most responsible of the siblings, would have contacted Chase by now.

"I'm okay. Please tell Lindsay that I love her. I couldn't get in touch with her and...I'm not sure what's going to happen to me yet, so just please let her know that you heard from me and that I'm okay and that I love her..." David looked up at the closed door. "Listen, I'm in trouble. Some pretty bad things are going on. Some people may be after me and I..."

The door opened and Henry came in, holding a six-pack of beer.

David said into the phone, "I'll call you soon." He looked down at the phone, and the time elapsed read over one minute. He pressed END and terminated the call.

Henry said, "You want one?"

David shook his head. "No, thanks. Not right now."

Henry hopped on the bed and grabbed the remote control, flipping on the TV.

David said, "Why aren't you more worried?"

Henry looked at him. "This *is* me worried." He cracked open his first beer, closed his eyes and took a long swig. "Ahh. But sometimes you just need to let it go."

David said, "We're going to have to set up a schedule so that one of us is always watching the street."

Henry was still looking at the TV. A soap opera was on. Henry seemed content.

"Henry."

"Yeah." He took a sip of beer, eyes still on the TV.

David sighed. "I'll take the first shift." David looked at his watch. Forty minutes until they needed to call Lundy back.

\* \* \*

Philippe's car pulled up on Peel Street outside the hotel. He looked down at the address that had just been texted to his phone.

"This is it."

He sent a text message on his phone. READY.

A moment later he got a message back. STAND BY FOR OUR ORDER. EXPECT A 10-MINUTE WAIT.

The driver said, "Are we going in?"

Philippe said, "Soon."

\* \* \*

David sat at the table and said, "Okay, let's do this."

Henry was over at the window now, sipping his second beer and half-watching the hotel across the street. The remote was still in his hand and he glanced at the TV every few seconds. At least he had put it on mute, David thought.

David dialed the number and hit send.

After a few rings, an intense-sounding voice said, "Is this David Manning?"

"This is David."

"And is Henry Glickstein with you?" Henry watched David now.

"He is."

"Good. Gentlemen, Mr. Lundy contacted my office about an hour ago and brought me up to speed. My name is Bob Crowley. I'm with the Central Intelligence Agency."

"Is Chuck there?"

"I'm here, David."

"And could everyone on the phone please introduce themselves?"

Six more men gave introductions. There were representatives from the Departments of Justice, State, and Homeland Security, and three branches of the military.

David said, "Okay, thanks, everyone, let me take you through the same information that I gave to Chuck."

David repeated what he had told Lundy, in a bit more detail this time. When he was finished, Crowley began firing questions away.

Crowley said, "David, please take no offense to my line of questioning. I'm not trying to ascertain fault, but to fully understand what went on."

"Okay."

"Was there a plan for Iran to attack the United States?"

"Sort of. The plan was to stage an attack on Iran and provoke them into attacking the US in the Gulf region. Then there were to be several different attacks on the US mainland to help ignite a large-scale war with Iran. The members of the Red Cell designed the plans so that all attacks would look like Iran was responsible. Eventually, one of the attacks on the US mainland would be a large cyberattack, which would actually originate in China. But it would still look like Iran was responsible."

"Alright, so this cyberattack would involve ARES, correct?"

"That's right."

"So can you confirm that everyone involved, including both you and Henry Glickstein, took part in planning attacks on the United States?"

David frowned. "We tried not to fully participate once we understood what was going on."

"David, I completely understand. Again, I'm not trying to determine guilt. I just want to understand how people were used. So you two, along with the rest of the members of this Red Cell, participated in planning attacks on the United States and its military?"

David looked at Henry, wondering why this was important. "Yes, Mr. Crowley, that is accurate."

"So this..." He paused like he was looking down at his notes. "Lena...she chose people to participate based on their areas of expertise and how they could contribute to planning attacks on the United States."

"That's correct. But, Bob, I think our time would be better spent here if we talked about how to save the Americans that are still trapped on that island."

"Absolutely, Dave. One last question—your area of expertise was ARES, is that correct?"

David said, "Yes, that's accurate."

"Okay, thank you, David."

"Now I have some questions I would like to ask if it's alright." He tried not to sound irritated.

"Sure, sure, go ahead."

"Is my wife alright? I haven't been able to reach her."

Lundy's voice. "David, I spoke with her less than thirty minutes ago. We've got her coming into our office for a brief on the situation. Obviously due to the sensitivity of this matter we didn't want to tell her everything over the phone." David wondered if Lundy had called her number at the same time he had, causing it to go to voicemail.

David said, "Thanks, Chuck. I appreciate that. Now about the Americans on the island..."

Bob spoke up again. "David, we can't go into details on this line, but rest assured that we intend to have all those Americans in our possession within the next forty-eight hours. Now that's probably more than I should share, but I want you to be able to sleep well tonight. Everyone in this room is fully committed to getting our people back."

David felt a huge wave of relief. Henry had a big smile on his face.

"What about ARES and the Chinese attack? They're planning to put the country into a communications blackout. And a lot more. I told you the basics of the plans. And there are supposedly Chinese agents in the American government already. Now we're not sure what to believe, but—"

"David, again...the men in this room are the good guys. You don't know us, but you know Lundy. And he can vouch for the rest of us. Just sit tight. Now that we know what's going on, we're going to be able to put our best people on it. US Cyber Command has already identified the ARES programs on many of our satellites and has begun operations to neutralize their ability to activate. And I personally am overseeing the personnel issues that you've brought up."

Henry held out his hand to David for a high five. David half-heartedly obliged.

Crowley said, "You did it, guys. Your warning came in time. I would hate to think what might have happened if it hadn't. And because we have you as witnesses, we can press the international community for unilateral punishment of those responsible. Please let me be the first to offer you a beer when you return."

A few men seconded the applause on the phone. Henry held up his beer in a mock salute.

"What about our protection in the immediate future? Where should we go? We're a little worried that Lena Chou's people might be looking for us."

* * *

Philippe got the message he was waiting for. EXECUTE ORDER.

APPREHEND MANNING AND GLICKSTEIN. LETHAL FORCE NOW RECOMMENDED. DELETE THIS MESSAGE AFTER READING.

He deleted the message, opened up the car door and stepped out toward the hotel.

"Stay here," he said to the men in the car.

Philippe unholstered his gun and was at the door before the men in his car knew what he was doing. He brought his pistol up to the lock of the door and fired twice. Two loud gunshots reverberated through the street. A few screams of surprise from the nearby streets. The sounds of his men, no doubt running to support him, regardless of his order. Philippe had to hurry if he was going to pull this off.

The door reverberated and opened slightly, the lock blown out. He kicked it hard, and it slammed open. Philippe ran into the room with his weapon drawn.

\* \* \*

David heard the gunshots coming from outside.

Henry sprang up near the window and waved his arm for David to come take a look. There were two sedans parked at the curb of the hotel across the street, right outside room 142, where Henry had placed the relay phones.

Henry ran to the phone on the table and ended the call.

David said, "What do we do now?"

"We call them back with this phone, without the relay this time. The app that I installed on the phones across the street worked as the decoy. But now we have to use this actual phone without any relay that would throw off our scent. We call them back right now and set up a meet time and place. Then we leave this phone here and run, because they'll trace this call as soon as we make it."

David said, "Okay. Set it up. Let's roll."

Henry typed on the phone and disconnected the application that had served as a relay to the phones across the street. He dialed the number and laid the ringing phone on the table.

"This is Lundy."

"It's David. We've got a problem. There are men across the street that are firing rounds and went into a room that we had set up as a decoy. I don't have time to explain further. We've only got a moment. We're going to have to leave this location. I'm going to give you a rendezvous point. When can you have someone pick us up?"

It sounded like Bob's voice again. "Yes, David. We can come get you. We will have people on the ground there soon. You tell us where to be, and we'll pick you up and bring you to a secure location."

David placed his finger down the map until he saw something that would work.

Henry, standing at the window, said, "They're leaving the room. There's two cars full of them. Shit, one of 'em's walking across the street and heading this way."

"Lundy, you said my wife's on the way?"

"Yes, David, she'll be here soon."

"Talk to my wife. Ask her to tell you her favorite aunt's name. We'll be on that street in one hour."

Lundy said, "Yeah, I hear you—"

David hung up the phone.

Henry turned out the lights and said, "Where are we going?"

"Beatrix Street."

Henry grabbed the bag with his new pistol in it. David brought the map.

They ran out the door as fast as they could go and headed toward the far staircase. Now David was wondering if a fifth-floor room made sense. The minute or so that they spent going down step after step and working up a sweat was also plenty of time to wonder what awaited them on the bottom floor. Thankfully the door at the bottom of the staircase emptied into a vacant parking lot on the side of the building opposite the men in black sedans.

Henry and David tried to look inconspicuous as they half-ran along the main street, taking the first turn onto a side road on their way to the meeting spot.

Henry said, "What will we do if those guys in black sedans are waiting for us on Beatrix Street?"

David thought about that and said, "Well, I guess you'll get to try that new gun you bought at the pawn shop."

Henry said, "Got it." He looked down at the piece, lying in the bag on top of a single box of ammo. He handed the bag to David. "You might want to take it instead. I'm a little low on my firearms experience. You should probably consider loading it too."

\* \* \*

Philippe looked at the empty phones on the coffee table and swore to himself.

The commotion outside was growing, until two men in suits that Philippe didn't recognize got past his men. One held up a badge.

"Are you Philippe Shek?"

Philippe looked at the badge. *ASIO.* It was like Australia's combined version of the American FBI and CIA.

"I am he."

The ASIO agent said, "Could you come with me, please? We'd like to have a conversation."

\* \* \*

Forty-five minutes later, David stood under the buzzing telephone wires of a small residential street. It was almost 11 p.m. local time now. No one was outside in the neighborhood. A slight breeze rolled through the coconut trees that lined the street. Henry hid behind one of them, trying to blend in.

A white Mercedes SUV with the word POLICE painted on the side turned the corner at the end of the street and headed their way. David's chest tightened as the vehicle approached. At least it wasn't a black sedan like they had seen earlier. A positive sign. He gripped the pistol inside of the bag, getting ready for whatever might happen next.

The SUV came to a stop directly in front of him. The passenger-side window rolled down and revealed a man wearing a button-down shirt holding a wallet ID. David could just make out the words *Australian Security Intelligence Organization*.

"My name's Wilson. I'm ASIO. Are you David Manning?" Australian accent.

David, not knowing what else to say at this point and still gripping the gun, said, "Who sent you?"

"Bob Crowley and your friend Lundy. I can get them on the phone for you if you like, but I'd prefer if you would get inside first so we can get you to Larrakeyah."

"Where?"

"It's an army base ten minutes away. We've arranged a secure place for you to stay there. Look, I'm not sure what's going on, but apparently you men are quite important and in danger. My job is to get you to safety as quickly as possible. If you would, please hop in. Bring the man behind the tree. Glickstein, I presume?"

David sighed in relief and called out to Henry, "Come on, Henry. Let's get in."

David slid across the backseat and Henry got in behind him. Wilson reached out of the window and shut the door with his hand, and the SUV zoomed forward.

Wilson said, "Gentlemen, Mr. Crowley asked us to tell you that we're your security for now. Like I said, we'll be taking you two to the Larrakeyah Army Base for the night. You'll be safe there. We've got armed guards outside, and we'll move you in the morning."

He held his hand out and said, "You don't mind if I take that weapon in the bag, do you? We're going to have to go through security to get on base, and they might not like it."

Henry looked at David and shrugged. David handed him the bag with the gun in it. He said, "What about the men that were after us?"

"We're on it. We've identified who they are and it will all be resolved shortly. They won't be bothering you any longer." He smiled and said, "You can relax, gentlemen." David saw the driver glance at Wilson as he spoke.

Henry slapped David on the back. "Phew. We did it," he whispered. He slouched back into the seat and closed his eyes. He looked like he had just dropped a fifty-pound pack that he'd been carrying for two weeks straight.

David was thinking of his wife and children. "You still got that phone?"

Wilson said, "Sure, you want me to call Lundy?"

"Actually, I was hoping to speak with my wife."

"Sure thing. Actually, we're almost at the base. Let's get to where you'll be staying tonight and I'll set you up."

"Alright."

The SUV slowed and came to a stop at a security gate. Beams of bright light shone into the car. David squinted as a man in a beige military uniform walked from window to window, shining his flashlight inside. The Australian driver said, "Come on, now. Important cargo here, let's get this moving." He held up a badge of some sort so the man could see. The security guard read the ID and waved them through.

The vehicle came to a stop outside a tiny single-story building that reminded David of a double-wide trailer. There were several more Mercedes SUVs scattered around the building, each with armed military men standing next to them. There must have been over a dozen men, almost all of them watching David and Henry get out of the car. Now this was security.

Mobile lighting units had been set up. The kind that were used for road construction at night. There were no other buildings around. David could hear the sounds of a marina nearby. The dings and clangs of the loose parts of boats bumping into the hard parts as they bobbed in the water.

Henry followed the two Australian men that had brought them there into the building. David was a step behind. His head ached and he was hungry. Wilson was telling them how they would be flown to a different location tomorrow.

They entered the building and two other men sat across from each other at a large wooden desk. They both looked up. Strange looks in their eyes. A flat-screen TV in the corner of the room was tuned in to a twenty-four-hour news channel. The sound was off. David caught a glimpse of the banner at the bottom of the screen. Something about Iran.

"Thank you, Mr. Wilson," the man behind the desk said. This one had a European accent.

Wilson said, "Quite alright. Mr. Shek, would you like them restrained now?"

"I think now would be an appropriate time, yes."

David felt Wilson grab his arms from behind and heard the click of handcuffs.

Henry wiggled and yelled, "What are you doing?" The man that had driven them there was handcuffing him too.

David, looking around the room in alarm, didn't understand. Then he saw tall black iron bars behind him. From the angle they'd entered the room, he hadn't seen it. Now he did. This building was like one of those old jails you would see in a John Wayne movie. Half office for the sheriff, half jail. These men had just brought them to a jail and handcuffed them. Not very standard procedure for people you were trying to protect. Pretty typical for people you were going to lock up.

The men were talking, telling Henry something. Reading the two men their rights, it sounded like. But David didn't hear any of it. He couldn't hear anything. He just stared blankly at the TV screen. The captions were on.

*"We can now provide you the names of the two American men that are considered armed and dangerous. David Manning and Henry Glickstein are believed to be somewhere in Australia or the Philippines. A global police manhunt is underway. Authorities say they have recordings of the men claiming responsibility for stealing US military cybertechnology secrets and selling them to Iran. They also participated in planning attacks against the United States. No word yet on whether any of this is related to the other major news coming out of Iran today.*

*"And a breaking news update on that other Iran story...the violent attack that has killed a top Iranian politician and his wife, who we have now learned is the niece of the Iranian Supreme Leader...The Iranian government has stated that they now have indisputable DNA evidence linking the American government to the attack. They have provided a name—Tom Connolly—a man Iran claims was the CIA operative who was behind the gruesome attack that left over two dozen dead. The US State Department has condemned the attack but has yet to put out a formal statement regarding this new DNA evidence."*

"Mr. Manning, do you understand what I have said, sir?" the man in the European accent was talking to him.

David was nodding, but he hadn't heard anything. Henry was screaming bloody murder about a lawyer.

"Mr. Manning, you are being charged under international law

for acts of terrorism. You have confessed to these acts. Would you like to make a statement?"

David was numb. "I...I would like to speak to my wife."

"I'm afraid that is not possible at this time. If you please, step this way."

The Australians helped to haul Henry and David into the jail cell. There was a wooden bench, two small foam mattresses, and a toilet out in the open. A roll of toilet paper sat on the ground. Iron bars on three sides. A concrete wall on the far side.

The European man said, "I am Philippe Shek and I work for Interpol. I now have custody over the two of you. You are not to speak with anyone but me. Anything you say can be used against you when you are tried." He walked out of the door, dialing a number on his cell phone as he left. Two Australian men remained, sitting at the desk. They turned up the TV.

\* \* \*

Outside the jail, Philippe spoke on his phone.

Lundy said, "Excellent job, Philippe. Lena was right about you."

"No problem, Mr. Lundy."

Bob Crowley's voice. "Mr. Shek, can you assure us that they won't be able to communicate with anyone for the next few weeks? This will be very important to us. If you have any doubt about that, we may need to look at more permanent measures to solve that communication problem."

Lundy. "What Mr. Crowley is saying is that we—"

Philippe said, "I understand perfectly what Mr. Crowley is saying. I have worked with Lena before. I assure you that I am one hundred percent reliable for her purposes. I'll need to transport them through multiple countries on the way back to the US. Manning and Glickstein will be tied up and unavailable for several weeks as many of these countries often will have jurisdictional issues, especially as additional criminal charges may crop up."

"Excellent. That will do nicely, Philippe."

* * *

The two Australian guards were glued to the news. So were David and Henry.

*Iranian authorities are claiming that weapons on the ground were made by both Israeli and American manufacturers.*

The headline at the bottom of the screen read MASSACRE IN IRAN and had a subtitle of AMERICAN CIA AGENT IMPLICATED.

David whispered to Henry, "None of that was supposed to happen for a year. I mean, this was all thought up just a couple of weeks ago. There's no way—"

The newscaster's voice said, "*Iranians are claiming that they have information linking US intelligence operative Thomas Connolly to the scene, where the Iranians were brutally slaughtered. The car carried...*" *The anchorwoman read off several Iranian names that David didn't recognize, then said,* "*The mother of the two children is the niece of the Ayatollah, Iran's Supreme Leader, and the wife of one of Iran's top political leaders. She was at the Iranian naval base in a naming ceremony celebrating Iran's newest submarine, which was...*"

Henry said, "They did this because of us."

"What do you mean?"

"Don't you see? They moved up the attack on Iran because they knew we were out here."

David shook his head. "We can still tell someone. We warned Lundy. This will all get cleared up. They told us—"

Henry shook his head, "David, it's over. If they moved up Iran, they will have moved up the timing for the rest of the attack plans.

Our credibility is shot. We're terrorists now. They've got us on tape saying that we provided a foreign government with information on ARES and planned attacks on the United States. We won't be warning anyone. Lundy and Bob and all those people on the phone...whether they really were who they said they were or not... they must be on Lena's side. It's over. We lost."

David, hands in his face, said, "So what happens now?"

On the TV, the newscaster said, "*And now we have even more reports of widespread GPS outages. Flights in the US have been grounded at several of the largest airports with no specific timeline given for a fix...*"

Henry said, "Now we watch our war plans come to fruition..."

THE WAR STAGE:
The War Planners #2

**A Chinese plot to destroy the US economy.**
**A growing threat of war with Iran.**
**One man's race to protect America, and save his brother...**

A US Navy destroyer sinks an Iranian patrol craft during a controversial exchange in the Persian Gulf. With tensions soaring between the two nations, an Iranian politician secretly contacts the CIA with a chilling revelation involving the Chinese.

Chase Manning is a rugged ex-SEAL working for the CIA's Special Operations Group in the Middle East. Now, he is tasked with uncovering the truth behind the Iranian claims before it is too late. But in the midst of battling deadly assassins and uncovering the layers of intrigue, Chase discovers that his own brother, David Manning, is right at the heart of the conspiracy.

**Get your copy today at AndrewWattsAuthor.com**

## ALSO BY ANDREW WATTS

**The War Planners Series**

The War Planners

The War Stage

Pawns of the Pacific

The Elephant Game

Overwhelming Force

Global Strike

**Max Fend Series**

Glidepath

The Oshkosh Connection

**Books available for Kindle, print, and audiobook.**

*Join former navy pilot and USA Today bestselling author Andrew Watts'*
*Reader Group and be the first to know about new releases and special offers.*

AndrewWattsAuthor.com

# ABOUT THE AUTHOR

Andrew Watts graduated from the US Naval Academy in 2003 and served as a naval officer and helicopter pilot until 2013. During that time, he flew counter-narcotic missions in the Eastern Pacific and counter-piracy missions off the Horn of Africa. He was a flight instructor in Pensacola, FL, and helped to run ship and flight operations while embarked on a nuclear aircraft carrier deployed in the Middle East.

Today, he lives with his family in Ohio.

From Andrew:

I hope you enjoyed The War Planners! The first drafts were written while I was on my final deployment on the aircraft carrier USS Enterprise in 2012. Now the series has developed into multiple novels, sold over one hundred-thousands copies, and made the USA Today Bestseller list. The adventure gets more exciting with each book! Book 2 in The War Planners series is titled THE WAR STAGE. Turn the page to find out more.

**SIGN UP FOR NEW BOOK ALERTS AT
ANDREWWATTSAUTHOR.COM**